A Murderous

Christmas

A Slice of Life Mystery

To Bob
The Holidays are fun!!
Sheryl C D Ickes

By Sheryl C. D. Ickes

Enjoy Other "Slice of Life" Mysteries

It Only Takes One Bite

Murder in the Woods

Look for "Becky and Rufus" Mysteries

Death of a Dispatcher

I would like to thank numerous people for helping me to get this book published. A big thank you to my husband, Ken, and daughter, Sarah. It took a bit longer to write this book and their support has meant a lot.

Pam and Hal K. for helpful input. Hal, a retired whittler, for information on whittling.

Thank you to Alan Tumblin, owner and manager of Castlerigg Wine Shop in Carlisle, Pa for information on wine.

Karen D. for the Todedes recipe and many years of friendship. A big thank you to the late Mrs. D for introducing me to different Christmas cookies.

Colonel Marland Burckhardt for military help.

Ben G. and Ken for drone information.

Jay Catherman and Deb Beamer for helpful input.

Any errors in this book are entirely of my own doing and should not reflect on any of the knowledgeable people that have helped me. This work is pure fiction. The people and the towns in this book are fictional. References to real locations are used to help bring this story to life.

Thank you to Joey Verderame, Toni Shindel, and Scott R. for character names and descriptions. We had a drawing at one of my jobs for anyone interested in being able to name a character.

I would like to thank Skye Kingsbury for her wonderful book, *A Dictionary of Flowers and Gems*. It is a great resource book.

Cover Design Art and Linden Tree Poem by Sarah Ickes

The Linden Tree

A tree
A special tree
A spear-shaped tree
Pointing toward God
Stood strong and fast
Against the hot, strong,
Blinding rays of the Sun
Lyndy was her name
She would capture the
Power and make it a
Slave
Slowly giving her energy
Silently, She suffered though
Her roots betraying this
Wonder
Pain swelled inside and was
Eating her away
Then a storm brew
There was lightning, thunder and
Rain
It showed no mercy
Lyndy stood still
No fear showed
Her branches danced
But, the storm knew
Her weakness
Wind came full force into battle
Charging at the tree
Lyndy yelped and fell
But, would not fall on the house
For she was noble
And she will always be

Cast of Characters

Slice of Life Bakery Employees and Family
Alexandra Jean Applecake "Alex"
Caitlin Farrell "Cat"
Maggie and Jake Marchetti
Montz Marchetti
Carol Marchetti
Carsenia Kreider
Joyce Hentzel "Jo-Jo"
Detective Thomas Baker "Tom"
Mike Porter
Aunt Gertrude
David Darr

Pets
Mikhail "Micky"
Jake
Conagher "Con"
Murdoch
Julia
Dixie
Cosmos
Doodles
Apollo
Carver

Police
Detective Thomas Baker "Tom"
Detective Johnathan Whitamyer "John"
Detective Joseph Vecchio "Joey"
Chief McPherson
Chief Watson
Officer Oscar Moorly
Officer Macklin "Mack"
Officer Kressler
Detective Rico

Victorian Carolers
Maggie and Jake Marchetti
Larry and Cathy Klinger
Mary Mumpert
Lincoln George
Richard and Lillith Tombow
Ethel Coover
Alexander Gavree Jr.

Cast of Characters conti.

Business Owners and Employees

Mavis

Milo

Jayne

Connie Hibsman

Cassandra Victorio "Cassie"

Ben Gifford

Mr. Nelson

Mr. Turnbaugh

Morgana

Mr. Nelson

Veronica Waters

Stan

Mr. Cutter

Steve Gunderson

Mr. Blaylock

Rufus Bridgewater

Becky Bridgewater

Jacob Carpathian

Rastus

Toby

Artisans

Alexander James Gavree Sr.

Leroy and Penny Winchester

Gray Sommerline

Sadie Sollenberger

Lincoln George

Lizzy Barnstable

Ornament

Sir Thaddeus of the Shire

"Thaddy"

Cast of Characters Conti.

Town Folk

Jody	Emily Ballantine
Chloe	Tommy Ballantine
Robbin	Twyla Ballantine
Mrs. Ava Ferrara	Tyler Ballantine
Alana Silverstone	Stephen Keefer
Mr. Jonas	Taylor Messimer
Irwin Seibert	Sedge
Santa	Mrs. Cavanaugh
Elf	Mrs. Roz Swenney
Marsha Winters	Cora
Derek Winters	Nancy
Ruby	Essie
Tasha	Diesel "Doc"
Xavier Scott Pierce	Mrs. Rutner
Bruce McDavy	Reed Wolf
Brick Oglby	Mrs. Shephard
Bryce Fencer	Letitia
Martiya	Jackie
Sylvia	Mrs. Rosenberry
Crystal Wycoft	Herbie and Georgette
Ronnie Metlamb	Carlin and Martha Birkman
Allie Caruthers	Pastor Lentz
Marshall Dustinger	Mrs. Morelander
Pastor Daniel	Mrs. Carbuncle

Chapter 1
December 1
Friday Morning

Alexandra Applecake, owner of Slice of Life Bakery, gazed out the window above her desk and smiled. Small snowflakes were gently floating down from the heavens, promising some snow for the Christmas tree lighting at the park this December first evening. She loved this time of year and the "magic" in the air that came annually every December. Her town of Creek Water really knew how to turn up the Christmas cheer. More holiday events than usual were planned for this year, and Alex smiled at the thought of checking them all out with her best friend and employee, Cat. Then, she sighed as her gaze returned to the paperwork on her desk to finish. "Soon done and then the fun!" She spoke out loud to herself and to her otherwise empty office room.

Alex had just started to review her last purchase order when, "You bitch!" rang out clear and strong from the intercom that connected her to the front register area of her store. Her eyebrows lifted and she froze, waiting to see if someone was joking or totally serious.

"Leave my husband alone or I will kill you!" A voice screamed that brought Alex out of her seat quickly and quietly jogging to the front. At first, she stayed out of sight, with a hand on her cellphone ready to dial 9-1-1.

"What are you talking about?" Jody replied. "I have my own man, I neither want nor need yours!"

"That's not what Mr. Dean and Wilbur implied in the paper."

"What paper?"

"The Town Crier, duh!"

"I don't usually read that paper. It used to be good under the old owner, but now it's basically gossip."

"Well, I still do and they said that you are fooling around with my husband."

"They are lying. It's not true. As I said, it's gossip." Jody patiently said.

"It has to be you!" She screeched.

"Excuse me, Chloe, but the clues can allude to more than one person." Cat explained. "Do you have your newspaper copy?"

"It's out in the car," Chloe seethed while staring at Jody.

"I have my copy in the back room." Alex stepped out into the room as she spoke. "Give me a second to retrieve it. And, I might also add, that my store is not the proper place to air out this dirty laundry. But, since you're here, let's end it here also."

After Alex disappeared, Robbin briefly stopped her shopping and asked Chloe, "The paper came out Wednesday, why did you wait so long to get mad?"

"I was away. I just looked at the paper this morning. Tony went to the doctors and I came looking for Jody."

"Why is your husband at the doctors?" Cat inquired.

"Because when I hit him with the lamp, he got cut. Now, when I get home I have to clean up his blood," she huffed.

Alex re-appeared and as she walked to the front counter, she flipped to the comic page of the newspaper. The ladies, except Jody, crowded around her. She reviewed the page with the Mr. Dean and Wilbur comic strip and handed it around. It was a 4x4 square drawing showing the back side of a brick house with a macadam driveway on the right side. A vehicle was parked in the driveway and a man looked to be going toward the front door. A woman in a bathrobe and a towel on her head was watching a man crawling out a back window.

"See, its Jody!" Chloe harshly repeated. "That is my Tony crawling out the window, he has that distinct ugly hat. That's Jody's husband's car parked there. I'd recognize it anywhere," she pointed her finger at the page, "and he's walking to the front door."

"Well…." Cat interrupted, "someone else came to my mind."

"I agree with Cat." Alex nodded.

"Of course you do." The irritated woman spit out. Alex and Cat quickly turned to look at the woman.

"Now, hold on a minute," Maggie, another friend and employee of Alex's bakery and supply shop, spoke up hesitantly, "I can think of at least one other lady." She added, "I do not condone this comic strip nor want to participate in a witch hunt, but there are probably others."

"Harrumph!" The woman scowled and stomped out.

"Please be careful Chloe! Think before you do anything!!" Maggie yelled after her. She turned to the other ladies in the store, "These comic strips are going to get someone killed."

"So far, they seem to be freakishly accurate. In the beginning, I thought they could do good. Remember that first one about the twenty-year overdo library book? It was funny, and they actually got the book back, in good shape I might add, with some money for the lateness," Robbin said.

"Yes, but they have turned nasty. They still have some humor, but you know someone did the deed in the comic strip. The whole town starts speculating and lots of people get hurt or relationships ruined over rumors and innuendos," Jody replied.

"I wish that one of those comic strips would expose who ran over and smashed Mrs. Ferrara's 'Little Library.' Being a retired librarian, she really enjoyed having that and seeing the faces of the children who borrowed books from it," Maggie said.

"I hear someone offered to replace it," Alex replied.

Cat turned to Alex with a concerned face, "Back to Chloe for a moment, do you think we should call anyone in particular and warn her to be careful before she opens any of her doors?"

"I will do that from my office." Alex stated and quickly left.

"The timing of these comic strips could not have been much worse," Jody observed.

"I couldn't agree with you more on that. It causes a dark cloud on the holidays," Maggie concurred and Cat agreed.

"Sorry, you had to go through that, Jody."

"Thank you for that, Maggie, and you too, Cat. It wasn't your fault. Chloe never was very good at cars. To her, they all look alike. She would make a bad witness to an accident. I, on the other hand, can tell the difference between a Honda and a Hyundai." She looked knowingly at the three ladies. "But thank you, just the same." Jody replied as she bought her candy supplies and left.

Meanwhile, back in her office, Alex had just reached Alana Silverstone on the phone. She quickly explained what happened with Chloe. "I am sorry if I am wrong in my thinking on this, Alana, but……. are you perhaps doing something that maybe you shouldn't be?"

There was silence on the phone for about a minute. Alex was about to ask if anyone was still there. "Yes, Alex," Alana quietly answered, "you are accurate. Do you think I should call the police?"

"I think that you might want to," Alex replied, "and soon!"

A short while later, Alex returned to the front of her store carrying a box, "Everything is done in the back." She looked around, "It looks peaceful out here for now."

Maggie and Cat smiled in agreement. "The last customer just left. What's next, boss?" Maggie asked.

Alex smiled at them and turned toward the tree, "We need to finish the tree and double-check around the shop to see if we are indeed totally done decorating. It is December first and the tree lighting at the park is in three hours. The kids' event of the Twelve Days of Christmas has started, have we had any participants?"

"I sure wish that they would change the name of that to something more accurate," Maggie said. "They get almost a whole month to complete the event."

"True, however, the town Christmas committee took into consideration all the holiday madness and people still having their regular lives and issues. Making families fit running around to twelve different businesses in exactly twelve days, would not be family friendly, nor the pleasant holiday event this is meant to be."

"When you say it that way, I can agree. My kids would not be participating either if that had been the case," Maggie chuckled, turning a small shade of red.

"As to your prior question, but on that same topic, we have had a few children, but you know how it is, the closer to Christmas, the more we will have." Cat answered.

"So true, Cat." Alex reached into a cardboard box and pulled some more decorations out of it. "I was getting worried that something had happened to this one. It was not packed in the correct box last year." She cradled a gorgeous glass dove in her hand. Alex placed it toward the top of the tree, just under the angel tree topper. The ladies were busy decorating and taking care of customers for the next hour. As Alex reached into the box again and pulled out a specially wrapped item, Cat groaned. Alex smiled knowingly, "Something wrong Cat?"

"Yes, and you know it. Do we really have to put that thing on the tree every year? It's ugly, it's nasty, and just gross. The dove," Cat looked up at it and smiled, "I understand. It's beautiful and represents your sister. It is a great way to have her with us each year." Cat waved a hand toward the item in her friend's hand, "But, not this one."

Maggie was briefly confused at her friends' reactions. She started chuckling when Alex finished pulling the item from the tissue paper. "Oh, yeah, I forgot about him."

"How do you forget about this thing, Maggie?" Cat gave her friend a strange look and turned back to Alex. "Come on, Alex, you know you agree. You just don't want to admit it."

Alex turned the item over and over in her hands. After re-examining the grubby looking, barefoot, freckled, green Santa troll figure with one leg a wee bit longer than the other, dressed in a light green tank-top, darker green pants and a Santa hat carrying a candy cane club-like in one hand and a red bag in the other, she chuckled. "Sir Thaddeus of the Shire is definitely unique. I remember a conversation like this with my Aunt Gertrude. She'd laugh and say that she liked candy canes. I'd agree, but remind her that I don't like the peppermint ones. I will agree that he wasn't blessed with beauty. She'd reply that it's a reminder to us........that beauty is only skin deep......that true beauty is on the inside. A person's true value is on the inside. She'd always get an unique look when she'd say that."

"What do you mean an 'unique' look?" Maggie inquired.

"I don't rightly know how to describe it. It wasn't sad....maybe introspective?" Alex shrugged, "I really can't describe it. She'd also have a glint or twinkle in her eye, and she would say, 'Don't lose this guy Alex! He'll keep you humble.'"

Cat quietly looked at her best friend of a bazillion years. "Don't you think this troll is too big to hang on a tree?"

"It's bigger than our traditional ornaments, but that doesn't bug me. Aunt Gertrude always put it on her tree. I put it where I do, because she always did, and it makes sense. Find a 'hole' or a 'gap' in the tree where you need something bigger and put it there. It's smaller than the decorative statues that I put out on display. It would get lost on my shelves."

"And that would be a 'bad thing?'" Cat asked. "It's an eyesore."

"That's pretty harsh, Cat," Maggie commented. "I agree that it's not the prettiest, but it's far from the ugliest, and Aunt Gertrude had a point, let it keep us humble. Besides, this has a lot of sentimentality for Alex and 'tis the season for sentimentality'."

Cat looked quietly at Maggie, "You actually like this thing don't you?"

"'Like' might be too strong a word. I see him as the guardian of the tree. He protects the tree and its inhabitants from harm with that bat-like candy cane," Maggie explained.

Cat turned to look at Maggie with a puzzled expression, "Has anyone ever told you that you have an overactive imagination? You could put that to better use," Cat suggested. Maggie just smiled as a reply.

Alex checked her watch, "Hey, it's later than I thought, we have to close. There's not much time before the tree lighting in the park."

Chapter 2
Friday Evening

Alex arrived at the town park at about six fifteen and looked around for Cat. "Hey there!" Her friend laughed. "Where's Tom? I thought that he was coming too."

Alex gave a quick hug to Cat and her main man Mike. "Where else? He had to work. He and his partner, John, have been assigned to find and stop the burglars that have been robbing these parts lately."

"Wow, that is not going to be easy," Mike commented and shook his head. "If it's the ones that I'm thinking of, they have been robbing people for at least three to four weeks, and not just here, but in at least two adjoining towns."

"Those are the guys. There have been only two robberies here so far, but the captain doesn't want anymore. He's insisting that they work with the detectives from the other towns, and catch these guys before anyone gets hurt. It's a complicated case. Tom and John had a brief meeting with one of the detectives from Black Water already." Alex answered.

"I would think that those other detectives should be pretty smart. Nothing against Tom and John, but I'm not sure that they'll be able to quickly catch them either," Mike opined.

"I concur, but I'll lay odds, Tom and John end up being the ones to figure it out. I believe the mayor might be in this mess somewhere too."

Cat changed the subject quickly. Looking around, she smiled, "Look at the lake this year. Isn't it fabulous?"

"Always!" Alex laughed as she surveyed the area. The sun had set awhile back, but it was far from dark. Luminaries outlined the entire lake and each walkway. All the surrounding trees were decked out in Christmas lights. Each tree was entirely lit in one color and in a different color from its neighbor on either side. The Victorian style streetlights were decked out for the holidays in evergreens and small white lights and red bows. A small band was playing Christmas music in the gazebo that was outlined in small white lights. People were happily buying hot chocolate and cookies from a decorated stand set in front of some festive evergreens. The trees helped to keep the slight wind that was blowing from being a problem.

The mayor, Irwin Seibert, stepped up to the podium positioned in front of the gazebo, "Please gather round folks. We are going to get things rolling here. First, some fabulous Victorian carolers are going to sing two songs to get us going, please feel free to sing along with them. Afterwards, a special guest will be arriving on the lake to help light up our floating Christmas tree." The carolers gathered around the microphone, the band started playing "The First Noel," and after a few minutes the crowd joined in. The second song, "Here Comes Santa Claus," set the mood for the special guest's arrival. Toward the end of the song, kids were pointing across the lake and gleefully shouting. All eyes turned to the boat driven by an elf carrying Santa Claus across the water to a Christmas tree floating about thirty feet from shore. Everyone clapped as Santa waved at the growing crowd. The elf stopped the boat alongside the man-made island that held the tree afloat. Santa stood up, extended his hands briefly to get his balance. He turned to the crowd, dramatically put a finger to the side of his nose and winked. He lowered his hand as he turned back to face the tree. He clapped his gloved hands and shouted "Merry Christmas!" The tree lit up and the crowd hooted and hollered and clapped their hands and rang Christmas bells.

Santa Claus returned to his seat in the boat beside a big red velvet bag. The elf brought him to the edge of a small wooden dock and the mayor helped Santa step up onto firm ground. The elf handed Santa his bag. "Everyone, please help me escort Santa to his hut and get in line to sit in his lap."

Alex, Cat, and Mike watched Santa for a short time and then headed to the train. Every year, the town's Chamber of Commerce sets up a temporary train that travels around the park. It takes people on a ride through Christmas light scenes and various comical ads by the different businesses throughout the town. "The competition is going to be tight this year, I believe, Alex," Cat commented as they disembarked the train.

"Yes, I agree. Which ad did you vote for?" Alex smiled.

"Ours, of course," Cat laughed, "but Connie has a good one. I'm already thinking of stopping at her restaurant on my way home."

"Don't forget Cassie's. Having a pet store gives her an edge. Everyone loves animals and hers is super cute."

"I told you to use animals," Cat teased.

"No, you said to use mice. They'll be cute, you said. Nothing cute about mice in a bakery! What do you want us to do? End up in one of those confounded comic strips? I thought the elves worked well."

"I liked them too. This competition is fun. There is no nastiness. People see humorous commercials and get to vote for their favorite."

Mike grinned, "I really liked the hardware store one." The two ladies turned to him quickly with their eyes opened wide, and he laughed. He raised his hands, "Don't hurt me. Don't hurt me. I voted for Alex's. I want to live." He laughed again as he put his arm around Cat and she playfully poked him in the gut.

After spending time with friends, Alex said good bye and headed off to complete some errands that needed done.

Chapter 3
Friday Evening

Alex pulled up in front of Alexander Gavree's place. Alexander was a friendly older man who whittled and did other woodwork for a living. She bounded up the front stairs and rang the bell. Alexandra, hearing him yell for her to enter, walked into his house, and found him in the back workroom. "Hi! I'm here for two reasons." She smiled.

"Just two?" He smiled and laid down the carving tool he was using on the project in front of him.

A wee bit surprised, she responded, "Yeah, just two. First, do you have your 'Little Library' parts done?"

"Of course, I do, as promised." He nodded his head toward the front door, "Everything is in the red box on the table by the front door.

Alex smiled, "Fantastic! Any problems?"

"No, I believe that you will like what I did."

"I'm sure I will, now two, how's the gift coming along?"

"Come and see for yourself." Alexander waved for her to come over to his table. "I've taken a small break from it." He stood up and turned around to get a box off a higher shelf behind him. He placed it on the table and smiled as he watched her face, "I take it that you are pleased."

"Oh, yes," Alex grinned. She placed her right hand beside the box as she traced the one shape with her left.

"I thought that you'd be," he commented confidently as he placed his left hand on her right and smiled as she slid her hand off the table.

Alex moved away as she spoke, "Will it be done on schedule?"

"Of course, dear Alex," he grinned. "However, I believe that you could convince me to have it ready earlier."

Alex was getting uncomfortable at the direction of the conversation. She slowly headed toward the front door, "No, the original date and time will do."

"Remember, the balance is due on the bill also." Alexander slowly followed her.

"I remember, as agreed, I paid half the bill before the work was started, and the rest is due when the project is completed."

"If you would like, I am sure that you could come up with an alternative idea for payment and save the money for other needs." Alexander had moved quicker than Alexandra had figured he was able and he stood between her and the exit.

"What's the matter, Alexander? You are acting odd!"

"I am fine, Alex, I assure you. You are too tightly wound, you need to let loose. Let's have some fun! What do you say?" He walked a bit closer to her and stumbled a bit, "Now, stop making excuses!"

Alex looked quickly around the premises, "I think I heard a noise. Is someone else here?"

"No, dear, that's just my dog, Carver, no one else is here," He grabbed her arm and shoved her backward against a bookcase.

"Oww! Alexander, that hurt! I'm not sure what your problem is tonight, but get a grip and knock it off," she growled. She gave a quick look around and noticed two bottles and a glass on a coffee table, "Are you drunk? You have carolers about to arrive any minute, and I know that you like to hand out your ornaments to them. I suggest that you get your act together."

"They will be a bit yet," he squinted toward a clock on the wall. "I am not drunk. I am in the mood for some great sex with a hot woman. Brunettes always turn me on. How about it Alex? One last fling before you decide to marry? Or is that detective guy of yours an eunuch?" He tussled with her a minute, Alex slammed her foot down on the top of his arch and he howled, "You bitch!" He grabbed her and she slapped her hand across his face, he howled again and leaned against a wall. He wiped his face with his hand and pulled it away. He glared at the blood on his fingers a second. Then, with a calm steely voice, he said, "I suggest that you take that box I'm working on and leave. I will not do any more work for you!" he finished vehemently.

Alex hustled to the work area and snatched the wooden box. She rushed to the front door and put it on top of the red cardboard box on the table. She quickly picked everything up and heard something fall to the floor, and hurried out the door. Alex could hear the carolers getting close as she concentrated on loading the boxes into her car.

She gave a quick glance to ascertain their position before getting into her car and missed seeing a couple wave to her. Alex was happy to be away from the house. She had never seen Alexander behave that way and decided that she would call tomorrow and check on him, but definitely from a distance.

Alex was on her way to a neighboring town to visit other artists when the carolers arrived at Alexander Gavree's home. She didn't see the carolers' concern as they sang to a closed door, nor did she hear the screams when a few carolers had entered the homestead, and found the artist lying on the floor dead.

Chapter 4
Friday Evening

Tom and John pulled up to the curb behind some police cars and observed the activity for a few seconds. "Pulling a new murder on top of the string of burglaries and our other cases is getting a bit unreasonable," Tom commented.

"The flu is not helping either," John responded. "At least they said something about witnesses. Let's hope that this will be a relatively quick wrap up. We have that meeting early tomorrow morning with the tri-town burglary unit."

As they approached the house, a young cocky officer recognized Tom, "What are you doing here?"

"John and I caught the case. Any reason that I shouldn't be here?"

"Because, as I hear it, your Alex is the victim."

Tom looked at the officer, paled a bit, unconsciously took a step backward and looked at the closed front door. "My.........Alex?" He swallowed. "Surely not," he thought.

John squinted his eyes as he looked from his partner to the officer. The front door to the house opened and an Officer Moorly stepped out. "Oscar, who is the victim inside?"

The middle-aged man replied, "The owner of this house, one Alexander James Gavree."

"Thanks a lot, Oscar." John glanced at Tom and shook his head and glared at the younger officer, on loan from a neighboring town, as they entered the house. "Don't assume anything, Officer Kressler," he warned.

As they entered the house, they were informed that the body was in the back half of the building and the coroner was on his way. The owner had converted two back rooms, basically the back half of the first floor of the house, into a workroom and office for his business. The tall, lanky artist's body lay in a pool of blood on the floor behind a work table on the right side of his set-up. Numerous bloody spots were visible on his shirt.

"Anyone else in the building?" John asked.

"No one, sir," Officer Macklin informed. "He was discovered by a group of carolers. We have them waiting for you in another room." He pointed toward the front of the house.

John and Tom stayed for a short time and observed the body, the room, and took notes as the crime team took photos and went about their job. "Any sign of the murder weapon?" Tom asked.

"No sir, the murderer must have taken it."

"Let's go see what the carolers can tell us," John suggested.

The two detectives entered the front room. Nine somewhat irritated people spread throughout the room trying not to look like they had been talking to each other, all turned their way. There were four men and five women in total. Tom looked around the group and was somewhat pleased when he recognized Maggie and Jake, friends of Alex's, for they should be worthy witnesses. They had level heads and were not ones for a lot of drama. As he approached Maggie, a tall thin man presented himself first, "The victim was my dad and your girlfriend killed him!" Tom froze momentarily and then turned toward his partner.

"Calm down a piece and let's sort this out," John commanded. He looked around the group, "Richard, please come and help out a bit here."

One of the Victorian carolers came over to help out and guided the distraught man to a less crowded part of the room. "Let's give these guys some room to work, Alex."

Tom asked Maggie to come into an adjoining room for questions. He looked over his shoulder at the sound of the man's name. "How many Alexes are there going to be in this case?" He muttered.

Maggie looked at Tom with watery eyes, "At least three, I'm sorry to say. The deceased, Alexander Gavree, is that man's dad," she inclined her head toward the upset man. "That man is Alexander Gavree Jr., goes by 'AJ' to many. And unfortunately, our Alex was the last person to leave this house."

Tom's eyes widened briefly, and quietly turned toward John, "John, we need you over here please." John came over as requested and questioned with his eyes. "Maggie, repeat to John what you just said to me, word for word, please." After she complied, Tom looked at John, "you need to take the lead on this investigation, but I will stay involved."

John studied his partner briefly, "Sounds like a plan." He turned to Maggie and asked her to explain her earlier statement.

"Our group was caroling as we do every year. We always stop here to sing, because Alex Sr. likes to hear us sing and then gives each one of us a specially carved Christmas ornament. As we were approaching, I saw Alex leave this house. She seemed to be in a hurry and was carrying a big box. I waved, but I don't think that she saw me. She opened the passenger door of her car and put the box in. After slamming the door closed, she hurried to the driver's side and jumped in and took off," Maggie used a Kleenex to wipe her face as she finished her statement.

"How far away were you when you saw Alex? Are you sure it was her?" Tom asked.

"We were about three or four houses away. But, I'm extremely sorry to say, that I am quite sure that it was her, and it definitely was her car. I know that she didn't ki..... hurt this man, but I didn't see anyone else. As we approached the house, we were singing and laughing. When Alex Sr. failed to come out onto the front porch like he always has in the past, a few of us went up the stairs and knocked. Nothing happened, so his son reached into his pocket and got a key to open the front door. He led the way into the house; Larry, Jake and I followed. We found the man lying on the floor in the back of the house. It looked like a workroom. AJ yelled his dad's name and ran to him, but didn't touch him at first. Larry hurried to Alex Sr.'s side and checked for a pulse. He couldn't find one, so

I called 9-1-1, while he tried CPR. Jake went to see if anyone else was in the house." Maggie started weeping a bit more as she continued, "Larry continued until help arrived, but they could not do anything to help him. He was dead."

"Alex Jr. had his dad's key in his caroling pants?" Tom inquired.

Maggie started to nod her head, when an angry voice shouted out from the door of the room, "Of course, Detective!" John walked over toward the man as he continued. "I had my car keys with me! I always keep a copy of dad's house key with them. What exactly are you accusing me of? Your girlfriend was the last one here. I was with this group for at least two to three hours before that!"

John waved a hand to catch an officer's attention, "Mack, please keep everyone away from this room. We will try to be as fast as we can." He turned back to Maggie, "Please give us a rundown on your caroling group."

Maggie re-adjusted herself to get more comfortable and to take a minute to think. "There is me and Jake, Lillith and Richard Tombow, she is our organizer, sets our schedule and stuff, Cathy and Larry Klinger, Alexander Jr., Mary Mumpert , her husband could not make it tonight, Ethel Coover, and…." Her forehead creased with puzzlement and she stopped talking.

"What is it, Maggie?" Tom inquired.

"Well, there is also Lincoln George, but he's not out there right now. He started the night with us.......so where did he go?"

"That is a question we will answer," John assured her. "Thank you Maggie for your statement. If you think of anything else, please let us know. We'll interview Jake next so that you two can go soon."

Jake entered the room a bit sheepishly, "Sorry, guys, I don't think that I will be of much help."

"Well let's get started and see where we go," Tom encouraged. "Start from where you all were singing a few doors down from this house."

"Okay," Jake agreed. "We were singing and Maggie bumped my shoulder and waved at someone. I turned to look and then we finished the song and walked a house closer. We sang a song or two at that house. They thanked us and we skipped the next house because it was dark. Then we started singing at Alex's house, I mean this one. He didn't come out on the porch, like in the past, so Alex Jr., Larry, and Maggie went to investigate and I tagged along. I didn't much care for the man, but I thought it better that I follow. When we found the man lying on the floor, Alex Jr. yelled his dad's name and ran over to him. Larry bent down, checked for a pulse and did CPR. Maggie called for help, and I went to see if anyone else was in the house. I mean, the man was lying in a pool of blood, it didn't look like an accident, so I went to see if anybody was hiding. I didn't find anyone," he shook his head as he spoke. "If I would have, I would have hustled Maggie out of this house in a hurry!"

"Let's back up a minute, when Maggie bumped your shoulder and waved, you said you looked. What or whom did you see?"

Jake shrugged his shoulders, "No one really."

"Can you elaborate on that?"

"I didn't get to as many practices as Maggie, and I didn't work too hard on the songs either because of work and family. We were singing a song that I am not too familiar with, but we carry song books along for just that occasion. I had my cheater reading glasses on so I could sing the song, they are great for close up, but horrible for long distance. When I looked in the direction that Maggie had indicated, everything was a blur. It was a dark night and the only light came from those Victorian style streetlights. They are not the brightest things. I can tell you that a person was there by a car. The car seemed to be a VW bug by shape and was a medium blue, but I cannot tell you any more than that," he shrugged. "Everything was really blurry. I feel bad, but at the time, it didn't seem important. I am sure Maggie could give you the details."

Chapter 5
Friday Evening

Detective Joseph Vecchio arrived at Alex Sr.'s house as the carolers were leaving with Tom and John trailing them. "Joey? Was there another burglary?" Tom inquired.

"Not that I know of. After our earlier meeting, I thought it prudent to get to know your town better. When I heard that there was a murder here tonight, I was curious to see if it occurred during a burglary. I thought maybe they be getting cocky, and switching things up."

"We didn't get a chance to really delve into anything yet. We just got here, observed the scene, and took witness statements," Tom responded.

"We will have to check out that possible angle though," John answered thoughtfully.

"That was a group of people just now, was a party going on at the time? With that many people, do you have a clear suspect?" Joey asked.

"It has been suggested that it was a woman who drives a VW bug."

"A medium blue one?" Joey asked quickly.

"Yes."

"Blimey! I might have passed her then," Joey started to get excited. "A medium blue bug went barreling by me on my way here. It was headed to my town. I'll call my guys and get them to keep an eye out."

Tom spoke up quickly, "You don't have to hurry on that."

"Why not?"

"Because I believe we already know the identity of that driver and she will be back."

Joey whistled, "Dang, you guys are good. You almost have it solved already."

"Not quite, Joey," John said. He turned toward Tom, "Let's not assume anything, Tom," John suggested.

Tom thought briefly and nodded his head, "You're right. Go ahead and alert your guys Joey."

"Do you know the license plate number?"

"Yes," Tom rattled if off without hesitation.

Joey just looked at Tom for a second, "I noticed that you didn't read that off of your notes. Is your memory that good? Are you one of those people with a photographic memory?"

"No, I just have a fiancé that has a tendency to get mixed up in things and drives too fast," Tom answered quietly to a surprised Joey. "Please put the APB out and then, let us clue you in on what we know so far."

Chapter 6
Friday Evening

"Where have you been?" an exasperated Cat asked her friend after Alex picked up on the thirtieth phone call. "I have been trying to reach you?"

"So I can see, now," Alex calmly replied. "What is the emergency?"

"If you are driving, pull over. I need your immediate and total attention," Cat urged.

"I just got into my car. I'm at Sadie's house. I just dropped off the items for her to paint. What's the urgency? Did something happen to one of my family members?" She asked worried.

"No, as far as I know, your family is okay, but something definitely happened. Sadie's house is in the middle of nowhere, so that's good. What have you been doing since leaving whittler Alex's house? Did you turn your phone off?"

"Yes, as a matter of fact, I did. I needed to visit two different whittlers and pick up their work that they did for me to help replace Mrs. Ferrara's smashed 'Little Library.' I got the stuff from Alex in our town and there was a bit of a situation there. I raced over this way and then decided I better chill a bit and clear my head. But it wasn't long, because I had to stop at Gray's and Leroy's and then get to Sadie's, so that she could get started on the painting. I'm aiming to get Mrs. Ferrara her new "Libby" by the end of next week. We discussed all of this earlier."

"What little situation at Alex's house?"

"He was acting weird. I ended up slapping him and he got scratched. I am a bit concerned about how that is going to work out. I grabbed my stuff and got out of there fast."

"Well, heads up! He's dead."

"What?! I just slapped him!"

"Well, he's dead. And, the cops are looking for you," Cat said. "But, I suggest that you call Ben."

"Cat, my shirt is ripped," Alex said seriously. "I think that could be a problem."

"What shirt?"

"My outer denim one," Alex answered. "I didn't notice it until I dropped the stuff off at Sadie's. She said I have some blood on the shirt at that spot too."

"What the heck did Alex do to you?!"

"It sounds worse than it is, but it's not going to look good."

"You have extra clothes in the car," Cat reminded Alex.

"Normally, yes, but they are at home in the wash. I knew that I would have them ready for tomorrow, didn't think that I needed them today."

"I can bring you something and meet you somewhere. Just pick a place. You need to get back to this town."

"Skip the clothes, but thanks for the offer. Please call Ben and have him meet me at the Black Water town cop shop," Alex urgently said.

"Why Black Water? Their chief doesn't like you, nor Ben!"

"Cuz, they're the ones behind me right now. So that's where I'll be. Please text Tom, tell him no matter the evidence, I did not kill Alex."

"Alex, what evidence...." The phone went dead to the sound of cop sirens blaring in the background.

Chapter 7
December 2
Saturday Very Early Morning

Ben entered the room, "Alex, please don't talk." He looked solemnly at Chief Watson and the other officer in the interrogation room. "May I have a few minutes with my client?"

"Of course, counselor," the Chief smiled as he passed the lawyer. "This time even you can't save her."

While the men were leaving, Ben observed Alex. She looked up with a questioning glance, but waited until they were alone. "What's with the look? I am innocent, but that look is different, what are you thinking?"

Ben waved his hand in the air, "I know that you are innocent. But really, Alex, this is the third time."

"Unfortunately, what comes in twos, usually comes in threes, good things or bad." Alex looked at her friend and lawyer again, "There is something else though, right?"

"Yes, something totally different and totally out there, we can discuss it at a later time." Ben rubbed his jaw briefly, "No, wait, this is going to bug me. I have to ask two things and then we'll put it to the side for a while.

"Okay, go for it." She encouraged.

"Have you ever been to Ireland?"

"No, I have not," she wrinkled her brow wondering where this was going.

"I have known you for quite a long time, but there is still a lot that I don't know, do you have an identical twin sister?"

"No, I don't," she added firmly and then got excited, "Do I have a doppelganger? Do you think that is why someone thinks I killed Alexander?"

"No," Ben shook his head, "I just wanted to confirm something to myself. We need to get you out of this town and back to ours. Then, I will need to see where you stand. For now, let's review a few things."

"Numerous people have said that they witnessed you leave Alexander's house and then found him dead. No one saw anyone else leave the house."

Alex sat back perplexed, "When I left him, he was very much alive. Ben, I went out the front. Could anyone see the back?"

"That is something I will be checking into. There is no mention of the back."

"That must be how the killer left. Maybe the witnesses were confused or are lying?"

"I don't think the whole group would be lying, especially because I know that two of them are your friends."

Alex leaned in toward Ben, but briefly looked at the large two-way window behind him. "What? No way! Who?"

"A group of Christmas carolers are the witnesses, or at least some of them are. In that group are Maggie and Jake, they firmly believe that you are innocent, but stand firm in what they saw and when. They are both very upset and have asked me to question them as often as I find necessary. Maggie saw more than Jake, but his information is still damaging."

"Who else in the group witnessed anything?"

"The victim's son, AJ and one other, he double-checked his notes, one Ethel Coover." He observed Alex scrooch up her face at the mention of the name. "I take it, you don't like the woman?"

"That woman has lied most of her life. We haven't really ever gotten along. She probably insisted that I killed Alex. In high school and since, Ethel used to start things and get others involved. If someone in authority would call her on some action or other, she would always throw someone else 'under the bus.'"

"Does she have a particular issue with you?"

"Believe it or not, it's all over a dress."

"Excuse me?"

"A couple of years ago, I made a couple of Victorian outfits that Maggie and Jake use. Ethel loved them and asked if I would make her one. I politely declined, and she got royally pissed. There's a lot of work in those outfits and I thoroughly enjoyed making them for my friends. But, I don't like Ethel, so there's no way in heck I would ever take the time to make her a simple dish towel, let alone a complicated Victorian dress." Ben gave her an incredulous look. "Look, you're a lawyer, you've seen how catty and petty women can get."

He nodded, "Seen it, oh yeah. Understood it, not in the least," he shook his head.

Chapter 8
Saturday Morning

"Morning, everyone!" Alex chirped as Cat, Maggie, and Carsenia entered the bakery.

"You seem awfully cheery for everything that occurred last night," Cat commented.

"Yes, it's weird I know, but I know it will work out somehow. Besides, we have a lot to do and no time to be glum."

"Where's your car?" Carsenia inquired.

"That shmuck, Chief Watson, from one town over, impounded it until Monday, so my lawyer loaned me one. Ain't it cool?" She grinned.

"Yes, who would have thought that he would have a VW bus?"

"I know! He seems to have a real quirky side. Apparently, he has a couple of vehicles. He let me choose between two different ones. He also has a Mini Cooper, but refused to let me use that one," she laughed. "I think that's his favorite."

"Can he really hold your car until Monday?"

She shrugged, "Ben is not happy about it and is checking into it. But, the weekend does not allow for much efficiency. A lot of official places are closed."

"Why not just use the bakery van?" Cat asked.

"I suggested that, but Ben wants me to just use it for bakery business.''

"He means that he doesn't want you using your business vehicle for investigative purposes. It kind of sticks out."

"And a classic blue and white VW bus in mint shape doesn't?" Carsenia inquired.

Alex laughed, "I know. Ben said that he doesn't drive the VW bus much and it needed attention. He also warned me to be careful with it."

Maggie waited until Cat and Carsenia left the room and she was alone with Alex, "Alex, are you okay with me working today?"

"What do you mean?"

"Well, I feel guilty about being a witness against you. I was afraid that it would be too awkward today and the foreseeable future."

"You just try to get out of work today," Alex joked. "As I have said, the holiday fun is in full swing now and we need all hands on deck." Alex got serious and hugged her friend, "You are an old and dear friend. Thank you for asking. I know that this is hard on you and you are concerned, but don't be. You have to do your duty and be honest. Please let your husband know how I feel. I did not kill that man. But once again, I have to clear my name, and I will."

Maggie smiled, "Thank you Alex. I know in my heart that you didn't do it. If you have any questions, or need me to do anything, just ask."

"Rest assured, I will," Alex laughed as Maggie turned to hurry out front and help start the day.

"You and Mags okay?" Cat inquired as she returned to the back room and found Alex at her desk.

"Yeah, she was worried, but I assured her all was well between us." Alex looked at her best friend, "We have four wedding cakes to deliver today. Jo-Jo will be in shortly to help out front. That will allow Maggie to come back and help finish a few late cake orders that came in yesterday." She observed Cat looking at a small bouquet of flowers on her desk, "Something wrong, Cat?"

She pointed at the flowers, "That's another one of your mystery bouquets isn't it?"

Alex nodded, "Yes, it is. It was in the split of the Linden tree," she smiled. "I always get a few around the holidays, you know that."

"I do," Cat replied. "I'm also surprised that Tom hasn't found the sender yet."

"He's had a lot on his plate lately. He is definitely not happy that someone has been giving me small bouquets of flowers anonymously since my Aunt Gertrude died. I've told him that I think it's a harmless and loving action of someone who probably had known my aunt. It reminds me of my aunt, in a good way, and I think that may be one of the reasons that he hasn't pursued it in earnest."

"I don't believe in flower language, but I know that you do. I find that it can be a bit difficult to make sure that you truly understand the sender's message. Some flowers are very ambiguous. So, what does this one mean?"

Alex picked up the bouquet that consisted of a red rose, baby's breath, greens, and some heather and inhaled the beautiful scents. "I believe it stands for joy and happiness, but also to watch out for danger."

"See what I mean. This person is too 'spot on.' I'm pretty sure the joy and happiness is about the holidays, which is real nice and all, but the watch out for danger? That must be about Alex Sr.'s murder."

"Yes, I think it is. This is not a threat, it's a reminder to me to enjoy the holiday, but also to keep an eye out for danger. I like the message and I love the flowers. They're gorgeous!"

"Are you expecting Tom or any other police to show up today?" Cat asked. "We could ask him what he thinks."

"I believe we will hear something, just don't know what and when. Ben said to keep my normal pace up until I hear from him or the police."

"If I remember correctly, the cakes for delivery, are all over the place and will take most of the day," Cat mused. "There are lots of things starting today Christmas-wise, are you going anywhere special?"

"I'm not sure. Mavis' Christmas tunnel opens today and Mr. Nelson's drive-thru Christmas light display will be unveiled tonight."

"I heard Mavis really outdid herself this year with her tunnel. I promised Mike I'd wait until he got back home to check it out. Do you want to go to the Nelson farm together?"

"Sure, Tom is busier than ever, especially with this murder added to his plate and another burglary occurred last night too," Alex quieted. "I hope that I won't be a distraction tonight. Ben told me to lie low a bit, but I am innocent, and I don't want the killer to ruin my holiday fun."

Cat bumped her shoulder against her friend's, "If you are a distraction, we will leave and return another day."

Chapter 9
Saturday Morning

Lincoln George was escorted into the police station. "Welcome Mr. George," John said and made introductions of himself, Tom, and Joey. "Let's go into another room and discuss a few things."

"Is this an interrogation room?" Lincoln asked as he entered the room with John and Joey following. Tom went into a neighboring room.

"Yes, it is," John answered. "We need to know your whereabouts last night?"

"I am part of the Victorian Christmas caroler group that sang last night, and that is where I was."

"Before your gig last night, where were you?"

"At work, I am a car salesman."

"So you act all the time," Joey commented.

"What do you mean act?"

"To sell cars, you have to act a bit to convince people that the car they are looking at is the best thing on earth, and if they don't buy it, they are losing out on a great thing."

He thought it over a second, "I guess you're right detective."

"So, you are pretty good at lying," Joey commented.

The man looked confused with anger on the horizon, "Exactly what are you getting at?"

"Just inquiring. Now, at some point last night you disappeared from the caroling group. Where did you go?"

The man fidgeted a bit before answering, "Okay, I will tell you, but it's a bit sensitive. I started out with my caroling group and then quietly left. I had planned on rejoining the group at Alex's house, but ran a little late. When I showed up, the police were there, so I went home. I just don't want my wife to learn of it."

The man quieted. "I thought that you said that you were going to tell us your location last night," Joey pushed.

"I was having a dalliance with a lady," he simply replied. "A married lady," he added quietly.

"We need a name," John responded.

"Marsha Winters." As the man answered, John looked at the large mirror on the wall. Tom wrote the name down and disappeared to find Mrs. Winters.

"Does your wife know that you're 'doing' someone?" Joey asked.

The man looked up sharply, "I don't like your language, detective. No need to be coarse."

"You're a married man fooling around with a married woman, not your wife, and you're trying to lecture me on my language?" Joey chuckled.

"Do you know of anyone who disliked Alexander Gavree enough to kill him?" John inquired.

"Yes," he turned toward John and answered adamantly.

John waited a second, "Care to elaborate?"

"Yes," the man just looked at the detective.

"Would you please supply some names," John patiently requested.

"Our entire local whittler group."

"Names, please," he said with a bit of an edge.

"I wondered when I'd start getting on your nerves," he smiled.

"Excuse me, sir?" John inquired.

"I was just having some fun," Lincoln replied. "Our local group consists of five whittlers: me, Alexander, Leroy Winchester, Lizzy Barnstable, and Gray Sommerline.

"Why would your group not like Alexander?"

"Because he did as he damn well pleased!!" he growled. "He stole designs from the different members and claimed them as his own. He had no honor."

"That's it?" Joey asked.

"In our world, that's enough."

"Enough to kill for?"

He thought a bit, "Maybe, but not me. He burned me once. I did not allow it again. And I didn't have the time."

"Any idea who else in the group might have had the time?"

"Not really," he finished. He looked at his watch. "Is this all? I need to get to work."

"One more question, do you all ever borrow tools from each other?"

"What kind of tools?"

"Woodworking tools?"

"I certainly don't! I doubt the others would either, but I cannot speak for them."

The detectives looked at each other, "Thank you," John said. A uniformed officer appeared at the door, "This officer will walk you out. Thank you again for coming in and talking to us."

Lincoln got up from his chair and headed toward the door. As he was about to leave the room, Joey added, "Oh, by the way, your wife talked to us earlier. I believe that you may have underestimated her knowledge on a few things."

It took a second for the news to sink in, "Damn it!" he said as the door closed.

Joey shook his head, "And my language was wrong?" He jerked his thumb toward the door and chuckled, "See, always acting."

Chapter 10
Saturday Evening

Alex and Cat thoroughly enjoyed Mr. Nelson's drive-thru lights. A plethora of light displays were set on what felt to be about ten acres of land. "I loved the penguin and polar bear snowball fight," Alex chuckled as she and Cat parked the car and walked toward the barn. "Wow, it's a bit brisk tonight!"

Cat blew out some air and watched the vapors disappear, "Tis the season you know. My favorite was the 'Twelve Days of Christmas' montage he created," Cat replied as they entered the barn.

Mr. Nelson had a small petting zoo set up on one side of the barn with hot chocolate and munchies on the other side, with plenty of hand sanitizer in the middle. Hay bales were set all around for people to sit on. As the ladies walked along and checked out the petting zoo, they heard a boy ask Mr. Nelson if he had any fairies for him and his sister to see. "No, son, I don't. I have never seen a fairy."

"We did!" the little boy jumped up and down and his sister nodded her head with a big smile.

The farmer looked at the two children, "Where did you see this fairy?"

"In our backyard last night, I was flying my drone and saw one, so I recorded it," the little boy said proudly."

The farmer looked at the kid's parents and smiled. "I bet that was fun."

"Yes, it was," the little girl half shouted.

Mr. Nelson looked behind the family and realized the line was growing. "Well, I don't have any here. I'm sorry, but I do have some nice animals. Have you seen my reindeer yet?"

"No!" they squealed.

"Just outside that door," he pointed toward the back of the barn and off they ran pulling their parents behind them.

Alex and Cat shook their heads and laughed as they walked up to the hot chocolate bar. They had just ordered their drinks when a masculine voice rang out, "So you're already out and walking about? You kill my dad and show up here."

"I didn't kill your dad, AJ," Alex stated quietly. "The police will find out who really did. They are working really hard on your dad's case. Don't you have faith in your local police force? I do."

Alexander Jr. looked around at the growing crowd, "Of course, you do, one of the detectives is your fiancé. I personally saw you leave dad's house, and then minutes later found him dead. Do you really expect me to believe that you are innocent?"

"Yes, I do. My fiancé is a true blue policeman, if he thinks I am guilty, he will arrest me," Alex looked around them and got a bit uneasy. "I am truly sorry for your loss."

Cat spoke up quickly, "AJ, we are going to go. The police are handling the matter. It would be a pity to ruin Mr. and Mrs. Nelson's opening night."

They got into their car and closed the door. "I opened the door for that one didn't I?" Alex sighed.

51

"Yes," Cat concurred, "a huge barn door."

"When will I learn to keep my big mouth shut?" Alex looked over at Cat smirking. "Shut up, Cat!" She grinned.

"I didn't say a word," Cat grinned back.

Chapter 11
December 3
Sunday Morning

"Thanks for opening up early just for us, Mr. Turnbaugh," Alex said to the Christmas tree farm owner. "Your trees look fabulous this year."

"Thank you, Alex," the older man responded. "I hear that you got yourself into a jam again with the law."

"Well, I had some help on that."

"Yeah, I heard," he said. "You can thank your friend here for me opening up. I had no problem doing it, but she is the one who called and made the request."

"Yes, she told me and I have," Alex smiled. "I don't think we will be too long."

"Take your time, ladies. But if you want to have the place to yourself, you need to be done in two hours. Otherwise, the rest of the world is allowed entrance," he explained.

They nodded, grabbed some saws, and headed out to find the perfect Christmas trees. After an hour of walking through a gazillion trees, they stopped in front of two trees side by side that "spoke" to them. They walked around them three times. "Can you believe this? Two trees, this great, side by side?" Cat squealed.

"Let me check one more time," Alex requested. She leaned left and right, looked under each tree for clearance, stepped back and studied them a bit more, and tilted her head, "They are perfect, I think I like....."

"I get the left one," Cat yelled as she ran to it.

Alex laughed, "Well...okay then. I'm glad that I wanted the right one." She sauntered over to it and started to saw it down.

"Did you two find your perfect trees?" Mr. Turnbaugh inquired as he watched the ladies come out of the field with their finds.

"Yes, it was a lot of fun!" Alex laughed.

"Do you want to bale them before you take them to your car?"

"Yes, I prefer them that way," Alex said. It only took a few minutes to finish the job.

"We'll take a couple minutes to tie the trees on my car and then we'll be in to pay," Cat said.

"Sounds good."

"Wow! You have made some nice improvements!" Cat said as she looked around his small building where people paid for trees and could shop and get some tree supplies and decorations. "I am loving the train set! It's fantastic!"

"Thank you very much. I am glad that you are pleased. Someone blessed me with it last Christmas."

"Come again?" Cat inquired.

"I found a wrapped gift on my porch last Christmas. Apparently someone knew I loved trains. It was my first Christmas without my Mable and I was feeling a bit low. Along with the train came two gift cards, one for the hobby shop and one for the hardware store. A note suggested that if I found idle time, I could design a fun train setup. It has really helped."

Chapter 12
Sunday Late Morning

Alex and Cat stopped at Cat's house and dropped off her tree first. "Do you want help getting it set up in your house?"

"No, I think I'm good."

Cat drove down to Alex's house next. They removed Alex's tree from the roof of the car, "I believe that this tree is a bit bigger and heavier than mine. Do you want help getting it into your house?"

"No, I'm good. I do feel a bit off this year. Normally, we tie the trees to my car. I'm glad that you could get them, Ben would have flipped if we used his vehicle to get these."

"It was fun," Cat said. "I can do it next year too, if you happen to find your car impounded again." She suggested and laughed.

"I certainly hope not," Alex replied. "Well, thanks again. Have fun decorating today and I will catch you tomorrow at the shop."

"Back at ya! Tom helping?"

"If he can get away for a short time."

Alex had just taken her tree into her house when Tom showed up. "Hey, great! How long can you stay?" She took one look at his face, "Uh oh, what's wrong?"

"Detectives John and Joey will be here shortly to take you in. I offered to do it, but the chief wants Joey to take a bigger role in this investigation and me a smaller role. His chief has agreed of course. Let's get this tree in water quick and set it up." He gave her a quick intense hug.

"Will I be coming home tonight?" Her voice trembled a tad. He gave her a longer hug.

"Yes, I believe so. I am really sorry that I have been so busy at work, that I barely have time to say hi and bye on the phone. I will make sure Ben meets you there. Please don't say anything, but later you and I need to talk." She nodded quietly.

No sooner had they set the tree, when her humongous red point Himalayan cat, Micky, took up his holiday job of guarding it, by lying under it, then the doorbell rang.

Chapter 13
Sunday Evening

Alex answered the door with a big smile. "It's good to see you! She bent down and hugged Con, a mix of Border Collie and Australian Shepard, and petted the top of his head. She laughed as his whole body jiggled as he wagged his stubby backend. "It's good to see you too, but you're looking a wee bit tired, sorry to say," she kissed and hugged Tom and waved them into her abode. Jake squawked as they entered the living room.

"You handled yourself well at the station house earlier," Tom complimented.

"That was more Ben than me."

"Any more said or said differently, you might still be there," he caught her eye briefly. "But, I fear, the captain believes you are guilty. He has a version of a story of your guilt that follows all the evidence, so far. To put it bluntly, it's pretty good."

"So, who is this 'Joey' guy?" Alex asked. "I heard you mention him a number of times."

"His name is Joseph Vecchio. He transferred down from New York City sometime back to Black Water. They had an opening for a detective and he wanted a change from the city. One might underestimate him at first glance as a pleasant stocky guy, which would come in handy at work."

"But what do you really think?"

Tom chuckled, "I think he's pretty sharp and could be a bulldog pugilist to be reckoned with, especially if you piss him off. I hear New York was not happy to lose him."

"I'm not sure I want him against me. So after the captain gave his rendition of my guilt, do John and this Joseph agree?"

"Not so much. Joey has doubt, but rest assured, John and I know you are innocent of this particular crime. With us working on the burglary cases, and this murder, and a few other things, I'm afraid each is not getting our best."

"So, what about the here and now?" Alex inquired.

"I'm taking a much needed break to see my true love," Tom exclaimed. "I needed to get away and come back with eyes anew. So I decided to bring Con with me and see if your Christmas tree needed any help. And yes it does, I see that it is still naked," he smiled.

"I was about to put on a Christmas movie and start decorating. Want to help with the lights?"

"Of course, but first, I brought you something for your tree," he handed her a gift bag with tissue paper sticking out of the top.

She smiled, opened up the bag, and pulled out a box, "A train?" She glanced toward her cat, "I hate to tell you this, I love trains, but Micky doesn't. He tackles them. The area under the tree is his."

Tom grinned, "I know." He glanced at Micky and chuckled, "This train doesn't go under the tree, but in it."

"Say what?" She flipped the box over and studied the picture. "This is so cool!"

"Do you want me to put it in? It goes in where your tree is approximately 3 foot across or less. It has to be installed before all other decorations."

"Sure. Do you need help?"

"Not really, but maybe something to drink?"

"No problem, I will get us some hot cocoa, and Micky and Con a treat," she said as she left the room.

"Sorry, I took so long," Alex said on her return. "Wow, you have the train installed already. It must be easier than it looks."

"Not really, give me a minute and I will set the train on the track," he chuckled, "I practiced on mine recently. I swore quite a bit before I got it set right," he smiled. Alex gave the animals their treats as Tom tasted the cocoa.

Jake screeched. "Okay, you're right," Alex answered.

"What?" Tom inquired.

"Jakey is jealous. Everyone got something, but him," she reached into a side cabinet and got her Nanday Conure a treat.

"Good cocoa, Alex, but the mugs are a bit odd, even for Christmas," Tom commented.

"Thank you for the cocoa compliment. It is my aunt's recipe. As for the mugs, they were a gift. What? You don't like drinking from Santa's pants?" She laughed and watched as he pressed the top of the engine's smokestack. It started to toot and move around the tree. "Do you want to sit for a bit? You do look tired."

"Sure. Just for a short time, then I need to ask you a few questions."

"Okay," they snuggled on the couch for a few minutes and Alex started the movie.

Tom stirred on the couch and watched Alex finish decorating her tree, "Guess I fell asleep for a bit. Sorry, I truly meant to help."

Alex laughed and rejoined him on the couch, "You needed your rest. I enjoy decorating the tree and quite used to doing it myself. You helped by adding a train this year, next year, who knows."

He watched the television briefly, "I believe I was asleep a bit longer than I thought. This is a different movie. I fell asleep to 'The Year Without a Santa Claus,' and this is not that."

She chuckled, "No, it is not. This is the third one." As he quickly checked his watch, she added, "'Twas the Night Before Christmas' was the second one, but it's not a long one. This is 'Santa Claus is Coming to Town'."

Alex and Tom watched the ending together, "Hey, do you want to do that?"

"Do what?" Alex looked at Tom and back to the TV.

He pointed to the TV, "That." He smiled at her, "Let's get married on Christmas Eve."

"This Christmas Eve?"

"Sure. Why not? If Santa Claus can do it, why not us?" His eyes sparkled as he looked at her.

She examined his face a few seconds, "You're totally serious, aren't you."

"Yes, I am," he smiled expectantly. "He picked the perfect night for the perfect reason."

"There are burglaries happening in three different towns, most of the police force has the flu, a murder took place that I stand accused of doing, the normal Christmas lunacy is currently happening, and now you want us to get married in like twenty-one days?"

He nodded and continued to smile, "Sure! Are ya game?"

"You're nuts," she laughed, "but, yes, let's do it. You do know that I have been accused a lot of times of trying to put 10,000 pounds in a 5,000 pound bucket. I'm always accused of trying to do too much."

"Want to try for 20,000 pounds in that same bucket?"

She laughed, kissed, and hugged her man, "sure, why not?"

"Then we need to solve this murder and clear your name," he declared.

"Easier said than done, I 'm afraid."

"This is probably the last time for a while that I can see you for an extended time. There was another burglary last night in the town of Cold Water. The boss is getting antsy and demanding results. Earlier today at the station house, you gave what I believe was a truncated version of the actual events of the night in question. I need you to walk me through that night from the time of your arrival to the time of your departure from whittler Alex's house. We need to dissect your visit and see if there are other clues to point in the direction of the murderer."

She studied him a moment, "Ben, would shoot me for doing this."

Tom looked into Alex's eyes, "Honey, because of our recent decision, I will be your husband in twenty-one days, you have to trust me."

"No problem, I do trust you, but you are a cop, and have certain responsibilities. But, let's do this." She took a deep breath, nodded her head, and began, "I knocked on his front door, he knew that I was coming and apparently didn't lock the door. He told me to enter."

"There was an 'A.A.' scheduled in his desk calendar to meet him that night. It was probably you."

"Not necessarily, I am just one possibility. There are others with my initials."

"Agreed. Next, there was a check from you on the premises. Did you pay him for something?"

"Yes."

"What?"

She was confused, "What what?"

"What was the check for?"

"That's irrelevant, so I'm not going to tell you."

"Any small thing could provide us a clue."

"This won't, so please move on."

"Ok, for now," he looked at her a bit unhappily, "please continue your run-through."

"He made a pass at me, which highly surprised me, because he's never done that before. I walked away and he pushed me against a bookshelf which ripped my shirt and apparently cut me a wee bit. I stomped on his foot and slapped him, which drew blood on his face."

"How would a slap do that?"

Alex lifted her left hand and turned it palm-side up. When I originally walked away from him, I took the time to turn my diamond engagement ring around to my palm. When I slapped him, my diamond cut him. I learned that in an old self-defense course I took. So, see, even when you were not there, you helped protect me."

Tom smiled, "I like it. That explains your blood and some thread that matched your one shirt at the scene of the murder, as well as the scratch on his face."

She nodded, "He seemed 'off' somehow, I asked if someone else was in the house and accused him of being drunk."

He held up his hand to stop her, "Why ask him about someone else?"

"I heard a noise from somewhere, he said it was his dog, but that didn't sound right. And speaking of his dog, why didn't I see him, and why didn't he protect Alex when he was attacked?"

"Very good questions, no one mentioned anything about his dog. I will have to check into that. Why accuse him of being drunk?"

"He was acting strange. He tripped when he walked. I had looked around and saw two bottles and one glass on the coffee table. The bottles were different shapes. One looked a lot like a wine bottle, but it was thinner than most wine bottles I have seen. There was something red in the bottom of it. I don't know what the other bottle was. It had an unique shape and looked like red wax melting down from the top. I am not real familiar with the different names for drinking glasses. All I can tell you is that the glass was not a wine glass."

"Alex, we only found one bottle. And it was not a wine bottle," Tom said.

"Well then, there was someone else in the house. For whatever reason, that person took the wine bottle," Alex stated. "Did the bottle you did find have some kind of red top?"

He nodded, "Yes, it did. It was a Maker's Mark bottle."

"Does one drink it with wine?"

"It doesn't seem like they would go well together, but since I do not drink alcohol," he admitted, "I will have to check with the guys as to if they can be companion drinks."

"Did you find a glass?"

"Yes, there was one on the floor, lying on its side."

"Alex told me to take what he had worked on for me and to get out and that is what I did," she stopped and thought for a moment.

"Did you remember something new?"

"Yes, when I picked up my boxes, I remember hearing something fall. I didn't look at what, because I just wanted to get out of there."

"There was a basket of something on the floor by the door," he carefully commented and observed.

She snapped her fingers, "That's it! I must have knocked over his basket of ornaments. Every year he hands the carolers an ornament that he's made. They were on the table with the box I grabbed. Then, I hurried from the house to the street. I looked briefly at the approaching carolers and then took off. And that is all that happened, when I left Alex, he was very mad at me, but very much alive."

Tom reviewed the events in his mind, "so we need to check if the guys found anything upstairs or elsewhere to indicate who else might have been there, and to see if there was any indication of a wine bottle or a wine glass lying around." At her questioning glance, he explained, "Two bottles might indicate two people, therefore two glasses. You only seeing one glass, doesn't mean that there weren't two." Alex nodded her understanding. "Where did you go between Alexander's house and when the Black Water police found you?"

"I stopped at Leroy Winchester's, Gray Sommerline's, and finished at Sadie Sollenberger's."

"Why make those stops?"

"I was running a few errands. I needed a detailed item made of wood in a relatively short time frame. Alex Sr., Leroy, and Gray each agreed to help make part of the item. I stopped at each place to pick up what they made. Then I went to Sadie's to drop everything off. She's painting everything."

"Did you stay long at any one place?"

Alex thought a moment, "No, not really. I made polite small talk with the men. I know each person, but not real well. I'd look around and mention something or other and we'd shoot the breeze briefly. I thanked them, they did really great work! I stayed at Sadie's a bit longer, but I do know her. She's the one who pointed out that my shirt had a hole."

"Did you go anywhere else or make any other stops?"

She hesitated, "Well, when I first reached Black Water, I drove around some to chill after my confrontation with Alexander. I was very mad at him and to be honest, a bit scared. I was not prepared for the way he treated me. But again, I didn't take too long doing that, because time was a bit short."

"Do you remember seeing anyone in particular or did anything stick out that you remember?"

"No, why does that matter? I was just driving around," she answered a bit irritated.

"I don't know just yet. Maybe you saw something that could help in some small manner. Time will tell just how important everything is."

Alex looked at her watch, "This has been my last full day off of work, until after Christmas. It is usually more mundane than this day has proven to be. I hate to repeat myself, but you do look tired. Why don't you and Con use the spare room for the night and I can take him home for you in the morning."

Tom gave Alex a hug, grabbed her butt lightly, and kissed her, "Sounds good. I will see you sometime tomorrow. Please try to lay low, so to speak, for a bit." After he took a few steps toward the guest room, he turned back to Alex, "you know, in about twenty one days, I won't be heading toward the guest room anymore. I am definitely looking forward to that," he grinned lasciviously and laughed as she turned a shade of red.

Chapter 14
December 4
Monday Morning

Alex bounded into the bakery about an hour later than planned, but her staff had everything running smoothly. She checked her watch, she still had an hour to review the cake orders for this weekend before a meeting with a bride. As Alex started her normal Monday check of the week's activities, Cat asked with a grin, "Any particular reason that you are late this morning?"

Alex looked at her friend and shook her head, "I can tell that you already know that Tom stayed over. Do you wait to see each morning, or do you get a nudge from a neighbor who's too nosey for his or her own good? You need to get a life, Cat."

"It would be too easy if I come right out and tell you. It's more fun this way. And I do have a life, thank you very much!"

"Whatever you say," she smiled. "Tom got a call from the mayor this morning, so he had to get back to work ASAP."

"Why the mayor?"

"There was another burglary last night, and this time the mayor was the victim. His wife is extremely upset at her husband, so he shared his irritation with Tom. Apparently, his chief is too sick to take the phone, but someone at the station house said that Tom was in charge of the burglary cases. That officer did not have the guts not to give the mayor Tom's personal cellphone number. He had his dog with him at my place, so I ran Con home. He was not happy to see me go."

"I forget, why does a police officer have a dog named 'Con'?"

"It's short for *Conagher*, one of Tom's favorite westerns," Alex replied.

"How's Con handling Tom's long hours?"

"Okay, I guess. Tom's one older neighbor suggested they kind of share Con. Tom keeps ownership, but Mr. Lombarty gets to enjoy animal companionship without the expense. Tom has a doggy door for Con to use. He can either run out to his own yard or use another doggy door in the fence to reach Mr. Lombarty. It seems to be working out pretty well for all concerned."

"Sounds like a good plan," Cat stated as she started to review the cake calendar, "Is that lady for the sixteenth finally fitting us in to finish her cake order?"

"Yes, she is. She'll be here shortly. Her wedding is in twelve days, I do hope that she's not going to ask for anything unrealistic."

The intercom sounded from her office, "Alex, your bride is here."

"I'll be right out, Maggie," she answered.

Chapter 15
Monday Morning

Alex briskly walked into the backroom and straight to her office. Cat put down her decorating bags and wandered over to Alex and found her searching their supplier's website, "That was a relatively quick visit and a quicker return. What's up?"

"The bride wants a simple set-up and a pretty simple decoration, except for the one item that I don't like when I make it. So I need to see if I can order any pre-made ones."

"Pinecones? Now?!" Cat asked. "That's a pain in the tush. While you check the computer, let me look in our supplies and see if we have any at all. I believe we were trying to use up the ones we had. We would have saved them if this woman would have come in sooner, like she planned," Cat replied irritated.

"Cat," Alex leaned out of her office and called out, "Did you find any?"

"Sorry, no," and she returned to decorating.

Half an hour later, Alex had just finished re-hanging the cake calendar when Cat returned to the office, "I ordered some pinecones. They promised them to me by Friday." Cat raised her eyebrows in surprise. "Seems like they had one box left. So I will think positive, but, come up with a back-up plan just in case."

Cat nodded and glanced at the calendar and did a double-take, "What's with the green pine trees on the twenty-fourth of this month?"

"I was putting the expected shipment on the calendar and accidentally dropped a green pen on the calendar. The marks were driving me nuts, so I turned them into trees. I like them," she turned toward her friend, "You don't?"

"They're alright, just different than normal."

Maggie entered the room smiling "You two should come out front and check out the Christmas tree," and then turned around and promptly left.

Alex and Cat approached the tree cautiously. "What did you do?" Cat asked.

"Not me," Maggie laughed.

"Nor I," Carsenia chimed in.

"Well, I'll be," Alex chuckled, "Thaddy has a friend."

Cat looked at the ladies, "How'd that happen?"

"One of our customers brought in her granddaughter, Ruby. Apparently, Ruby heard at Mr. Nelson's farm that fairies are living somewhere in town. She saw a beautiful fairy ornament at the card shop and asked her grandma to buy it. She wanted to give it to someone who was lonely. The grandma thought it was a hoot when she found out who the lonely 'person' was. Her granddaughter is young and she wants to encourage her thinking of others, so she agreed to stop by here and help the poor lonely soul. So now Thaddy has a friend," she smiled.

"Oh, brother," Cat shook her head.

Alex smiled, "I like it. Next time Ruby is in, let me know. I'll give her a thank-you gift." Cat looked wonderingly at Alex. "What, Cat? The girl was thinking of others, that is commendable."

"It's an ornament, Alex, an ornament!"

"And I like it," Alex laughed. "Kids can be interesting, Cat. Now, let's get in the back, we have gingerbread houses to bake for this Saturday. Don't forget you promised to help me get my car back and return my current ride to Ben."

Chapter 16
December 5
Tuesday Early Evening

"I think that this was our first normal day of this harried season," Alex told Cat and Maggie as she locked the door.

"I rather enjoyed it," Maggie chuckled. "Very busy, but just holiday business."

"Well, I'm glad that you two reveled in those brief joyous feelings for a moment or two, because tomorrow is Wednesday," Cat said knowingly.

Alex and Maggie looked thoughtfully at each other. "Comic day," Alex and Maggie said simultaneously, and they all laughed.

Chapter 17
Tuesday Early Evening

"Tommy, I don't think that you should be flying your drone again!" His sister, Twyla, whispered.

"Why not? It's fun! Don't you want to see the fairies again?" Tommy asked.

"Of course, but it's starting to snow. If rain can hurt your drone, can snow?"

His face scrunched up as he thought about it, "I don't know. It was okay the other night when it was snowing. Will you go ask mommy?"

Twyla hurried back into their upstairs room, "Mommy's doesn't know much about drones and daddy's at work. She said to bring it back inside for the night and to ask daddy tomorrow."

"Okay," he reluctantly agreed. "I didn't see any lights out there anyway, but I will check my new recording, just in case." The boy concentrated on getting the drone back inside and never noticed the man in the shadows watching him. He waited until the kids shut the window and turned out the lights before slipping away.

Chapter 18
Tuesday Evening

Tom came through the bakery shop's door with a pizza and some garlic breadsticks. "Dinner's here if you're interested."

"Wow! This is a nice surprise," Alex replied. "What's the occasion?"

Tom laughed, "I wanted to see you babe!" He put the pizza on the table and gave her a hug and kiss.

She laughed as she got paper plates and drinks, "And?"

He smiled in return, "This is a bribe and I need some information or input?"

"Okay, I accept your bribe. How can I help?"

"I have been mulling over these burglaries. We have a number of theories we're sorting through, but I thought of another and wanted to hear your thoughts. Every now and then, I hear about somebody or something called 'The Dove.' It's more like a whisper. Whenever I try to inquire, I'm told it's basically a do-gooder and that's it. Do you know anything about it?" Tom inquired.

"Of course, 'The Dove' has been around for some sixty years, give or take. It is a benevolent thing that only shows around Christmas time. You hear from time to time how a family received money, presents for the kids, or a needed item from 'The Dove.' Only a few people receive something each year. It's not a lavish amount, but it helps. Is this the information that you are looking for?"

"Somewhat. Do you think this 'Dove' could be involved in these burglaries?"

"No, definitely not. These burglaries are happening this year. As I said, 'The Dove' has been helping for about sixty years."

"Maybe it's running low on money."

"Then why not just stop? 'The Dove' is good and helps, like churches do at this time of year. These burglaries are the opposite."

"You said that this 'Dove' only shows up around Christmas, and it is that. The burglaries are happening at homes of the affluent. Maybe it sees itself as a modern day 'Robin Hood.'"

"I understand what you're saying, but I believe that you are totally off base. "The Dove" is very low key. If it enjoyed the limelight, I would say that you might have a possibility. I suggest following your other ideas and forgetting about 'The Dove,'" Alex replied. "This pizza is hitting the spot. Thank you for bringing it tonight," she purred.

Chapter 19
Tuesday Night

Penny Winchester, a "holiday widow" due to her artisan husband's need to work, was about to enter her shower when she heard some glass break and froze. She heard some more glass hit the ground and guessed it was her back door. She reached over and turned on her radio and glanced around her bathroom. What a night to leave her robe in her room. She quietly locked the door to the room and glanced at the window. She grabbed her bath towel, tightly wrapped it around her body and slipped into her bath slippers. She raised the window pane, leaned out to see if anyone was watching while the cold wind instantly caused coarse goose bumps up and down her body. After climbing onto the toilet, she crawled out the window, and slowly lowered the pane down. She looked around at her neighbors' houses as she re-adjusted her towel. "Not too many lights on," she mumbled to herself.

Penny scurried over two houses after remembering her next door neighbor was gone for three days. She pounded on the door to no avail and kept moving on to other houses trying to remember which neighbors said they were leaving to visit family and who stated they were not. Half-frozen and frightened out of her wits, she looked behind her to see if she was being followed. She looked forward and saw a stone house with lights ablaze. She ran up the stairs and pounded hard. A tallish stocky man opened the door, his eyes widened a bit at her appearance, and asked her what was going on. She hurriedly explained as she shivered and begged to be let in. "Of course, get in here," he quickly looked around outside as he shut the door. "Go over to the fireplace and I will get you a robe to put on."

The man quickly went to his spare bedroom to get a robe and reached for his cell phone. The phone was picked up after one ring, "Alex! I need your help!"

"Sure! What can I do?"

"Get over to my house immediately. Is Tom there by chance?"

"Yes, by dumb luck."

"Bring him too!"

"Ben, what's wrong?"

"I have a naked woman in a towel in my house and I need your help!"

Alex started laughing, "Excuse me?!" She couldn't remember her lawyer friend ever sounding this distraught.

"You heard me." He briefly clued her in, "I don't like it," he replied sternly. "Stop laughing, this is NOT funny. You owe me, now please get your butt over here, pronto!"

"We are on our way."

"Hurry! Jackie will be here shortly and I don't need a naked woman here with me ....alone."

Chapter 20
Tuesday Night

Not fifteen minutes later, Alex and Tom parked in front of Ben's house. They got out of the car and just as they entered his walkway, Jackie came busting out the front door. She flew right past them. "Jackie!" Alex turned and shouted. "Wait up!" Since Jackie did not even slow her pace, Alex started after her and shouted again, "Jackie, stop!"

The woman spun quickly, "Why?! He's got a naked lady in there!"

"We know," Alex simply said. "I believe that she's in a robe now."

Jackie stopped and stared, "How would you know?"

"He called us. He apparently answered his door and she was there shivering. I guess he didn't want her to freeze to death on his front porch. But once in his house, he didn't want what just happened to happen."

"No, I did not, on both counts." The ladies turned to see Ben standing on his porch at the top of the stairs.

Alex walked to Jackie and put an arm around her, "Come on girl. Let's go check out this naked lady issue." And Jackie nodded and laughed with her.

Chapter 21
Tuesday Night

The group entered to see a woman standing in front of the fireplace dressed in a robe, a towel around her head, slippers on her feet, and a glass of wine in her hand.

"Penny?" Alex was surprised at the woman's identity. "What is going on?" Alex inquired. Alex made introductions around so that everyone knew everyone.

Penny told the group everything that had recently taken place. She looked at Jackie, "I am sorry to cause so much trouble for you and Ben. I did try at a few other places. No one seemed to be home. I am glad that Ben let me in. I was getting quite cold."

"That's alright. I totally understand now. Sorry, I got so upset."

Penny laughed wholeheartedly, "No, don't be sorry. I would have been plenty upset myself, if our places had been reversed."

"I think it's time to wrap this up here," Tom said. "Penny, let's get you home and see what's going on at your house."

Ben and Jackie walked their guests to the front door, "Penny, please keep the robe." She started to object. "This is one that I keep for guests to use, and I have others."

Penny smiled and hugged it to herself when she stepped out of the house. She turned, "Thank you again, Ben. It was fantastic of you to help me in my time of need. I wish you both a great night."

Chapter 22
Tuesday Night

Penny and Alex waited in Tom's car while he entered her house and checked it out. "Penny, do you have any idea who this may have been?"

"Maybe those burglars that I keep hearing about?" she guessed.

"No," Alex shook her head, "they have been real careful. No one has been home when they attack. This doesn't feel right for that." She watched the woman getting a bit antsy, "There's something else, isn't there?" She thought over the past half hour. "You were the one upstairs at Alex Sr.'s house, weren't you?"

"Why would you think that?" Penny asked scared.

"Something to do with wine," Alex answered. When the woman looked confused, Alex continued, "Tom will be out here soon, please just answer me."

"Yes, I was there. I got plenty pissed when he made that pass at you."

"How did you know about that?"

"Sound travels weird in that house."

"Was he acting odd before I got there?"

"What do you consider odd?"

"Like drunk or something?"

"No, not that I remember. We had just gotten something to drink, when we heard you pull up. I scurried upstairs quick so that you would not see me."

"Wait a minute," Alex thought briefly, "what happened after I left?"

"What do you mean? I left after you did."

"Was Alex alive or dead when you left?"

Penny got real uncomfortable and wiggled around quite a bit.

Alex glanced toward the house, "Penny, please answer the question?"

"He was dead. I decided to wait a few minutes after you left, for me to leave too. But, then someone else entered the house and had a major discussion with Alex."

"A discussion or an argument?"

Penny shrugged her shoulders, "There were some raised voices, some other noises, and then silence. I started to freak out because it got way too quiet."

Alex thought a second or two, "If I heard you, then the killer might have also."

"But, I don't know how Alex died, nor who killed him. So, why go after me?" Penny whined.

"Because the person doesn't know what you do or don't know. Think a minute. Do you remember anything that could help identify this person--- a smell, noise, sound of any kind."

She thought a second, "nothing really, just that the person used the secret passage, but nothing else comes to mind."

"Secret passage?" Alex asked, she was intrigued and had no patience at this point.

"Yes. There are actually two depending how you look at it. There is one from the outside into his work area, but it also connects to one that comes up to the second level."

"How could you tell someone used the lower part?"

"Because, I felt the wind and heard the bump," she simply answered.

"Come again?" Alex inquired. "Felt what wind, heard what bump?"

The woman smiled, "When one shuts the outer door below, you can feel a draft and sometimes hear a 'bump-like' noise. The system is not sealed is what I was told."

"Who all knows about these secret passages?"

She shrugged again, "I really don't know, he didn't exactly advertise it.

"How do you know about these passages?"

She ducked her head, "well, I am... err... was kind of seeing Alex. His dog, Carver, did not like me, so he would put him in another room. He had to use the passage to access that room."

"I didn't hear Carver bark or anything."

"You wouldn't, Alex didn't like hearing him bark, so he sound-proofed the room."

Alexandra looked at Penny for a minute, "Aren't you married?"

"Yeah, I am, to Leroy. But, he barely gives me a minute of his time, so I found someone who did when I wanted attention."

"Does Leroy know?"

"I don't think so. I would only see Alex every now and then, I believe I have been pretty good at keeping it a secret. Leroy really doesn't pay much attention to me, especially at Christmas time."

"Till now, maybe," Alex tipped her head toward Ben's house.

"Yeah, till now."

"Where is Leroy now?"

"He had a two day trip." Headlights shined behind Tom's vehicle, before changing direction into the house's driveway. Alex and Penny turned to look, "He's here now." She turned to Alex, "As far as I am concerned, this was a burglary or an attempted burglary. If you say anything about Alexander to my husband, I will deny this whole conversation. I will sue you for slander and own your bakery. Do you understand?"

Alex was momentarily taken aback, "Yes, I hear you. First, two quick questions. Were you drinking wine at Alex's house?"

Penny nodded her head as she looked toward her husband's car again.

"Did you take the wine bottle with you?"

"No, I took my wine glass, but not the bottle." Penny gave her one last look, and opened the car door to run to her husband as Tom walked out their front door. He stopped over at the couple briefly and then returned to the car. He looked at Alex, "What's up?"

"I don't understand," she absently muttered.

"You look like you're mulling something over," he stated as he pulled away from the curb and headed toward Alex's home.

"Did you find anything?"

"Looks like maybe a burglary. They will have to check around and see if anything is missing. Mr. Winchester said that he would look first, and then decide if it was worth calling the police or not. I told Penny's husband that a window of their back door was broken. I offered to help, but he turned me down." He looked over at Alex briefly, "And I'm quite thankful that he did. There's something off with that woman."

"Do you think that maybe she could have been upstairs at Alex Sr.'s?"

"Do you have any proof?"

"Not at this time, but she....."

Tom turned to face Alex, "Be careful. You are not the police, we have guidelines that we try to follow. You accuse this woman of something, she could yell slander and go after you," Tom warned. He was about to pull into Alex's driveway, when she suddenly gasped. "What's wrong?"

Alex turned toward Tom and put her hand on his arm, "I think we need to go to Alexander's house."

"Why? I'm not sure that's a good idea."

"We have to. I believe Carver's in that house. I will explain on the way."

85

Chapter 23
December 6
Wednesday Morning

Maggie came in Alex's door waving the local paper in her hand. "Did you see today's comic?"

"Yes, I did," Alex said. "Apparently, someone is stealing Christmas gifts being delivered to homes when people are away."

"I believe that is a yearly threat, is it not?" Cat asked as she entered the room.

"Yes, but now there is a drawing and I believe I know who this porch pirate is," Maggie stated.

"Porch pirate? I like that term," Cat replied and Alex nodded in agreement. "But are you sure about his identity? There are a number of guys that look like that drawing," Cat replied and again Alex nodded in agreement.

"Unfortunately, today is not going to be a good day for some of those men," Alex said.

"Do you all remember when these comics started? Some were just funny, some gave helpful hints, and then they changed," Maggie shook her head.

"Yeah, but even when they first changed, they encouraged people to right some wrongs or to try to make better choices. The people in the comics were general, now if one studies the pictures close enough, one can figure out a real message about real people," Cat stated.

"Too bad some people see what they want to, or add two and two and get ten," Alex regrettably.

"It might make your class tonight on last minute Christmas treats a bit more entertaining," Cat suggested.

"I will keep it on track," Alex assured her. "I added a few more ideas and there won't be much time available for gossiping." Alex raised her right index finger, "And that reminds me to find a few more items for tonight's class."

"There are twenty-four people signed up," Maggie said. She looked around the back room, "With all our extra Christmas orders and preparations, will it be tight back here?"

"It will be fine. There will be some cancellations, there always are," Alex stated. "But, if any more people call in, tell them we are full." Maggie nodded. "By the way, it's the first Wednesday of December!" Alex said with a big smile.

"You seem really chipper," Maggie observed. She smiled when she saw Cat shake her head and she looked toward the wall calendar in Alex's office. "It's Welsh cookie day!"

"Yes, it is!" Alex laughed. "And I am ready! I wait all year for these!"

"Mrs. J made you some not too long ago," Cat reminded her friend.

"Yes," Alex nodded, "too true. But that was a bonus time for this year."

Maggie was confused briefly, "Oh, that's right. When you all went to Mr. and Mrs. J's campground this summer to make their daughter, Darby's, wedding cake."

Alex nodded gleefully. "Come on, Cat. Just because you don't really like them is no reason to be glum. You're making Todede's Friday." Cat's face lit up with that remark and Alex and Maggie laughed. "And they are all yours to make." As the women turned to start their various tasks, Alex drew their attention back, "I forgot to fill you in on Carver."

"Alexander Gavree's dog?"

Alex told them how she and Tom found Carver in his hidden room. "Was he there since Friday?" Maggie asked aghast.

Alec nodded her head, "He was very hungry and thirsty, but otherwise okay."

"That room must have smelled pretty bad," Cat commented and wrinkled her nose.

"After four and a half days, actually, it wasn't as bad as you might think," Alex answered. "Apparently, he spared no expense. There were pee pads and an air system, but it was still on the potent side."

"So where's Carver? Did you take him?" Maggie asked.

Alex chuckled, "No, showing himself to be a typical Chow Chow, Carver likes me, but he definitely did not take to Tom. I called Cassie to help out for the night. She brought her van and took him to the pet store for the night. This morning, Cassie was going to take him to her vet."

"Then what? If I remember correctly, Alex Jr. doesn't particularly care for the dog," Maggie said.

"I believe it's mutual," Cat smirked.

Alex shrugged, "I don't rightly know. I'll ask Tom later." The ladies separated to handle their duties.

Chapter 24
Wednesday Late Morning

A couple hours later, Maggie and Alex were in the middle room of the store re-stocking shelves. "Maggie, I believe that you are out of sorts today." Alex observed.

"What exactly are you saying, Alex?"

"It's Christmas, Mags. Everyone overdoes it at this time of the year. In fact, Christmas can be murderous. You have three kids, family activities, work here, and aren't you helping out with your church's Christmas program? You have a full plate and it can be distracting."

"I'm good Alex. Really I am."

"Then, if I may ask, why did you re-stock milk chocolate for dark and vice versa? I mean, the shades are close, so I can see it. But, I am not exactly sure how to explain your colored chocolate refills." She chuckled as she waved her arm toward the candy shelves with the different colors all mixed up.

Maggie's eyes grew big as she tuned into her work results. "Oh, boy, I think you might be right." She smiled, "I'm sorry, I'll have it fixed shortly."

"No, you won't. I'll help as you tell me what has you at sixes and sevens."

"Basically, it's the church Christmas program right now. I'm making all the costumes."

"Ok, but you have been working on that for some time. I thought everything was on schedule."

"And it was. But, a group of people from another church are coming to ours for a while and bringing all their children. That's like fifteen more kids. I'm trying to figure out how to get all the kids dressed."

"Why are they coming to your church?"

"Because their pastor has been getting weirder and weirder," she responded. "The latest things he's insisted on are no jewelry with crosses, and contribute or tithe only in cash. People have stayed as long as they can, but things are getting worse, not better."

"I believe I know which church you're referring to. That's unfortunate, and I fear something unsavory is taking place. I hope someone is contacting the higher-ups."

"I heard that they are, but nothing seems to be changing. People are wondering if it's falling on deaf ears," Maggie commented.

Alex looked at Maggie, "Your children's practice starts at seven, am I right?" Maggie nodded. "Can you swing by my place before practice, say around five thirty? I will take a quick run to my house before returning for the class tonight. I believe that I might be able to help a wee bit. But, don't get your hopes up."

At Alex's insistence, Maggie left a couple hours early. She stopped in at Alex's at the pre-arranged time later that day, "Thanks for leaving the shop to help me out."

"Not a problem, I just got home a short time ago. I brought the costumes up from the basement. You might want to shake them out a bit. They have been in these tubs and they're a bit crushed."

Maggie walked over to the tubs and beamed, "These are great!" She continued to check out the outfits as Alex talked.

"Take the tubs with you. Use what you can. I believe that you could mainly dress the kids as more shepherds or angels. However, there are a few animal costumes in there as well."

"These are going to be a huge help. I have one little boy who's insisting on an Angry Bird costume. His mom is bringing it tonight to show me."

"So?"

Maggie rolled her eyes, "Do you remember the Angry Birds? It's the big red one."

"And?"

"It looks like a cardinal, Alex," she added a bit exasperated.

"And............?"

"There were no cardinals at the stable when Christ was born."

"Who says? I wasn't there, were you?"

"Alex, I don't believe cardinals live in that part of the world, but I admit I haven't truly checked it out yet."

"Is the boy from the other church?"

"Yes."

"Then make the boy happy. It would be hard to be thrown into a new church at this time of year. Let it help him with the adjustment," Alex suggested.

"But an Angry bird?"

"Why not? It was a time for miracles. Besides, you need to pick your battles. Some people might smile."

"Some people might complain to me later."

"Who cares? Tell them to help next year, that will shut them up. The same ten percent of people at any given church seem to do all the volunteering. People like to complain. Maybe someone will be encouraged to pick up their Bibles to check it out. That's a good thing. Maybe people will realize that the Wise men were not there when Jesus was an infant. Lots of people put them at the stable in their Nativities. I don't. I have them starting over from a more distant location. Maybe someone could put it into an informative speech at school and thereby bring a healthy Christian discussion into school."

"I think that you're reaching now," Maggie smiled.

Alex shrugged and laughed. "So, I'll reach. Let someone prove to you that there were no cardinals at His birth. Lacking a time machine, I don't think they will be able to."

Alex helped Maggie take everything out to her car. "Thank you for everything and I will see you at work tomorrow," Maggie hugged her friend and left.

Alex had just re-entered her house, when she felt a vibration in her back pocket. She smiled when she picked up her cellphone and saw Tom's photo. "Hello! What can I do for you?"

"Nothing at the current moment, I just wanted to hear your voice," he replied as she sat in her papasan chair.

Micky jumped into her lap and she quietly pet him as she listened to the phone.

"That's nice. Thank-you. At the risk of sounding like a broken record, you sound a bit tired," she observed. "Catch any bad guys today?"

"I wish, catch the local news tonight, and you will hear about poor Mr. Jonas.

"Mr. Jonas?" Alex thought briefly. "It was him in the comic strip this morning wasn't it? Did someone whup him?"

"No, but almost," Tom chuckled. "I can laugh only because he came to no harm, or at least so far. He ran into the police station around noon with a small horde of people chasing him and screaming for the return of their packages. Once we figured out what had happened, we tried to get the word out for the poor bugger. He even asked for a signed note for him to carry in case someone accosts him."

"A note for what exactly?" Alex inquired.

"A note clearing him of any criminal activity, with the captain's signature, and a contact number at the police station."

"Can he sue the newspaper? Did the comic strip lie?"

"He can try, but I don't know if it would get anywhere. He did take a number of packages off a porch approximately two blocks from his house."

"He admitted it? Did you all have to beat it out of him?"

"No, we didn't beat him and you know it. And yes, he freely admitted it. His friend had set up the delivery date on a day that he knew he would be home. Apparently, a family emergency changed his plans. He had to leave town for a couple of days. He called his buddy up, informed him of his predicament, and asked him to get the packages, and hold unto them until his return. Mr. Jonas did just that. He tried not to act furtive when he did it and thought all was well. His friend came to his house three days later and got the packages. 'No harm, no foul,' or so he thought."

"I take it you checked with the friend and everything checked out?" Alex laughed. "Just playing 'devil's advocate,' now. Do you know for a fact that he didn't do it elsewhere?"

Tom chuckled, "One hundred percent? No. We contacted the newspaper to see if they would play nice, and give us their source for this comic information, and they refused. Can you imagine?" He ended sarcastically.

"The old owner would have helped out, not this new one. What am I saying? The old owner never would have added these comic strips to his paper in the first place. Just being curious, any other guys come running for help? The drawing looked like a number of guys I know."

"A few called in saying that they were worried for their safety and that they were innocent. John and I checked on the one, because we felt he protested a bit too much. I think we will continue to keep an eye on that one."

Alex checked her watch, "Speaking of keeping an eye on things, I have to get back to the shop. I have a class. If I hear anything of interest, I will let you know."

Chapter 25
December 7
Thursday Morning

Maggie rushed into the bakery all excited. "I'm glad that you and Cat are here!" Last night, I had children's play practice, "Little Tommy said that someone broke into their home the other night, but nothing was taken. He was understandably scared. Then he asked if his drone could record the play, he had brought it with him to show me. I let him show me how he could control the thing inside the building for a short time. When he turned it on, it sounded familiar to me for some reason. I told him that I was sorry, but I didn't think the drone would be a good idea. We do video the play each year. I also explained that they had no drones back when Jesus was born and that the audience's attention might be on the drone and not the play. Some people might even be afraid that it would fall on them, no matter how good the controller was. Most of the way through practice, the sound bugged me. I knew that I had heard it before. Then it hit me, it was the night of the murder. I heard that sound when we were caroling outside the Alex Sr.'s house."

"How did you hear it over the singing? A drone is not usually loud," Cat inquired.

"At one point, we were slow switching songs, in the silence, I heard a strange noise, akin to a mosquito, but it's the wrong season for those. I started to look around, but then the group started the next song, and I joined in and forgot about the noise. I asked Tommy if he had flown it outside that night. He got excited and told me yes he had. He was a bit worried that the snow would cause some issues, but that he had seen some fairies with it. I'll save you the whole discussion, in a nutshell, he flew the drone the night of the murder and caught a fairy flying around. The fairy was in Alex Sr.'s backyard. It's a white light that "floated" about."

Alex and Cat looked at each other and then at Maggie. "You think he really saw a fairy?" Cat asked.

"No," Maggie glared at Cat, "but maybe a flashlight, or as Jake suggested a headlamp. I think Tommy caught Alex Sr.'s murderer leaving the scene of the crime. And," she paused for effect, "it's recorded!"

"Holy crap! Serious? Where's this recording?" Alex jumped up.

"Tommy has it," Maggie responded, "unless that's what the burglars wanted and they try again."

"We can't let that happen. Where does this boy live?"

"His backyard abuts Alex Sr.'s backyard," she answered looking Alex directly in the eyes.

Alex looked at Cat, "Are you in the middle of something or can you go?"

"Give me five minutes to clean something up and I will be ready to go."

Alex and Cat pulled into Tommy Ballantine's parents' driveway about fifteen minutes later. Tommy's mom, Emily, answered the door and they explained that they were curious about the fairy Tommy had caught on his drone's camera.

"Oh, that?" She laughed, rolled her eyes merrily, and swished the air with her right hand. "It wasn't a fairy, ladies."

"You sure?"

Emily looked over the top of her reading glasses and raised her eyebrows, "You do know that fairies do not exist, right?"

"Possibly, but I don't count them totally out either." The woman gave Alex a pitying look at that response.

"Is it possible to see the 'fairy'?"

"Sure, why not, let me get Tommy."

The boy leapt into the room with his drone and a computer tablet, "Mommy told me that you wanted to see my fairy!"

"Yes, we do," Alex said intrigued.

He showed them the video on his tablet. "That is totally awesome!" Alex said and looked sideways at Cat, "May I have a copy?"

Tommy beamed at his mom, "Can I share it?"

She smiled back at him, "Yes, you may."

Ten minutes later, Alex and Cat were leaving the Ballentines. As soon as they got in the car, Alex handed her phone to Cat, "Please find that video and copy it to your phone." As the ladies left to return to the bakery, they failed to see two men sitting in a car observing them.

"Oh, great, those two ladies must have heard about that kid's fairy," Xavier growled as he started the vehicle and slowly followed after them.

"Ya think?"

"Yes, I do. Why else would those two just make a quick visit in mid-morning during the busy Christmas season? They didn't bring anything with them and I didn't see them carrying anything away. Did you?"

"Now, that you put it in those terms. You might be right. I didn't see them carrying anything. Xavier, we searched the place and didn't find the drone."

"The kid probably had it with him, now the ladies have seen his so-called fairy."

"Why the fuss? You know that fairies don't exist. You haven't told me why you are so upset."

Xavier glanced briefly toward his companion, "You guys were doing a 'job' that night, not far from his place. Who knows how long he was flying his toy. I think that he caught you guys on some kind of recording. For some reason, he's calling you fairies, but if the cops examine that recording, they might find a clue that puts our activities at risk."

His companion looked at him, looked at the ladies several cars ahead, and thought quietly. "What do you think we should do?"

"Let me think on this, I might have a mission for you," Xavier replied.

Chapter 26
Thursday Early Evening

Later, after work, Cat was running a quick Christmas errand, when she developed a case of the heebie jeebies. She felt like someone was following her. Cat slowed down and nonchalantly looked in the store window on her right. In its reflection, she noticed a black-hooded man with a limp. He was approximately twenty feet behind her. She went in one store's front door and out the side door, the guy followed. Cat thought a second, and headed toward the bookshop to go through the "Christmas Passage Tunnel." It was crowded and she ducked away quickly at the end of the alley. She had intended to walk home, but she called Mike. Thankfully he had been able to pull a trucking run that allowed him to come home for the night. He came by and picked her up. "What have you and Alex been up to today that would make someone worried?"

"Nothing that I know of........." she drifted off.

"Cat,........?" He glanced worriedly at her.

"Alex and I got some fairy film to check out." At his incredulous look, she explained.

"Where's this fairy recording that you are talking about?" Mike inquired. "I'd like to see it, if you don't mind."

"Sure thing, I don't mind. When we get to my place, I'll show you," Cat answered.

As soon as they entered her house, she quickly turned her television on and blue-toothed her phone video to it.

"Alex and I just got a quick look earlier. We had intended to study it more, but the shop got very hectic today. I figured that I would take a better look tonight using my TV. It will let us see things so much better." She got the video started while Mike moved an ottoman close to the set for them to sit on. About ten minutes into the recording, Cat pointed at the small white light that meandered about the screen. "Alex and I don't understand why the white light is moving about, it's not staying in one steady direction. And no," she looked at Mike, "we don't really think it's a fairy. We think someone used a flashlight to leave Alex Sr.'s house after his murder. You'd think it would head in one steady line away from his house, but it doesn't. It meanders to the left and then the right and back again of sorts." Cat watched Mike study the video and noticed his eyes narrowing, "What are you seeing that I am not?"

"The red fairy," he answered.

"The what? Where?" she restarted the recording and quickly scanned it again. "I'm not seeing it."

"You are studying the wrong area of the video. Back it up again and I'll show you." When the video restarted, "look in the background, what do you see?"

"Hey," she excitedly half-shouted, Cat tapped the screen with her finger, "here it is. I see it, but what exactly is it?"

"Not sure, we need to be able to zoom in on it. There's a lot of dark here and just two pinpoints of light. Since this is a young kid's drone, I'll lay odds the camera has low resolution. You need to talk to Tom and see if the police can do anything with this video."

Chapter 27
Thursday Evening

Alex pulled into Ben's driveway and jogged up to his door, "You wanted to discuss a matter of some urgency?"

"Yes," he welcomed her into his house. "Are you going to inform Tom of 'The Dove'?"

"Most of me says yes, but, I admit part of me is hesitating."

"Why?"

"Marrying a person is a risk I take. 'The Dove' is bigger than one person, there is a much bigger risk. I feel I could fail my aunt."

"I don't think anything you do could fail your aunt. I do need to ask you a simple question, for you are marrying this man. Do you not trust Tom, and think this will not work out?"

"Yes, I trust him. But, what if I mess up again? I trusted David, and as history has proven, I can divorce. If we would have informed him of 'The Dove,' he would have spilled the beans and ruined everything."

"But, as you have pointed out to me in the past, Tom is absolutely nothing like David," Ben rubbed his jar. "If you want, I could draw up a confidentiality paper for him to sign, a non-disclosure contract, if you wish."

"Oh, I'm sure he'll like that," she sarcastically responded.

"I believe that he will understand if properly informed. From all I have gathered, your Tom is a smart man. He will understand that whereas the trust is a nice amount, you are only allowed to distribute so much each year, and that you only receive so much for handling your part. The trust is not for your personal use and never will be. David would not have understood. You need to think and pray on this. I believe that you will know what to do. When you decide, just let me know," Ben smiled.

Alex hugged her friend as she prepared to leave, "I will take your suggestion."

Chapter 28
December 8
Friday Morning

Cat returned from making a delivery and passed a delivery man shaking his head as he walked out the side door of the bakery. "That man seems a bit upset," Cat commented when she saw Alex.

"Good!" Her friend spit out.

"What happened?"

Alex stepped to the side and flourished her hands toward the boxes on the table, "Take a look."

Cat's mouth dropped open in dismay as she surveyed the damaged boxes. "What happened?"

"Swifty out there," Alex pointed toward the delivery/office door, "that's what. He forgot to close his delivery doors properly after the last delivery and a number of the boxes, these, and apparently only mine," she pointed at the table and fumed, "fell out. He realized what happened, pulled over and retrieved them. Apparently, one or two got nipped by cars that had been behind them. I called the company that we order from and complained. They told me to check out the order, take pictures, and let them know of the damage. They will try to replace the damage, but can't totally promise anything, because some of it is Christmas stuff and they are not getting more in. I told them that I understood and would be getting back to them within two hours. We received six boxes, how about we split them up and see how everything is."

"Awesome, let me wash up and I'll start," Cat responded.

After a bit of time, Alex spoke up, "I believe that driver got very lucky. I can't wait for our regular guy to get back from vacation. Whereas some of the outside boxes were damaged, the inside boxes aren't too bad, and the product inside those were not damaged at all. There are a couple of odds and ends that will need replaced. How about you?" She turned expectantly to Cat.

"Well, I concur. There are a few odds and ends that got smashed. The one item that got majorly smashed, I don't believe was totally the driver's fault. It was at the bottom of a bigger box with other stuff piled on top of it." Cat picked up the white cardboard box that had been flattened to half its original height. "Someone somehow missed the 'Fragile' warning stamped at numerous spots on the box."

"What was in that box?" Alex inquired.

Cat stared at her friend a moment, "The pinecones."

Alex closed her eyes momentarily, "Sure, why not? Of course, the pinecones." She shook her head and chuckled, "I'm glad I came up with a back-up plan." She glanced at the wall clock, "Let's get pictures of the damage and get everything put away. There is still a lot of cake work to do."

"Anything pressing? I was going to make the Todedes shortly."

Alex chuckled, "How did I forget? Go ahead, I got this."

Chapter 29
Friday Evening

Penny and her friend Tasha left the Singing Tree event at the church. "Where's your car?" Tasha asked.

"Just back there, I'll see you tomorrow. This has been fun," Penny replied. She said good-bye to her friend and headed through the building's pedestrian tunnel to her car. Penny had just emerged when movement to her right caught her attention. Before she could react, someone grabbed her right arm, and twisted her to the left, pulling her right arm up behind her back, and slammed her against the brick wall.

"Shut up!" He hissed in her ear, "I want your purse!"

"Take it!" She cried, "Just don't hurt me."

He grabbed her purse and leaned in closer, "Remember this…. You know nothing about anything! Don't talk to anyone, especially the cops. I know where you live." He pushed her hard into the wall, and turned to run, just as he heard someone scream.

Alex and Tom came running around the corner and past an older man comforting an older woman. The man pointed toward Penny crying against the wall. "Penny?" Alex inquired. "Let us help you!"

"Mrs. Winchester, are you hurt?" Tom inquired. When she looked at them, Alex involuntarily gasped, "I'm calling 9-1-1."

Alex grabbed a bandana from her handbag, "Here, it's clean. I would just hold it carefully against your cheek.

Your face got scraped up a bit. Tom's called for help, the EMTs will do more. Are you hurt elsewhere?"

Penny took the bandana and did as suggested. She cried as she nodded, "My arm hurts something fierce!"

"Mrs. Winchester, can you tell me what happened?"

"Only a little. A man grabbed me, shoved me into the wall, and took my purse."

"Anything else?" Tom heard a siren approaching. "Let's walk a bit into the parking lot," Tom suggested as an ambulance and police car pulled into the lot.

"No, that's it," she shook her head and then started to shudder all over.

Tom looked at Alex and nodded toward Penny, "I'll go talk to the officers for a minute."

Alex stepped a bit closer to the woman, "Penny, the EMTs are coming. Can you tell me anything about your assailant? Height? Weight? Did he or she say anything?"

"It was a 'he,' but I know nothing else. It happened too fast."

"Call me if you need anything," Alex urged and gave her one of her business cards.

"Thank you," she cried and went into the willing attention of the EMTs.

Tom searched the area and didn't find any clues. Officers searched and found nothing.

"It seems like an average purse snatching," Tom said when he joined Alex later at her house.

"Is that what you think it truly was?" Alex asked, "Because I don't."

"No, but we have nothing else to go on, but guts," he replied while enjoying some Christmas cookies and cocoa. "She didn't tell you anything else other than it was a man?" Alex shook her head. "How did she ascertain the assailant's gender?"

"She didn't say and then the EMTs took over." Alex looked at her fiancé a moment, "Tom, I have something real serious to discuss with you, totally unrelated to Penny and her mishap."

"Okay, what's on your mind?" Tom plopped down on the couch beside her and gave her his full attention.

"All families have secrets, both good and bad. I found out a doozy when my aunt died. She always felt that to truly keep a secret, you could tell no one. I believe that she practiced that well. My aunt never married, or I would have a precedent to follow or at least guide me. I feel that a spouse should know this kind of family secret. I need you to contact Ben and set up a time to chat. Some things should not be taken lightly or discussed with other possible ears listening. He has a special room in his house built for such discussions."

"As a reminder, I love you deeply, but you, as numerous people have pointed out, haven't known me as long as some think you should. I take marriage quite seriously and plan on ours lasting 'til death do us part.' So would you rather wait for a bit?"

"No, I also believe that we will grow old together. This is very important. I know your deep sense of justice and believe that no matter what might happen, that you won't share this knowledge. And in a state of full disclosure, I must tell you that Ben has checked you out to the max."

"Me? Why? When?"

"Apparently, as soon as he got back from our camping trip where you proposed to me. He was going to talk to you in the spring or summer, but our choice of December twenty-fourth has changed that. I contacted him after we set a date. And Tom, not all secrets are bad, they just need to be made clear and understood."

Tom kissed her and said no problem. "When I met you, I heard all kinds of rumors both bad and good. I know what you may or may not have done in the past. I have a feeling not all of it, and I have made peace with it."

"That is why you need to have this talk with Ben before Christmas Eve."

"I will call him shortly," Tom assured her.

Chapter 30
December 9
Saturday Afternoon

After an energetic and bustling morning, Maggie found Cat putting some supplies out on the shelves, "Cat, did you move Thaddy?"

"Why would I voluntarily touch that thing?" Cat turned to face Maggie, "Why do you ask?"

"He's missing."

Cat looked around for Alex, "Since when?

"I just noticed now."

"When was the last time you remember seeing him?"

Maggie thought for a few seconds, "Somewhere around noon, I believe."

"Did you mention this to Alex?"

"No, I didn't want to alarm her. I was hoping that you decided to quietly move it for some reason. Since, that is not the case, I guess I will go tell her."

Cat touched her shoulder, "Let's wait till morning. She has a lot on her mind. Maybe it will show up somehow."

Maggie raised her eyebrows and tilted her head, "Do you think he went for a walk and will return by morning?"

"Not on his own of course."

"Then......you think someone took him?"

"We just had a group of children leave with their gingerbread creations," Cat answered.

Maggie was horrified, "But they were Girl Scouts! I am pretty sure that they are discouraged from stealing."

Cat chuckled. "Maggie you tickle me with your naiveté at times. Yes, they were Girl Scouts, not angels. Besides, didn't some of them have siblings that came along to get them?"

"Now, that you mention it. Yes, a few did."

"Did any of them mill around the Christmas tree? Touching things as kids are prone to do?"

Maggie eyes widened, "Yes, they did, a number of them."

"I think someone's mom might be getting upset about now and hopefully will give a call in the morning."

The two looked up when the front door opened, "Thank goodness you are here, Cat!" Mrs. Ballantine entered the shop with Tommy and his drone in tow.

"Is something wrong Mrs. Ballantine?"

"Emily, please," she smiled, "Not wrong really, but, Tommy found another fairy."

Cat caught motion outside on the driveway, "Let's go join Alex in the backroom. I believe that we won't be disturbed back there."

Cat called out for Alex as the small group entered the bakery area and the walk-in cooler door opened. "Coming," Alex answered. She put some baking supplies on the one table as she took note of the group, "Do you all need something?"

"I found another fairy!" Tommy blurted out, "An older one!"

Alex turned her head slightly and made a questioning face, "When did you tape this fairy?"

"The same night as the other fairy, just later in the night," he replied. "I was watching my video again and remembered that I had more recording to watch. I watched it and found her!"

"And how do you know the fairy is older?"

"The light is not as bright. Mommy says that grandma's 'bulb' is not as bright as it used to be, because she's old, so this must be a grandma fairy!" He finished with a bright smile.

Emily choked as her son spoke and turned bright red as Alex and Cat looked at her with wide eyes and huge grins. She chuckled, "Out of the mouths of babes," was all that came to mind and they all laughed. "I guess I should watch what I say a bit more," and they all chuckled again.

"May Cat and I see this old fairy?" Alex asked the boy.

"Sure!" Tommy played his recording.

Alex and Cat looked at each other and then the mom, "Tommy, please send Cat a copy of this recording." Alex guided Emily toward her office and explained that the recording might be important and why. She suggested that they place the drone and recording in a safe place. She noticed Tommy and Cat walking their way, "Emily, if it's okay with you, I would like to gift Tommy and your family with a box of cookies."

Tommy's eyes lit up with joy as he realized his mom was accepting the offer.

Maggie came back at the end of her shift to find her friends studying a computer screen. "What all has your attention?"

They explained the situation, "We believe the fairies are really people exiting out the back of Alex Sr.'s house using flashlights or headlamps, but we don't understand all their meandering?"

"What do you mean?"

Alex reversed the screen and then replayed it, "See how the lights move and curve around? Both fairies end up seeming drunk or something." Mags nodded.

"Why not just walk straight out the back and away from the house?" Cat asked.

"Because of his yard set-up," Maggie answered.

"What do you mean?"

"He has a curving stepping-stone walkway that twists and turns. The land on either side is covered in pebbles, mulch, prickly shrubs, and statues. If you try to walk straight out, you will trip or probably get injured."

"How do you know this?"

"Alex Sr. donated money to the Cub Scouts to help him install everything. Jake and our son, Montz, were some of the workers."

Alex smiled, "Thanks Maggie. Looks like we need to check out his backyard."

Cat checked her watch, "After we deliver one more wedding cake."

"Maggie, how's it going out front? Can Carsenia handle things"

She nodded, "I believe so. Things were hectic earlier, but it has slowed a bit."

Chapterr 31
Saturday Late-Afternoon

Alex and Cat delivered the last wedding cake and headed over to Alex Sr.'s house. Alex parked two houses down from the actual house. They took a quick glance around and scooted to the whittler's backyard. "Wow, this is actually quite nice," Alex commented as they headed to the base of the walkway.

Cat got out her cellphone and glanced around one more time, "I suggest we go to the backdoor and follow the path and see if we can match it up to the old fairy's flight path."

"How about I get the young fairy's flight path going on my phone and we can look for any discrepancies there also?" Alex added. When Cat nodded, Alex got out her cellphone and they slowly made their way.

The two had gotten about two-thirds of the way down the path, when Cat spoke up, "I believe the older one hovered at this next bend briefly, does the younger one?"

"No," Alex shook her head, "Let's see if we can figure out a possible reason." When they reached the bend, they stopped and observed a gnome diorama. "This is cute, but not what I would expect Alex to have."

"I believe that he has two granddaughters."

"That would make sense." They studied the gnome family setting. Numerous gnomes of different sizes, color, and dress were placed around a tallish skinny house with colorful ceramic tree mushrooms, a few smaller houses, and a pool complete with pool furniture.

"These buildings look like they're made of gourds. They're awesome!" Alex commented. "I especially like the windmill. I wonder where they got them or if they grew them themselves. From what I know, that would take some patience."

"There's supposed to be a really neat gourd place down near Carlisle. I think it's called Meadowbrooke Gourds. I heard Carsenia talking about it. We should take a road trip there one day and check it out." Cat squatted down and looked closer to the ground, "Alex, look! The ground coverage is polished glass that you can find at the craft store."

"OK, what about it?"

Cat pointed, "Look closer, some of the glass is not polished. It looks like someone smashed a glass here." She reached into some nearby grass and pulled out a tube-like piece of glass, "looks a bit like a small glass tootsie roll."

Alex's eyes lit up, "I bet its Penny's wineglass. That looks like part of the stem to a wineglass. She said that she took the wine glass with her, just not the bottle. Maybe once she left the house, she realized that she still had the glass in her hand and needed to get rid of it. I mean, why keep the glass, someone might ask about it. "

"Well, she picked a great place to try to hide it," Cat concurred. "This would also mean that Penny was the old fairy. Now, all we have to do is figure out who the young one was."

Alex smiled, "You make that sound so easy. Let's finish the walkway and get out of here."

As they returned to the car, Cat spoke up, "Sorry we didn't figure anything else out, Alex."

"Maybe yes, maybe no. We are still figuring out the puzzle pieces, Cat. I feel we did good here today," Alex responded. As they headed home, Alex's cell phone rang.

"Hi, Alex!" Tom said. "I need to talk to you, but I can't get away. Do you have a minute or two? Or am I interrupting something."

"No, I'm good. Cat's with me. What's up?"

"Earlier I talked to my mom and I want to warn you that she might cause some hassle."

"About what?

"She hates that we are getting married Christmas Eve. She doesn't believe that we have been dating long enough. She has a tendency to believe that her opinion is the only right one and voices it."

Alex thought it over, "Okay, is that it?"

He was quiet for a moment, "Isn't that enough?"

"I'll let it go in one ear and out another. Besides, I don't like to fight at the holidays." Cat looked at her friend and shook her head.

"I just wanted to give you an out. Do you think you might want to change anything?"

"No, I don't. But, one thing, how long is long enough for your mom?

"She believes that she should meet a future in-law at least fifteen times before anything becomes permanent."

"Why fifteen?"

"No one really knows, and she won't explain."

"What about your dad?"

"Oh, he's cool with it. He especially likes that Santa Claus picked the date," Tom chuckled. "Sorry, but I have to go."

"Okay, bye," Alex replied. She looked at Cat, "Tom's folks are a bit odd. We're planning on seeing them over the holidays. I'm thankful that they don't live next door, but also glad that they live only a couple of hours away."

"Mike's folks are pretty cool," Cat replied with a grin.

Chapter 32
December 10
Sunday Morning

Maggie, Jo-Jo, and Carsenia were manning the store, when a customer rushed in to get some last minute supplies. As she passed the Christmas tree, she seemed to be studying it. "Did you guys decide to replace that horrid ornament with a ballerina? I didn't think that Alex would ever part with that," Veronica inquired.

"No," Maggie replied. "Someone took it."

"What?? No way!!" Jo-Jo and Carsenia hustled over to the tree.

"And........." The ladies turned back to Maggie, "Alex, doesn't know yet. It went missing yesterday. We hoped that it would get returned today. In fact, I was kind of hoping it would be here by the time Alex got back from church. She's running a bit later than expected."

"Not bloody likely," the woman continued. "I saw it at church today, in the White Elephant Gift Exchange. Someone got it as a gift."

"Do you remember who?"

"Let me think on it for a moment?" she said. "Nobody fought for it, so.......yes! I remember, Sally Brady took it home."

"I will contact her and see if she will part with it."

"You better hurry, she did not seem pleased. She might even have thrown it away. I wish I would have known that

Alex really wanted it, I would have easily gotten it back for her." Veronica said. She purchased her items and left the store.

Jo-Jo called Sally immediately. "I'm sorry, I no longer have it. I really didn't like it, so I gave it to the dry cleaner man, Toby."

"The dry cleaners are open today? It's Sunday," Jo-Jo questioned.

"Yes, just like you guys are opened these last Sundays before Christmas," Sally answered. "But, he was about to leave for a visit with someone, his one employee was going to keep the shop open. Good luck!"

Jo-Jo called the dry cleaners and found out that she was indeed too late, so she left a message for Toby to call the store the next day.

"Girls," Maggie spoke up, "I propose a plan if you two are willing. Let's handle the case of the missing Thaddeus for Alex. Are you two game?"

Jo-Jo and Carsenia looked at each other and nodded. "This could be fun!" Carsenia chuckled.

"We will keep our ears and eyes open and follow his trail. Hopefully, we can secure his return to Alex before the strike of midnight on Christmas Eve as a gift for her." Maggie's eyes sparkled.

"Do you think that we can do it?" Jo-Jo asked.

"Tis the season for miracles," Maggie responded. "I will inform Cat of our mission. It will be up to her whether to tell Alex or not. All agreed? Should 'Operation

Thaddeus' commence?" Maggie put her hand out in front of her and looked with joy at her friends.

Jo-Jo and Carsenia enthusiastically put their hands on top of hers, "Yes!"

Carsenia looked around, "I got here after Alex and Cat left. Where are they now?"

"Cat took gingerbread ornaments to the library for a community event foodraiser. Alex was going to meet her there. Each family that donates non-perishable food to the library gets a chance to sit down and put together a three-dimensional ornament. It's similar to making mini gingerbread houses, but without taking as much time."

"Oh, yeah, I remember seeing the finished examples. They were really cute!" Carsenia replied.

Chapter 33
December 11
Monday Morning

Alex arrived at the bakery a couple hours earlier than normal to get a start on things. She was pleased with the amount of work she was able to finish by the time her employees showed up for the start of their work day.

"Thank you anyway, but I believe I will pass," Alex finished the phone call and hung up the phone.

As she re-entered the bakery, Cat looked up from some cookies she was working on, "Well?"

Alex shook her head, "No good. They said that the pinecones are backordered. I told them that we would pass." Alex looked around the table, "How we doing?"

"Just finishing up the Holtry order."

"Great! We still have a lot to do," Alex commented with a big smile. "I will check on what all we need for this weekend's cakes." Alex spent the day making needed flowers and snowflakes for cakes and prepping the wedding cake set-up supplies.

Chapter 34
Monday, Mid-morning

Maggie answered the phone to find Toby returning Jo-Jo's call. She explained the situation. "Sorry, Maggie, I re-gifted that item already."

"To whom?"

"To my mailman, Herbie. He was looking a bit down, so I gave it to him. I had only planned on gifting him with a gift card to the coffee shop, but it seemed a bit bland. That troll was so ugly, he's cute. I had hoped maybe it would brighten his spirits a bit," Toby explained. "He left about an hour ago."

"Okay, thank-you. In which direction does he go from your place?" Maggie waited for an answer and called Carsenia. "Did you get your mail yet?"

"Let me check." Carsenia set the phone receiver down on the table for a minute and then returned. "No, not yet." Maggie clued her in on what Toby said. "I could wait, but he could get rid of it before getting to me. I'll go see if I can find him."

No sooner had Maggie put down the phone then it rang again. She picked up the phone and before she could get one word out, a feminine voice spoke, "I need to talk to Alex please."

"Let me see if she's available, I know she's super busy in the bakery. Tis the season and everything."

"Tell her it's Penny and it's important."

"Yes, ma'am. Please hold for a few minutes." Maggie hurried to the back and relayed the message. "Plus, I think you need to look at the intercom, I tried calling back and nothing happened."

"Will do, thank you Mags," Alex picked up the bakery's receiver, "Alex here, how can I help you?"

"Alex, its Penny. I need to talk to you, can we meet?"

"Yes! When and where?"

"Tonight, at the park."

"Are you okay?"

"For now, yes, for much longer, I don't think so. That purse snatching was really a threat, I wanted to tell you, but I was warned not to. I'm scared!"

"Then come here right now or I will meet you wherever you want. Don't wait!" She implored.

"I want to get something first. Tonight nine o'clock at the park, by the Holly bench. Do you know where I mean?"

"Yes, I will be there! Penny please be careful!" Alex hung up the phone worried.

"What's up?" Cat asked. Alex clued her in. "I'm coming too!"

She glanced at the clock, "Good, I was about to suggest that very thing."

Later, Carsenia called Maggie back, "Herbie already gave it to his wife, Georgette. She had come by his route to ask him a holiday-related question so he gave Thaddeus to her. She told him it was ugly, but she would take it."

124

"I will call Jo-Jo. I think she lives out their way," Maggie said. She hung up the phone and quickly relayed the request to her.

Jo-Jo shortly reported back, "I went by their house and no one answered when I knocked. When I returned home, I called and left a message. I come in to work in a couple of hours, hopefully I'll hear something by then."

Chapter 35
Monday Night

As Alex and Cat headed for the rendezvous, they glanced at each other quickly and jogged toward the flashing lights.

Joey V. stopped them before they reached their destination, "What is the purpose for jogging this way?"

Alex furled her brow, "That's odd wording. We're here to meet someone."

"Who?"

Alex looked over his shoulder, "Please, tell me that's not Penny Winchester."

"I honestly don't know who it is. There is no ID," Joey responded. "Tom and John will be here shortly."

"Does she have a scraped face and an arm in a sling?" Alex inquired.

Joey glanced over toward the lights and back at Alex, "You are a person of interest in a murder case. I cannot confirm your ID?"

"But you didn't deny," Cat added.

"I am not saying who this person is. What business did you have with Mrs. Winchester?"

"She called me earlier at the bakery and said that she wanted to tell me something."

"Did she specify what it was?"

"No. Penny had been burgled and roughed up lately. I happen to know that she was upstairs at the time of Alexander Gavree's death. She said that she was scared

126

and wanted to talk to me. She said that she had to get something and set the time and place for this meet. I need to know what she wanted to tell me. I asked that she come to the bakery immediately, but she would not have it."

Joey glanced toward the heavens, "Ladies, please come over, but do not cross the police tape."

Alex and Cat stood with others by the police tape. They observed Tom and John arrive and meet with Joey. As Joey spoke, Tom and John glanced their way and slightly shook their heads. They all walked down to the barricaded area where the body lay. Tom hunkered down to see the face and talked with Joey and John a few more moments.

Tom walked up to Alex and Cat, ducked under the police tape, and led them a distance away. "Review with me why you two just happened to be here." They obliged and then he continued, "As you know, we just got here. Please go to Alex's house and wait for me. I need to sort some things out and I will want to talk to you two."

He turned to go, but Alex touched his shoulder. He stopped and turned her way, "Is it her?" Alex inquired.

Tom gave a slow nod, "Yes, it's her."

Chapter 36
Monday Night

Christmas music regaled Tom, John, and Joey as they entered Alex's house. Cat and she had been at the dining room table drinking soda and playing cards as they awaited their arrival. "Alex, we need to check some facts with you," Tom started. "Let's sit down and talk."

She looked around the group and stopped at the one, "Joseph, I did not hurt Penny," she declared.

"I didn't say that you did, but some higher ups think you did."

"How and why? I have been busy today for my business. I was at the shop, I received her call, she set the time of our meet," Alex pointed at Cat and then herself, "and then we went to the park."

Joey turned to Cat, "Did you actually hear the call?"

"How would I?"

"Speakerphone."

"No, Alex told me of the discussion after she hung up, and I insisted on accompanying her. She agreed, end of discussion."

"Did you two stay together until the time of the meet?" John inquired.

They both shook their heads, "No, we worked on shop holiday orders until closing at six. We did our own things and then Cat came to my house and we set off for the park." Alex looked around the group, "Now, what?"

Tom spoke up, "Alex, you need to talk to Ben. We need

to know where you were in the time frame that you were separate from Cat. Because, for now, you had opportunity and knowledge of Penny's whereabouts. Some would say, that you just might not have told Cat everything from the phone call. For example, Penny might have picked an earlier time, you met and killed her, and then you met up with Cat, returned to the park as planned, and pretended to not know what was going on."

"Even if Cat was with you, she's too close to you. What would her value as a witness really be? Your alibi would have been shaky at best," John added.

"Why would I kill her?" Alex asked Tom. "She was going to help me clear myself."

Joey spoke up, "Some would say that if Penny was indeed upstairs at Alexander's house, she saw you kill Alex, so therefore, you needed to get rid of her. Maybe she threatened to blackmail you."

"But, that's not what happened," she sternly replied. "Out of curiosity, how did she die?"

"She was stabbed, like Alex Sr.," John responded.

"I believe that you all need to leave and I will contact Ben." She got up, walked to her front door, opened it, and flourished her arm and hand from right to left to encourage them to leave, "You guys do your best, you will not find me guilty of this."

Chapter 37
Monday Night

As the men walked from the house, Joey spoke to the air, "Why does Alex call me Joseph, not Joey?"

"Because she's not happy with you," John answered.

"Does she ever call you Jonathan?"

John smiled, "A few times, but, I believe Tom will be hearing 'Thomas' numerous times in the years to come."

"Hey, I don't agree," Tom spoke up.

John and Joey looked at each other and smiled knowingly. "Naïve, man. For being a cop, you can be real naïve," Joey commented. All three laughed as they got into their cars.

Chapter 38
Dec 12
Tuesday Morning

Cat arrived at the shop to get things going and noticed Alex over at a far table looking at something. "What'cha doing Alex?"

Alex turned around and smiled, "Come see what I made. Let me know what you think?"

Curious, Cat walked over to see some brown items on a tray. She looked a bit closer, "These are nice! They look like chocolate."

"They are."

"But, I don't remember us having chocolate molds to make pinecones," a perplexed Cat replied.

Alex looked at her friend a moment and grinned, "Why didn't I think of that? Awesome idea." She knocked on her head with her knuckles, "All of those molds we have out in the shop. Sometimes I can be such a ditz." Alex glanced at her friend, "Shut-up, Cat." She laughed at the glint in her friend's eyes. "I will order some when I can." Alex pointed toward the table, "These are not edible. You could suck on them I suppose, but not chew on them."

Cat screwed up her face, "What in the world did you make exactly?"

"I found some detailed plastic pinecones at the one store. I washed them, sterilized them, let them completely air dry, and dipped them in chocolate. What do you think?"

Cat chuckled, "I like them a lot! Cool idea, but you know, the ones you make from royal icing are nice looking, Alex."

"Thank you, but no. A pinecone should not be hard to make, I know the gist of them, I just don't like my finished product. It's really irritating, but one day I will perfect it, just not this year. This time, I will use these and just tell the cake cutters at the banquet hall that the pinecones are not to be eaten." Alex's watch alarm went off and she quickly quieted it, "I have to deliver some cookies across town. I shouldn't be too long."

Chapter 39
Tuesday Late Morning

Alex was returning to the bakery when she passed a house with two people outside that she hadn't seen for some time. She continued up the street to safely turn around and come back. Alex pulled into their driveway and parked behind their car. "Hi! May I help you take your packages in?" She asked the gentleman.

The older man turned slowly around to see Alex walking up to his car. "Hey, Alex! It's been a bit. And yes, you can help."

As Alex and the man approached the side door to the house, it was opened by a slightly younger light brown-haired woman. "Did you say something Carlin? Oh, Alex, I didn't realize that you were out here."

"Hi Martha! I saw that you two had a lot of stuff to bring in, and thought that I might offer some help."

"Thank you, dear. We have been away for some time, so we tried to do all of our holiday and grocery needs in one day. Unfortunately, we will have to wait until another day to finish up, but we do have plenty of time yet."

"Where have you been?"

"Arizona, visiting some relatives. We left just before Thanksgiving. It will probably be our last visit out that way, so we decided to really spend some time."

"Really? I didn't notice. Lights have been on at this house at different times. Didn't seem like they were timer set. There was a car in your driveway at various times."

Alex pointed over her shoulder toward the driveway, "Oh, wait.... it was a different color from the one that's out there now."

Martha smiled, "That was our granddaughter, Olivia, house-sitting. All we asked was that she makes the place looked occupied. If she wanted to stay over, she could, it was up to her."

"She did a great job!"

"Thank-you," Martha beamed. "I'll let her know. The only night she couldn't help was our first night we were to be gone."

"As it turned out, she wouldn't have needed to come over. We had a bit of a rocky start," Carlin said. "There was a bad storm out west, so we delayed our start for one day."

"Did that cause you much trouble, the delay, I mean?" Alex inquired.

Carlin shook his head, "No, not at all. Our vehicles were in the shop for work and maintenance. So we just went with the flow. The only real difference is that we let our friend who was taking us to the airport, and the kennel that was taking care of Apollo, know that we would be a day later than scheduled."

"Even the change in plane tickets went smoothly," Martha added. "The only real thing that was odd was our last night here before we left. Remember Carlin?"

He looked at her a moment, "Oh, yeah," he nodded his head and looked at Alex. "We were in the basement enjoying a great game of Scrabble when Apollo went nuts!

He popped up off the floor and raced up the stairs and started barking. By the time we got to him," he smiled at his wife and then returned his gaze to Alex, "you see, we don't move as fast as he does." Everyone chuckled as he continued, "Apollo was still jumping and agitated, but not quite as much as before. We opened the door, but didn't see anything. I petted Apollo to calm him and Martha gave him a bone. We turned the light back off and returned to the basement to finish our game."

"That was a great game, too," Martha added and her husband agreed. "After that, nothing out of the ordinary occurred. We went to bed and Apollo was fine."

Alex glanced around the room, "You all have a real nice place here. I don't believe in all the years that I've known you, that I have been inside before."

"Well, we mainly talk outside, dear," Carlin said. "We're usually puttering around outside, I especially find it helpful when you help me prune my apple trees. We were fortunate, after some long years of working and having a family, that we were able to retire early. We live a comfortable life. We are quite blessed."

"A few relatives passed away without children, so we benefitted that way and our children will too," Martha smiled. She lightly touched Alex's arm, "They left us some nice trinkets and odds and ends." A twinkle in her eyes made Alex smile.

Alex looked around and realized that these people had some great "trinkets" and laid odds that they had enough in their bank accounts to live comfortably the rest of their lives. There was nothing super showy in their belongings, but if you knew your stuff, you could see that the mantle clock, the secretariat, and some of the chachkies were worth big bucks. She was sure they had a lot of high quality items throughout the house. An idea started to tug at her brain.

These two people were humble and helped out others in need. She knew the town could always count on some help from them when it came time to raise funds for one project or another. Something was definitely niggling at her brain. "Out of curiosity, the next day, when you were leaving in a brighter light, did anything stand out amiss to you two?" The loving couple looked at each other and thought, "Even a small thing?"

"Well, I told Carlin that the door lock had a scratch on it," Martha said.

He waved it aside with his hand, "I probably did that myself the one night I tried to bring in a gift for Martha. I was unlocking the door, the gift in my arm started to fall, and I moved quick to catch it."

Martha gazed at her husband of fifty-five years, "He made so much noise that I came to investigate. He made me close my eyes so that I didn't even get a peek."

"It would be my luck that she would see something that would give the surprise away. I don't like that," he grinned.

"I totally understand," Alex returned the smile. She looked around a second, "Did you notice anything else before leaving your driveway. At your neighbor's for instance?"

Martha reached out and touched Carlin's arm, "Ava's box thing." At his questioning look, she shook her head, "that little library box thing that she liked so much that she nicknamed it 'Libby.'" She turned to Alex, "someone had vandalized it."

He nodded quickly, "that's right. Somebody smashed it. We couldn't understand who would do such a nasty thing like that. But, it was pretty early and we had to get moving. I can't believe we forgot about that." He looked chagrined.

"I think it's understandable," Alex stated. "It happened before Thanksgiving and you two have done a lot since then."

"We'll go over today and inquire," Martha suggested. "I liked it a lot. Someone had done such a swell job of making a small replica of her house. They even had put a small 'Ava' on the porch. I wonder how she's going to replace it?"

Alex smiled, "I believe that I heard something about it being looked into, a replacement or something is being built."

"Well, that's great!" Carlin enthused. He looked at his wife and she nodded. Carlin took out his wallet, "Here, we'd like to donate a small something toward book replacement." He took out some bills and gave them to Alex.

"Thank you so much!" Alex accepted the money. "I'll give this to Mrs. Ferrara."

"Alex, we'd like to stay anonymous," Martha quietly said. She looked at Alex a second, "I believe that you understand that feeling. Could you choose some books at Mavis's shop and get them to Ava somehow?"

Alex mutely looked at Martha and Carlin for a moment and then nodded her head, "I believe that can be arranged."

She hugged Martha, "Thank you for looking out for us, Alex. You are such a dear."

Alex nodded her head to Carlin, he only liked his wife to hug him. "Thank you again! I wish you both a fantastic holiday season. If you need anything, please contact me." Alex left the house and got back into her vehicle. She gasped when she saw the "small" something Carlin had casually taken out of his wallet and given her, three one hundred dollar bills. Mavis could certainly do a lot with that kind of money. "Dang!" She looked upward, "Thank you Lord!"

Chapter 40
Tuesday Late Morning

Jo-Jo called Maggie at the shop. "I hate to inform you, but Georgette gifted Thaddeus to her Pastor. There was a holiday-related meeting at her church Monday night and she gave it to him."

"What church? What's the Pastor's name?" Jo-Jo gave her the requested information and Maggie called Creek Water's First Church of God and requested to talk to Pastor Lentz.

"Hi Maggie! How can I be of help?" Pastor Lentz pleasantly asked. Maggie explained briefly about the ornament. "I'm sorry, Maggie, I no longer have it. It wasn't quite my taste, so my secretary offered to take it off of my hands."

"So Nancy should have it then?" Maggie asked hopefully.

"All she said was that she would take it off my hands. Her intentions were unknown to me," the Pastor clarified.

"Is she there?"

"No, she's running an errand to the grocery store for some parishional needs."

Maggie looked around the store and thought for a few minutes. She picked up the phone and called Jo-Jo back, "I can't leave the shop for a few more hours. Can you go to the grocery store, find Nancy, my Pastor's secretary, and ask about Thaddeus?"

"Sure, no problem getting to the store, but I'm not sure who Nancy is."

"At this time of year, she always wears a Kelly green long jacket with a dark red scarf and a gold angel pin," Maggie assured her friend.

"Always?"

"This is a woman of routine. Trust me, but if for some reason you are in doubt, just give me a call here at the shop," Maggie instructed.

Chapter 41
Tuesday Early Afternoon

Alex entered her office as the phone started ringing and she answered it, "Alex, it's Ben, you've been cleared!"

Alex was stunned, "How?"

"The police arrested Leroy Winchester."

"Leroy? But why? I mean I'm glad that I'm in the clear, but why Leroy?"

"Apparently he found out about Alex Sr. and his wife and went nuts. They found the murder weapon at his house. The DA figures that Leroy had motive, means, and opportunity. Police Chief McPherson agrees. That's all I need to know. You're in the clear. I have a few other issues to handle so I will sign off, but I wanted you to know as soon as possible. I wish you a fantastic Christmas!"

Cat found Alex sitting in her chair and staring at the phone, "What's up?" Alex filled her in and Cat's face lit up, "That's wonderful!" She studied her friend's face for a moment, "But, you don't believe it?"

"Oh, I believe it, I just don't buy it," Alex stated.

"Alex, let it go," Cat recommended. "It's not your problem anymore."

"I guess you're right," Alex smiled and got up to delve back into the holiday frenzy at her shop.

Chapter 42
Tuesday Early Afternoon

Maggie picked up the phone to the sound of the Salvation Army bell ringing loud and clear, "Hello?"

"Sorry, Maggie, you picked up quicker than I thought you would," Jo-Jo explained. "I found your church's secretary. You're not going to like this, but she gave it to her dog, Cosmo. She suggested that I swing by their house and see if her husband, Mark, knows where it might be. So, I'm on my way and will call you back in a little bit."

Chapter 43
Tuesday Early Evening

Maggie grabbed the phone as she was preparing to leave for the day, "Maggie, I got to the church secretary's house. I explained everything to her husband. He said that Cosmo, their black shepherd, buried it in the backyard."

Maggie inhaled deeply and smiled, "So did you unbury it?"

"We tried, but failed. Apparently, another dog must have come into their yard and dug it out of the ground."

Cat rounded the corner to bring more supplies for the register area. "Do we know which dog?" Maggie inquired quietly. Cat took note of her lowered voice.

"No, sorry," Jo-Jo answered. "We are at a dead end."

"Maybe for now, but this is a time for miracles, we have time yet," Maggie thanked her friend and hung up the phone. She stared at it for a moment before turning to leave and found Cat blocking her way.

"Everything okay Mags?" Cat asked.

"Yes, or it hopefully will be," Maggie replied. Cat just stared at her and waited. "I hate that stare." Cat just slowly smiled and continued to stare. "Knock it off, please."

"Just tell me, I won't stop until you talk."

Maggie took a deep breath and looked to the ceiling for a second and then back to Cat, "Okay, maybe you will hear of something or have another suggestion." Maggie briefed Cat on Thaddeus' adventures.

Cat chuckled, "See, no one wants to keep this thing."

"You know, re-gifting is permitted," Maggie said quietly.

"This seems to be at turbo speed," Cat replied. She looked at Maggie and they both started laughing. "You guys are nuts! But, a big thank you for everything. I will leave it in your capable hands. If you need anything, let me know. If I have any ideas or hear anything, I'll let you know."

Chapter 44
Tuesday Evening

Alex was just closing the door to her office for the day when the phone rang, "Alex, this is Milo, can you swing by my office sometime tonight?"

"See you in about fifteen minutes," Alex replied.

Alex entered Milo's office and grinned, the place was festooned in Christmas decorations, "I love it!" she grinned at the man who just rolled his eyes. "I'm glad that you let Mrs. Rosenberry decorate this year. Between Mavis and her you'll never forget whatever holiday is happening," she laughed. "You know you love it." She plopped down in a chair, "Now, why am I here?"

"I took on a client and he has asked me to ask you to do him a favor, if you be so inclined," Milo replied.

Alex replayed the sentence through her head, "Okay, shoot."

"My client is Leroy Winchester."

Her eyes widened, "No offense meant, but this is not your normal thing is it?"

"No, I would have suggested Ben, but he's your attorney. I don't want any conflicts of interest. I believe Leroy to be innocent and that he was arrested in error, an error that will be found out in time. And that is where the favor I mentioned earlier comes in. He has a piece of woodwork that needs to get to a competition. It's a time sensitive event. It's bad enough he's lost his wife, whom he did not kill, he doesn't want his work wrongfully damaged. He will be proven innocent, but he truly believes he can win this competition. He has been working on it in total seclusion, no one, not even Penny knew the design. The past few years, Alex Sr. has always seemed to know what it would be. I guess now he knows how that may have happened. If he can't enter the competition, then the killer wins in at least two ways. The prize money could come in handy. He was hoping to win and take Penny on a cruise, but, of course, that's out now. He wants to compete, he wants the bragging rights, winning would help his business and that's all he has left right now. You truly understand the importance of this competition, and that is why he would like you to make sure his piece gets there in time and in perfect shape. I warned him that you might not have the time seeing that it's one of your busiest seasons."

"When's the deadline?" Alex asked.

"Friday by five. He doesn't want to trust the mail. He was planning on taking it to its destination in person. You can take it in early starting Thursday morning, it just cannot be late."

"I believe that I just might be able to fit in it. Let me look at my schedule tonight and I will get back to you. I never believed him guilty, even the cops aren't sure." She stopped and her eyes widened briefly, "Oops! You did not just hear me say that. But, I do want to make sure that he has a fair shot at this competition."

Chapter 45
Dec 13
Wednesday Morning

"Alex, did you see the latest comic strip?" Maggie asked as she entered the bakery to start her day.

"Yes, unfortunately it's the first thing I do now. But I have decided that I'm not doing it anymore. I have a tendency to like gossip and try to figure out if it's true or not. That's not really a good thing. I wouldn't want any of my mistakes to show up in the paper and have people chase me around town or give me dirty looks. I am super glad that we did not grow up with cellphones and the internet."

"I know what you mean," Maggie agreed. "I keep telling my kids that they have to be mindful of where they are at all times. Any mistake could be recorded and put out on the internet by anyone, so try not to break the law or do something stupid, especially with others around. It's not the best way to grow up. It's almost like you have to look over your shoulders all the time or else be a 'goody two-shoes."

"Well, that definitely would leave us out," Cat commented as she entered the room. She looked back and forth between her best friends, "What are we talking about?"

The ladies laughed and brought her up to date. Maggie put her copy of the comic strip on the table in front of them. Cat laughed, "Well, you definitely know that Alex couldn't be any help." She shoulder bumped Maggie, "As you know, if it isn't a VW bug, she won't be able to tell you anything about these cars and their possible owners. It isn't even in color, which is her favorite way to identify cars," and the ladies burst out laughing.

"I am so glad that I could provide you both with such enjoyment," Alex sniffed.

Maggie and Cat laughed even harder, "You're welcome! It's true and you know it!"

Alex laughed, "Yes, it is. Now tell me who all is involved here please."

The ladies looked at a drawing containing two vehicles. One car with a dent in its side was parked along the curb properly. Another car was driving away. Using drawn sketched lines, the cartoonist showed that the second car hit the first car and kept going. Before the car hits, the lines weave to indicate a possible DUI. In the bottom right corner of the sketch shows the cartoons main characters, Mr. Dean and Wilbur, horrified at what they had seen. Maggie looked at Cat a second and Cat nodded, "I believe it's Stephen Keefer."

"I concur," Cat replied.

Alex looked between the two women, "Would that be Councilman Stephen Keefer?"

"I think so," Cat replied.

"That's my guess," Maggie answered.

"Wow," Alex said. "I wonder if this one is accurate."

"Well, if it's not, someone is going to be sued big time."

"This could be awkward, he's supposed to come by tonight and finish paying on his bill. We are delivering the desserts for his Christmas party this Friday night.

Chapter 46
Wednesday Evening

Alex followed behind the last of the group of children and their parents as they filed through her store to leave with their handmade Christmas treasures. "See y'all!! You've been great! Take care!" She waved as she closed the door and turned to see Maggie standing behind the counter, "That was really really fun! But, boy did they make a mess! Who knew that making chocolate dipped pretzel rods rolled in different sprinkles could make my bakery look like Willie Wonka's factory exploded?"

"You did," Maggie laughed. "You added more sprinkle choices and had a pretty large group of kids."

"Yes, but these were tweens, not elementary kids."

"So did you stop any food fights or sprinkle storms?" Maggie laughed.

"Yes!" Alex looked at her friend. "How did you know?"

"Alex, I am used to all ages. You usually work with younger and older and you are really good with people. But, tweens can catch you off guard a bit especially in larger groups. If you remember, I did suggest a bit more help," she chuckled.

Alex laughed, "Yes, you did, but I really did have a lot of fun. As a whole, they listened well, sprinkles can get messy even with the best intentions."

"If it's alright with you," Maggie glanced at the clock, "I'll go back and do clean up. I have a bit of a headache and some of our customers are already showing signs of holiday burnout." When Alex looked at her with concern, she continued, "Nothing I couldn't handle, but people need to learn to chill better."

"Yes, they do. I can take over the front area. Do you want to leave a bit early? I can clean up later."

Maggie gently shook her head, "No, I want to help. There is only one more hour. I'll just pop a headache pill and chill out in the back." Alex agreed and Maggie took off for the backroom as rain started to pelt the shop's tin roof.

Alex had just started to refill a cake pop display when she saw headlights turn into the bakery's driveway. She looked out the window of the front door and hurried around the counter to open the door as the customer rushed in. "Wow! The weather is brutal tonight. I believe the weatherman got it wrong again. I heard storm, but I thought it was to be snow, not pouring rain!" He stood over the front doormat and shook the water off his jacket.

"At least we don't have to shovel it," Alex replied with a smile.

"There is that, but take care, it hurts when it hits you. There's a bit of ice in it!" The man looked up and walked over to the counter. "I'm here to pay off my bill."

"No problem, Mr. Keefer." She turned to get his order out of a small drawer. She reviewed the order with him to make sure that there were no changes and he paid the final amount owed. As she gave him the receipt, she asked, "Everything else going well, sir?"

The councilman took the receipt and looked her in the eye, "Why don't you just ask me what you really want to know, Alex? I promise that it won't interfere with current or future business with you. My family is addicted to your baked goods."

"Okay, sir," Alex returned his look, "I will. I saw the comic strip this morning," the man lowered his gaze as she spoke, "and figured out who all might be involved. Councilman Keefer, did it actually happen the way it was shown?" She lowered her voice as she spoke. He looked around briefly. "There are no other customers currently here," she assured him.

"Yes, unfortunately. I was stupid and I'm really glad that no one got injured. But, I thought that I had stopped him from printing anything."

"Who him?"

"That slimeball who bought the newspaper, Steve Gunderson."

"How would you have stopped him?"

"I paid him off, if you must know."

"You paid him off? You mean you offered him a bribe?"

"Bribe? No! He blackmailed me."

"I didn't want the hassle. After he contacted me that he had received some damaging information, he inferred that money may persuade him to stay quiet. I didn't want any doubts, so I confirmed that if he received payment, he would not print anything. So I paid."

"Then what happened?"

"About a week later, he paid me a visit. Steve wanted me to vote on a town issue in an upcoming meeting in a manner that would help him at some later point business-wise. I said that I could not. The whole town knew where I stood on the issue. If I voted the other way, people would think that I accepted a bribe or such. He got a bit nasty, but I reminded him that he had a lot of 'dirty laundry' himself. I knew about it and would talk. I also reminded him that I paid him a lot of money to stay quiet and he had agreed that that would be the end of things. Now, when the time is right, I plan on burying him." He looked outside, the downpour had ceased, "And, just to let you know, I did make things right with the owners of the vehicle I hit. They are fine with everything. Now, I have to go. I will see you Friday. Please don't spread around what I have said." Alex watched him run out to his vehicle and leave.

Chapter 47
Dec 14
Thursday Morning

"Alex! Phone call, hysterical bride," Maggie called back on the intercom.

"Hello? How may I help you?"

"Oh, Alex," a woman cried, "my fiancé just now told me he wants a motorcycle on our wedding cake!"

"Calm down, I hate to ask, but who is this?"

"I'm so so sorry, this is Taylor. Taylor Messimer. You are doing my wedding cake this weekend," the woman started bawling.

"Yes, I am," Alex rolled her eyes, "let me just go grab your order." She got up and took the remote phone with her, "Take a deep breath, Taylor. We can work something out."

"But, it's THIS weekend," she wailed. Alex could hear her audibly take a deep breath. "I'm sorry, Alex. My future mother-in-law is on my case again about getting married in December. She keeps yelling 'who does that?' all the time. She thinks it rude that we aren't waiting for a hot month, because she hates the cold. We like it! But, now, Sedge is demanding a motorcycle on our cake. I think he's getting cold feet and to tell the truth, I think he, with his mom's help, might call off the wedding."

"How about if I talk to him? Can I talk to him over his lunch?" Alex offered.

"Yes, I will let him know and get back to you," she answered happily and hung up.

Cat entered the office, "What's with the Jayne Sparrow cake? When did that pop up?"

"Just this past Monday," Alex replied. "I was extra early, and the girl called to see if she could place an order. She had a full day of work ahead of her and asked if I could take her immediately or much later in the day. I agreed to the early time."

"I don't know a Sparrow family," Cat commented, racking her memory. "Do you?"

"She said that she was in charge of getting her friend a cake, brought a few pictures, gave me some directions, paid for it and left. She didn't waste any time. It was one of the fastest wedding cake orders that I have ever taken." Alex was concerned, "Did I put it in the wrong week? I believe it's for Christmas Eve."

"You put it away in the right place," Cat answered. "I was just checking on how many cakes we have set this year for Christmas weekend."

"The cool thing is that the woman will be picking up the cake on the twenty-fourth. She knows that we are only opened for four hours on the day of Christmas Eve for last minute holiday pick-ups."

"Sounds good to me."

Alex answered the phone, checked her watch, "Sure, I can be there around twelve thirty."

155

Chapter 48
Thursday Afternoon

Alex pulled into "Stan's Garage" and parked. She walked in with a big box of cookies for the shop and asked for Sedge. The receptionist made a call and a twenty-something man came forward from the back of the garage and invited her into their break room. She took a copy of his and Taylor's wedding cake order out of her handbag and sat down. After about a fifteen minute discussion, they worked out a solution that would sit well with him and did not change the bride's wedding dream cake. "I'm sorry to cause you trouble, Miss Applecake. I don't know what got into me," he apologized.

"Don't worry about it, everything's good," she smiled. "Answer me one question, if you will?"

"Sure, if I can."

"Why is there a pile of stuff sitting on that shelf?" She pointed to a plain wooden shelf attached to the wall about a foot above the picnic table they use for eating.

"That's our 'weirdest find-of-the-week' collection. In our business, you find all kinds of unique things. For instance, last week someone brought in his car and one of my co-workers found french fries in the air filter." He glanced at her and grinned, "Don't look for those, we don't include food in that pile."

"How would that happened?"

"The people had taken their car to one of those oil-and-lube chain franchises a bit ago. I guess someone was eating their lunch while working on the car or such. They didn't just show up out of nowhere." He walked over to the shelf and pointed, "See this little dog head? I had a vehicle up on a lift yesterday and was working on a problem, when all of a sudden I saw this cute, almost smiling, decapitated dog head looking at me. It was weird, but funny, so I brought it in and added it to our pile."

"That really is odd. It doesn't look like it would get caught on anything. I mean, it's on the small side. May I touch it?"

"Sure," he shrugged.

Alex picked up the head and a green and light tan mound came with it. She turned it over in her hands, "Oh, I see. There seems to be part of a green bush or tree attached to it."

"That's right; there was something with it, that's the actual piece that got jammed between the spare tire and the car frame. I actually broke it a bit getting it out. I believe it's made out of wood."

"Nice work. I wonder what it belonged to," Alex muttered.

"Who knows, there are all kinds of trash along the road and such," he looked at his watch. "Could have been a toy," he suggested.

Alex took the hint, "Well, thank you Sedge. I wish you a fantastic wedding and a great marriage."

He nodded and smiled, "Thank-you, back. I am looking forward to seeing the motorcycle."

Alex was a few minutes out of Black Water when an idea struck her; she did a quick check for cops and did a "U-turn." She walked into "Stan's Garage," and asked if she could see their oddities collection. A man who introduced himself as "Stan" readily agreed, "Any time that you would like to drop off more cookies or need some guys to taste-test a new recipe, just come our way. These cookies are fantastic!"

"Thank you very much! I will keep that in mind," Alex replied with a smile. "Do you mind if I take a picture of your collection?"

He shook his head and chuckled, "I don't mind at all."

She took a couple of photos from different angles, thanked the man, and started on her way back to the shop.

Chapter 49
Thursday Mid-afternoon

Alex re-entered her bakery to a bit of pandemonium ringing through-out the store. "Now what are you going to do?" An older woman said quite loudly. She reached the front room to see a child struggling to get off a smashed white cake box on the floor.

"Sorry, Mrs. Cavanaugh, it was an accident. She didn't mean to hit you," a frazzled-looking young mom of two apologized. She bent down to help her daughter up off the floor.

"You mean, run into me. Honestly, parents now-a-days do not control their children. I never let mine get out of hand, especially in public," she glared. "And now I will be short on my promised donation of cupcakes for the church tonight." She was about to say more, but stopped when she saw Alex enter the room.

Alex surveyed the area, "Oh, my," she looked at the little frightened girl, "are you okay?" The little girl nodded mutely and her eyes filled with tears as she held onto her mom's left leg. "You sure?" and got another mute head nod in reply. "Okay, then. I hope that you learned that when you are in a store, you need to be careful, especially around other people," she smiled as she spoke and little girl calmed down.

"Yes, ma'am," she replied as Maggie picked up the smashed box.

"I'm going to let Carsenia help you, your sister, and your mom, while I talk to Mrs. Cavanaugh in the other room."

The older woman "harrumphed" as she passed the young family and followed Alex.

Twenty minutes later Alex was in the back room asking Cat to add twenty-four yellow cupcakes to her baking for the day. "I noticed that you didn't come out," she chuckled.

"Hey, I was about to, but it happened as you entered your office and you headed out there immediately. How many people does it take to handle a situation? Maggie and Carsenia were already on the spot."

"So, it had nothing to do with our old math teacher?"

"That old bat was a nasty crank then, and she did not age well," Cat laughed, "and you know it. So what's the agreed upon remedy."

"We're going to remake the cupcakes and I will drop them off at the church on my way home."

"I find it intriguing that she doesn't see a problem with her attitude toward people and that the cupcakes were a donation to a church."

Alex just shrugged, "The church is not filled with perfect people, just a bunch of sinners trying to change their ways."

Cat rolled her eyes, "Speaking of church, are you going to the live Nativity tonight at St. Mary's?" Cat inquired.

"I was thinking of it," she answered. "Is Mike back yet?"

"Nope, is Tom available?"

"No, how about seven o'clock? It gives me some time to spend with the animals. I believe they're getting irritated with me."

"Sounds like a plan." After Cat finished the baking, she looked up Alex. "I forgot to inquire earlier, what happened with the motorcycle wedding cake?"

Alex swished the air with a hand, "Took care of it. I told the groom about a groom's cake and he was all for it. He liked the idea that we can place it on the bridal party table by his seat. I just have to double-check with the bride, but I don't see a problem."

Chapter 50
Thursday Night

Alex and Cat took Cat's car to the live Nativity drive-thru at St. Mary's. It was a fun event especially when the two cows started picking on the goats. Alex checked her phone to see if she had any more availability for photos, "Geez! I forgot!"

"Forgot what?"

"I think I have a clue to help out Tom on something. Do you remember Mrs. Ferrara's library box?"

"Yes, it got smashed and now 'we know who' got it replaced. What about it?"

"Do you remember the design?"

"Not really, it wasn't really my thing. I know generally that it was supposedly a duplicate of her house."

"Look for Maggie or Jo-Jo, I think they could help us."

"I see Jo-Jo at the hot cocoa stand," Cat replied and they hustled over that way.

When they caught up with her, they asked her to follow them off to the side and asked her about the "Little Library." "Yes, I know all about it. Everyone is super excited, the new one was installed yesterday. Have you two seen it yet? My kids were one of the first to check it out. Each side is beautifully decorated in a different genre. Even the pole that holds it up is decorated. Mrs. Ferrara is extremely pleased. The new Libby is absolutely fabulous! And this one has three shelves! She doesn't know who gifted her with it and all the new books, but she is planning a thank-you notice of some sort. Normally, she does a twenty-four day advent countdown, but this year, because of the old one getting busted up, she's doing a twelve days of Christmas countdown. She added a new blow-up yard decoration and balloons to draw attention."

"I'm glad that someone was able to help her out. We will have to drive by and check the new one out," Alex replied. "Do you happen to remember the old one detail-wise?"

"Yes, in fact I have pictures of it with my kids. Why do you ask?"

"There was a little Ava in it, was there a little dog in the design too?"

Her eyes lit up, "Oh, yes, a black and white one that represented her dog, Dixie. She was not amused when it got destroyed. I mean, who would do such a thing?"

Alex showed her a picture of the dog's head that she taken earlier, "Does this look familiar?"

Jo-Jo smiled and nodded, "That's it!" She took a closer look, "At least part of it." She took one look at Alex's face and decided not to ask any more about it. "Did that help at all?"

"Oh, yes, a lot. Please thank your family for letting us borrow you for a few minutes."

"Now, what?" Cat asked.

"I contact Tom."

Chapter 51
December 15
Friday Morning

Maggie and Carsenia were breaking bulk chocolate down into two pound, one pound, and half pound bags in the small room behind the front register area, "Carsenia, will you be bringing Stone with you to Alex's for the Christmas Eve party?"

"No we split up......well, actually, I decided it was time to split up?"

"Should I be happy or sad for you?"

"He was getting a bit controlling and I was feeling suffocated. I mean I'm on the younger side and don't have much to compare him to, but I thought he was getting weird."

"How so?"

"If I was running a bit late, he would call me and remind me that late was not good. Or he would ask me why I was stopping at a pizza shop or the deli?"

"How would he know where you were?"

"He would check where my phone was and therefore where I was?"

"Come again? He would check up on you? Like track your phone?"

"Yes," she nodded.

"You can do that?"

Carsenia smiled, "Yes, parents use it or can use it to keep tabs on their children."

Maggie thought a minute, "That could come in handy, but you're not a child."

"No, I'm not. Recently, he asked me to get rid of my cats."

"But, you love Thelma and Louise," Maggie protested.

"Yes, I do, but he does not. And they don't really like him."

"Cats know."

"Last week, he told me that he didn't like my friends and that I should stop visiting them."

"Wow," Maggie shook her head shocked, "Just, wow."

"So, I discussed things with my mom. She pointed out that if he really loved me, he wouldn't want to change me so much. In the beginning, he was cool and mom thought he was the one for me. But he's been changing, and she suggested that I re-think things. So I did. I also listened to you and the other ladies here at the shop and how your guys treat you. They worry about you, but they don't track you or try to control everything you do. I decided that he was not right for me and dumped him. It hurt at first, but not for long. I'm enjoying being me again," she smiled.

Maggie smiled back, "Then, I'm absolutely thrilled for you. You deserve so much better."

Cat came through a side entrance with another box of chocolate. She set the box down and looked around, "You two are doing a great job! This one is dark chocolate and I'll be back with another box of milk chocolate. That will be all for today, of this particular task," she smirked

"You're enjoying this," Maggie grinned. "Thanks, Cat."

Cat looked at Carsenia, "I didn't mean to eavesdrop and I'm sure that I didn't hear your whole story, but I got the gist. I'm really glad that you left Stone. He sounds like a control freak that would have only caused more and more problems. If he has trouble accepting your dumpage, make sure you let people know, don't hide it."

Carsenia grinned, "Thanks Cat! I really appreciate what you both have said." The phone rang and she took off to answer it. "Hey, Cat, when's Alex expected back? Someone wants her on the phone, and only her."

Cat glanced at her watch, "Probably around one."

Chapter 52
Friday Afternoon

Alex parked in front of Mavis' store upon her return to Creek Water. "Hi Jayne, I'm here to pick up the book you called me about. While I'm here, is Mavis free for a few minutes?"

"Cool, I'll get the book." Jayne returned with the book and just stared at Alex a moment. "The boss is here somewhere, but whether she's free or not is up to her."

Alex laughed, "You're right, I deserved that look."

Alex found Mavis in the History room finishing a conversation with a customer and motioned her to the side. "Your hubby is busy with someone, would you please let him know that I did my errand for his client?"

Mavis' face lit up, "Yes, I will. Thank you for helping out on that. He was going to do it himself if you couldn't, which means I would have went along and did the driving. I'm getting ready for an event tomorrow and didn't really have the time, but for Leroy I'd of done it. That man is too milquetoast to commit murder."

Alex looked around the room they were in, "Can we go somewhere quiet? I'd like your take on something."

"Sure, let's go to my office." After they got settled, "What's up?"

"You hear a lot of things. Have you ever heard of Steve Gunderson blackmailing people?"

"I know for a fact that he does."

"How would you know that?"

"Simple, I've paid him to keep quiet."

"What? Why?" Alex was highly surprised.

"One of these days, your nose is going to get you into big trouble," Mavis commented. She laughed when Alex turned red, "I love it when you do that. I paid because I didn't want to lose business. Someone gave him information on my store cameras. This is a small town, nobody wants "big brother" watching their every move. I understand that, I also understand safety. Me having gargoyle cameras in each room has really come in handy. I made Mr. Gunderson sign a non-disclosure contract. I knew that he really needed money for something , so he signed the contract and I paid. I figured it was a small price to pay in the long run. We each got something out of the deal. But, make no mistake; I made sure that he understood that if he said anything, anything at all, or printed anything in his newspaper, I would sue his arse to the max. I also made sure that he understood that he would be hurting in numerous ways. I would make sure he was penniless and lying hurt in a gutter somewhere."

Alex listened to her friend and absorbed what she said. "I believe that it would be very prudent of me to stay on your good side."

Mavis looked at her and smiled a shark's smile, "Why, dear, of course it would be. You have never given me a reason to think otherwise." She then smiled a smile that reached her eyes, "Thank you for helping me and Milo."

Alex had stepped out of her office momentarily and then peered back around the corner, "Will you remember to tell Milo that message? Or do you want me to write it down?"

Mavis smiled self-deprecatingly, "Thanks for the reminder. One of these days my head is going to return to normal. I'll write a note now and send it on the train to him."

"I love that you can do that! I am sooooooo jealous! See ya!"

Chapter 53

Friday Evening

Alex had two packages stacked in her arms as she waited with a few other holiday shoppers preparing to cross the street when the signal allowed. The lady on her left turned her way, "I hope that you're not parked too far away, that bottom package looks a big unwieldy."

She smiled, "I'm just across the way. I should have asked for a bigger bag I guess, but it's not heavy. There were only a few minutes to closing, so I wanted to get out of the store. I was only going to get one item, but you know how it goes."

The lady lifted her two bags lightly, "Indeed, I do. But, at least I......." The woman screamed as Alex pitched forward toward the street. Strong hands hauled her back onto the sidewalk before she hit the ground. A car rushed past with its horn blaring.

"Damn!" Alex uttered shakily as she looked at her smashed packages on the road.

"Alex! You should not swear around children!" An older female voice chided her. "Are you drunk?"

Alex turned toward the voice, "No, Mrs. Shepard, I do not drink."

"You should pay better attention to where and how you are standing," the lady sniffed, and continued to admonish Alex as the light turned in their favor, and she walked away with her two teenagers.

"Like those two kids don't know how to swear," the man behind Alex commented. As Alex turned to face her saver, he asked, "Are you okay? I didn't hurt you when I grabbed your arms did I?"

She thought for a second and smiled, "I'm not sure to tell you the truth, but I don't care. A bruise here or there is still so much better than what could have happened. While my packages are smashed, I'm not, and I could have been. Thank you so much for saving me. I'm not sure what happened."

"A man bumped into you is what happened," the gentleman responded grimly. "And you might think I'm nuts, but I swear he also had a cane and used it to help trip you forward," the man frowned. "I'm just glad that I could help."

"I am too," Alex looked around slowly to see if someone seemed to be watching her. Her attention switched back to her rescuer when she heard glass tinkle as he picked up his own dropped packages, "Oh, no! I'm sorry that your items got broken!"

He looked over his glasses and smiled, "Its okay. Items can be replaced, people can't."

"I'm Alex," she introduced herself to the man as she held out her hand.

"Pleased to meet you, Alex," he shook her hand. "I'm Marshall." The distinguished-looking man had a trimmed beard and mustache and was dressed in blue jeans, a red and green plaid scarf, a black bowler hat and a long black overcoat. He bowed slightly.

"Are you new to the town?"

"Yes, I have relatives here. They convinced me that this would be a great place to live and the area could use a computer guy. I think that they just want my help," he laughed.

"Please let me pay for a replacement for your broken gift."

"Unfortunately, I don't believe that is possible, this was a special order and I don't believe there is time for another to arrive." He saw the dismay on her face, "Don't worry, I will get another for another occasion. I have plenty of gifts for my people, this was an extra." He looked toward the road, "How about yours?"

She looked up and down the road before leaning down to pick up the broken packages, "I can replace these easily enough." They walked over to a public trash can and threw their stuff away, "I just wish I understood what happened."

"Not sure, myself. I must be going, Alex, please be careful. I hope to see you around," he inclined his head, touched the brim of his hat lightly and started to walk away.

"Excuse, me …err, Marshall," the man turned her way, "Do you have any business cards? I have a business and am a bit computer stupid myself." He obliged with a grin and she thanked him again before he left.

Chapter 54
Friday Night

Alex contacted Tom as soon as she got home and told him of her experience. "Why didn't you call me sooner?"

"I was going to let it go, but the more I mulled it over, the more I think someone really meant to hurt me."

"But, you really are okay?" He asked concerned.

"Yes, I was pretty shaken, but I'm good now."

"I believe one or two of the companies in that area have cameras. John and I will check it out. Please read me the name off that business card again."

"Did that information I gave you about the dog head lead anywhere?"

"Yes, but one lead leads to another. So, we're working on it." She heard someone call his name. "I'm sorry, Alex, I need to go. Please keep aware and be safe."

"I will try," she replied to the dial tone.

Chapter 55
Dec 16
Saturday Morning

"I can't believe I forgot that Maggie is off today. I have a feeling this is going to be a busy day!" Cat forecasted.

"I don't doubt it," Alex grinned. "Historically, next weekend won't be so busy, but this one is. Thankfully, we don't have our usual amount of deliveries." She pointed at the four boxes on the counter, "we have these cookies this morning and then two wedding cakes in the late afternoon."

A light tap at the door grabbed their attention. Alex checked her pocket watch, "Too early for anything that I know about."

Maggie opened the door, "I gave a warning tap because I didn't want to scare anyone into possibly dropping a cake or gingerbread house."

"Did you forget you don't have to work today?"

"You look great! Where are you going? I don't recall what you said," Alex inquired.

Cat laughed, "With everything going on, I wouldn't expect you to." Maggie joined in.

"You seem a bit nervous or something, is everything alright?"

"Well, I thought it best to tell you both something about something that's been in the works a bit, that I haven't clued you in on," Maggie replied.

Cat had to re-run that statement through her mind again. She grinned as she observed Alex do likewise. She backed up a few paces and looked her friend up and down, "You're not pregnant again are you?"

Maggie smiled and laughed, "Heavens no!"

"But what then?" Alex inquired. "I'm dying to know!"

Maggie looked at her two questioning friends and took a deep cleansing breath. She picked up her huge handbag and pulled two items out. She handed one to each of the ladies, "I wrote a book."

"A book!?" Cat repeated without looking too close at first.

Alex was dumbfounded as she read the front cover, "A Small Bite Can Kill by Maggie Marchetti!"

"Wait! What!?" Cat looked at her friend and then back to the book in her hands.

"Holy cow, that's fantastic! But how......?" Alex hugged her friend. "I didn't know that you wanted to be an author."

Maggie smiled shyly, "I had an agent briefly, but to make a long story short, I don't believe he was a good one. So, I ditched him and self-published. It's a growing area and gaining respect in the book world."

Cat had quieted as she read the back of the book and looked up at her friend. "Really?" she deadpanned. Alex flipped the book over and read the synopsis on the back.

Maggie blushed and laughed, "Well, why not? Write about what you know people say?" She looked at both friends and nervously asked, "I know it's a bit late, seeing as it is already published, but are you okay with it?"

"Just a wee bit late," Cat concurred and looked expectantly at Alex.

Alex finished reading the books' synopsis, a groom dies after eating one bite of his wedding cake. The cake decorator, who is also the business owner, is accused of the murder. She works to clear her name and find the killer before her career and life are ruined. "Sounds a bit familiar, I must agree."

"Ya think?" Cat asked sarcastically.

"To be honest, I'm not sure how I actually feel. I will have to read it first."

"That's only fair," Maggie agreed.

"I take it that I'm the cake decorator in the story?"

"Yes and no, no one character is totally based on any one person in the real world. I did change the names and a number of the facts. This way no one can get mad that I have a character do something that they wouldn't do. Well, they can get mad, but I can do what I feel is needed. And, since you are my friends, and I want to keep working here, I believe that I treated you well in the story," she smiled.

Cat grinned, "So, now I understand that smile awhile back, when I said that you needed to channel your over-active imagination. You already did."

"I didn't realize that you saw that," Maggie responded.

"I see a lot of things," Cat chuckled.

Alex looked at the book again, "Congratulations Maggie, this is awesome! So where are you going so nicely dressed?"

Maggie ducked her head momentarily, "A kick-off for my book, Mavis is helping me."

"The cookies!" Cat exclaimed. "That's why they are wedding cake shaped and have a bite out of each one design-wise!"

"Mavis just ordered them earlier this week," Alex stated. "You're the up and coming new author!"

"Yeah, one man's troubles are this woman's good fortune, or at least that is how Mavis explained it, when she asked me if I was interested. It still seems a bit wrong, so I hope all goes well."

"What do you mean?"

"Well, my book kick-off was originally going to be around mid-February, close to Valentine's Day. I had planned to tell you two about this book in a totally different way. Mavis had a different author scheduled for this event; actually it was a writing team that writes under the pen name, M.J. MacAllen. One guy, Joseph McDonahue, lives here in the United States and the other guy, Mason MacDonald, has been living in Africa. The one in Africa recently got killed by a lion."

"A lion," a wide-eyed Cat repeated.

"Yeah, a horrible way to go," Maggie shuddered slightly. "So, naturally they couldn't make it today."

"Understandable," Alex agreed.

"Would be a bit hard," Cat concurred.

"Mavis was upset. She felt really bad for the guys and their families and all, but here, far far away from the tragedy, she had her own problems. She had had the date set for quite some time and had already advertised. Since she already would have to send out corrections, she looked at the next author event. It happened to be mine. She doesn't schedule events for January, and usually not February either, due to our high chances of snow, but since I am real local, we were going for mid-February. Anyway, she pitched a good sale and I eventually agreed. The other guys were great and unique for our area, so I hope that this doesn't backfire on me," Maggie said with concern.

"I'm sure it will work out fine," Alex encouraged.

"Mavis will have your back," Cat seconded.

"And so do we," Alex and Cat simultaneously stated.

"Thank you both so much. I've signed them both," Maggie checked her watch and squawked, "Oh, man, I've gotta go!"

"Yes, don't be late! Have fun! We'll see you there!" At Maggie's questioning look, Alex continued, "Mavis told us we would want to meet the author, so we planned for it time-wise today. We just didn't know who it would be. Normally, I would have scouted it out, but tis our busy season, and it escaped my mind."

They hugged their friend and Cat helped her take the cookies out to her mini-van.

Cat found Alex at the front of the building getting ready to open up the shop. "Wow! That was interesting. What do you really think of Maggie's book?"

"I am truly happy for her, but I believe I need to read her book."

"Concerned?"

"That's too strong a word I believe. She's smart so I don't think she would include the 'wrong' stuff, but……," she widened her eyes briefly and shrugged.

"We might want to be even more careful than usual when speaking in this place," Cat suggested and Alex agreed.

"I think it was an interested choice to base her murder mystery book on the case of the groom dying from eating one piece of his wedding cake. Who would have thought that possible? Kill one person with the same cake that killed none other. And with Maggie being a witness against you for Alex Sr.'s death, she has a lot of fodder for a second book."

"Oh, great, that's too true! Not sure I needed one more interesting thing in my life right now, but it is what it is. Maybe we'll learn more at the book signing," Alex checked her pocket watch. We need to leave in one hour. Please handle the front until Carsenia and Jo-Jo show up. I will double-check our orders and make sure all is right in the back so we can leave.

Chapter 56
Saturday Early Afternoon

As soon as Alex and Cat entered the bake shop office, the intercom started squawking, "How'd it go? How'd it go?"

The ladies walked to the front room, "It was really nice." Alex smiled. "Mavis really outdid herself with the decorations and food."

"Being Christmas, didn't hurt," Cat added.

"You're right there. Mavis even surprised Maggie with some out-of-town visitors. She had Maggie's favorite aunt and uncle there and a few others. She figured since the rooms were already booked for the other authors, and there are no refunds at this time of year with the B&B she had used, it was a great opportunity to surprise Mags."

"Did a lot of people show?"

Cat looked at Alex, "I think so. The main event took place upstairs, but there were more than normal on the first floor also."

"I'm glad for her!"

"Mavis was smart to put a lift in when she renovated," Alex said.

"A lift?" Carsenia asked.

"Are we in Britain?" Jo-Jo smiled.

"It's an elevator. Mavis was calling it that today and now it's stuck in my head for the day."

"But why is she calling it that?" Carsenia persisted.

"You don't really know her too well do you?"

Carsenia turned a bit red, "No, I pop in from time to time. To be honest, she scares me a bit. I like Jayne more." Everyone chuckled.

"I really don't know who's more dangerous," Alex replied. "Mavis is cool, but ever since she got that concussion, she'll use one word for another or forget the word she wants."

"That's sounds very frustrating."

"For her, it can be. As long as I can understand what she wants or is trying to say, it's good. Sometimes you just need to wait a moment or two, but she gets it done."

"What all do they do at a book signing? I've never been to one," Jo-Jo inquired.

"It varies. A while back I went to one about two hours away and all the author did was sign the book, no real interaction with the author. I didn't really like it. Mavis does it differently. The author is introduced, they talk about their book for a short time, and sometimes they do a short reading, then answers questions, and finally the actual signing of the book. I think Maggie did really well, and I believe she did pretty well on sales."

"Some people missed the change of author notices and were a bit upset because Maggie's book was not an adventure in Africa, but Mavis smoothed things over. I don't even know if Mags knew it."

"There was a minor ruckus while Maggie was signing her books, but that was downstairs and it was handled. Tom was there to see Maggie and was slightly involved in the issue. He and John took care of it. And again, I don't

181

think Maggie knew anything about it. She was on cloud nine," Alex grinned.

"Mavis also had a trivia book game and a few raffle baskets," Cat added. "Something tells me we weren't as busy here."

"Oh, we had our share of business," Jo-Jo replied.

"Super busy a number of times," Carsenia said, "and it was fun!"

As customers entered the shop, Alex caught movement outside her building toward the rear and glanced at her watch, "That's awesome, but we need to get delivering those two wedding cakes."

As the ladies entered the backroom, Cat stopped for a moment before giving her boyfriend a big hug, "What are you doing here?"

"Taking you away for an overnight surprise!" Mike grinned.

Cat was nonplussed, "But,.......I can't, Alex and I have two cakes to deliver."

"You can and you will," Alex laughed. "Now, go have fun!"

"But I don't have any clothes!" Cat said.

"Yes, you do," Mike replied. "I stopped and picked up the overnight bag that Alex packed for you this morning."

"That's why you arrived about thirty minutes after me this morning," she glared at her friend. Alex gave her a smug grin in reply.

Cat looked at Mike, "Not that I don't want to go, but, that one cake is a bit of a bugger to set up alone."

"That's why I'm here." Connie stepped out from around a corner in the kitchen and flourished her arm and bowed.

Cat just looked around the room and smiled, "It looks like everything is set then."

"And I got your cat covered," Alex added. "Now, git out of here," she made shooing motions to which Connie joined in laughing. "See you Monday or Tuesday if you want. Just let me know."

Cat stopped and turned before getting into Mike's pick-up, "Thank you everyone!"

John parked the car behind numerous other official vehicles lined up along a country road leading to a farm just outside of town. As Tom and he got out of the car, he commented "I sure hope we don't have to walk through too much cow dung."

"Great day to wear your new shoes," Tom chuckled. As they approached an officer, Tom asked, "Where's the body?"

"Over this way, sirs," the officer replied. They followed him over to a pond located just off the road in a farmer's field. "The farmer, a Mr. Blaylock, was checking his fence line when he came across a man floating in one of his ponds. He said that he immediately called 9-1-1, and then his wife, and stayed here until help came. He said that he was sure that the man was dead, so he didn't go into the pond for any reason. The coroner should be here shortly."

Tom and John interviewed the farmer and were just finishing up checking over the whole scene, when an officer pulled the body from the lake. "Oh, crap! It had to be him."

John quietly nodded his head as he looked at the dead man, "It's definitely not a plus. What do you think?"

"I think it would be one heck of a coincidence for this man to be dead of an accident less than twenty-four hours after the incident at the book store. We need to see if we can learn of Ronnie Metlamb's activities during that time frame." He watched the coroner show up, "And I am real curious as to his cause of death."

Chapter 58
Sunday Morning

"Alex, great to see you here! Did you decide to change churches?"

"No, Eleanor, I came to see the Children's play. Our church usually does one, but the lady who handles it had to go back home this year. Our children did a great singing program, but I really enjoy the plays."

"Maybe, if it happens again, you could offer to handle it."

"I'm a bit busy at this time of year, but I will think it over."

"It doesn't take much, just a few hours," the older woman stated.

"I don't think you realize how much time and effort goes into one of these plays, Eleanor," Alex carefully replied.

She lightly waved her hand back and forth in the air. "You could handle it easily," the woman assured her.

"Please don't dismiss all the hard work that the children and adults have put into this," Alex requested as she looked past the lady and caught a glimpse of Maggie. "Excuse me, please. I need to go congratulate a friend."

Chapter 59
Sunday Early Afternoon

Tom and John entered the bookshop "Passages of Time" and asked for Mavis. The clerk told them to go back to the History room and they found her restocking some books. "Hi Mavis! Quick question, do you have cameras throughout your shop?"

Mavis looked up at the men, "Sorry, only in the register area and outside perimeters. Would that help?"

"Perhaps, can we see the footage from yesterday?" John asked.

"Yes, of course, give me five minutes to finish up here and meet me in the back right corner of the shop in the horror thriller room, please," Mavis replied and returned to her work.

"Very good, sounds like a plan." John commented as he watched Tom walk forward to welcome Joey to the shop.

"This place is splendiferous," Joey commented as he looked around the bookshop. "The amount and the quality of artwork are awesome."

"Yes, it is," Tom responded. "When you get a chance, each book is in an area decorated to match its genre. You already walked through and seen the fantasy and children's areas. I like the mystery area in the back room next to the horror.

Ten minutes later, after introductions were made of Joey to Mavis, the men were following her down a short hallway with coat hooks on the walls that led away from the main room. The men were curious as they came up behind her at the end of the hallway. It just appeared to be a dead end with a beautiful wooden intarsia eagle and tree art piece on the wall. Mavis pushed a few pieces in the artwork and the end of the hallway swung inward into a room. "Impressive door, Mavis," Tom said. "I can honestly say that I didn't see it coming."

Mavis chuckled, "That's the idea. You can thank my hubby for it. I love it too. Hidden rooms and passages excite me."

As the men looked around and checked out the video room, Joey spoke up in awe, "Nice set up. I wish everyone had this set-up."

"My computer guru had input when we set this place up. He got together with the contractor and they worked out this neat room that can hold a lot of monitors and computers and yet not take up a lot of space. It was an added plus that my husband gave them more of a budget than I would. He worries about me and wants me safe." She smiled and looked around at the guys.

"Good man," John replied. He noticed a small opening in the wall that looked like a tunnel with train tracks coming out. The tracks were visible for about six feet before disappearing into another tunnel. "Cool train, too."

"That can definitely come in handy," Joey agreed rubbing a hand on his bearded chin.

Tom looked at the various monitor screens, "You have more cameras than you let on, Mavis."

"We were in the shop area with people around. I don't want the world thinking 'big brother' or in this case 'big mother' is watching everything they do. Each room has a gargoyle of a different design, but with one major similarity, each of their eyes is a camera. My husband says I trust too much, he requested the cameras."

"Good man," Joey agreed with John.

"Yes, he is, but we are a small town where people believe in trust and friendliness. These cameras don't set that tone." She looked befuddled a second, "'Alex's guy,' what time frame are ya'll looking at?"

"Just yesterday as a whole," Tom responded.

Mavis set the men up with their own monitors for viewing; made sure they were good, and headed back out to the shop. "There is a small fridge with drinks and munchies in the back corner. Feel free to indulge. Let me know if you need anything else."

Joey waited until the door closed behind Mavis before asking, "What's with the 'Alex's guy,' doesn't she know who you are?"

Tom smiled as he checked his monitor, "Yes. Get used to it, Joey, but hopefully only for a bit yet. Mavis is a cool lady. Two years ago, a woman driving behind Mavis wasn't paying attention to the road and rear-ended her. Mavis got a concussion. Apparently, women in general take longer to recover from a concussion then men, older women even longer. Mavis is in her mid-sixties. So the doc told her it might be six or seven years before she heals totally. So, she sometimes forgets names of people, doesn't

189

matter how long she has known you. One never knows what nickname you might get for a while. When she gets tired, her speech can be affected and she has trouble reading information out loud. Sometimes she means one word, but says another. It can get very frustrating for her and sometimes very humorous for others. It's a good thing she has a sense of humor. Her husband, Milo, is real supportive and she has good staff people. Her main staff person is Jayne. She is loyal to Mavis, works in the shop, handles her website, and is an artist. She helped to design and paint the different rooms in this shop."

"Was Jayne the one running the front register when I came in? A twenty-ish woman with long dark wavy hair?"

"Yes, that would be her."

"When you get a chance, check out the 'Christmas Passage' tunnel," John suggested. "Mavis and Jayne outdid themselves this year."

"Where's that?"

"If you go out front and look at the bookshop. There is a connected building to the left of it and one on the right of it. The right one is a teahouse. The one on the left is where Milo has his law practice. Where Milo's and Mavis's meet, there is a pedestrian tunnel that leads one from the front sidewalk to the back parking lot. It's about four foot wide. Right now, it's decorated for Christmas. It's great anytime, but especially at night. They used plexiglass and lighting on the walls to make different scenes. The plexiglass is painted with scenery and such. There are lighted figure designs between the plexiglass and the brick tunnel walls.

You can't see them until they turn the power on and it's really cool. At one place, it looks like reindeer jumping from one side of the tunnel to the other. They play Christmas music as you walk through and one can see different action holiday scenes. There are snowmen dancing, elves building toys, and loading a big sleigh, and Santa Claus with his reindeer to name a few."

"And they use some kind of projection technique to make it look and feel like it's snowing as you walk through the tunnel. Even the glass panels on the streetlights in this shop's area are decorated with some sort of Christmas design. The newspaper did a great article on it last week," John added.

"Sounds really interesting, I bet my grandkids would love it," Joey grinned.

The men went to their different monitors to view the events in the bookshop of the previous day. After about twenty minutes and some general comments of seeing Ronnie coming in and walking around, Tom called the guys over to him. "Watch this. "Here's where he starts to boast about the criminal mind being superior to ours and that the police won't catch the boss man. Right after he starts spouting out, a man brushes up against him. Ronnie turns like he is about to say something, but doesn't."

"He kind of looks a bit scared of the man if you ask me," Joey observed. "And he leaves shortly afterwards, in fact they both do."

"Agreed, but this angle is bad to identify the man. He's dressed pretty basic and the hat that he's wearing is not helping at all. Let's re-check the recordings for a better view of that guy," John offered. "I am beginning to think that this guy knew about the cameras in this store," John stated. "We have been at this for a while and I have yet to get a clear view of this guy. Anyone else?"

Negative grunts answered him. "Let's expand to checking out the book signing as a whole. We might catch something else," Tom suggested.

A bit late Joey spoke up, "I think I see our man come in." The other two joined him, "He has the hat on that keeps getting in the way of our sight. He enters wearing a denim overshirt, but removes it before bumping our guy. I don't see any logo, so I don't know if the reason for removing the shirt is important to our case."

"Is he with anyone?"

Joey rechecks his monitor. "He came in alone and then I lose sight of him for a while. He rounds that corner and then doesn't re-emerge for about ten or fifteen minutes." Joey fast forwards the recording a bit.

Tom taps Joey's shoulder, "Stop a second. Mavis came out of wherever that man was. I am not super familiar with this shop, where is this taking place?"

John stepped out of the room briefly and then reappeared, "it appears to be just outside this room we are in. Remember, we followed Mavis out of the main area, through an archway, and down a short hallway to the door to this room. "Joey, anyone leave after our man, let's call him Mr. Hat for now?"

Joey fast forwarded briefly and the men waited. A middle-aged man with short brown hair that was combed upward and had a goatee casually walked out of the observed area. He looked around for a few minutes until he appeared to find someone. "I wonder what he is staring at?"

"Or whom?"

"We need to check out different angles and look for Mr. Goatee here." Tom and John returned to their monitors.

"Whoa, what the heck?" Joey jumped and yelled causing Tom and John to turn his way to see what was going on. Joey was squatting down and looking under the counter. "Geez, you guys made me jump."

"What's going on over there Joey?"

Joey motioned with his right hand encouragingly to something. Tom and John walked over to investigate. A big black short-hair cat and a wee bit smaller black-striped tabby carefully walked out into the room and looked at the men. "No one told me that there were cats here."

"You don't like cats?" Tom asked.

"I don't favor them, that's all," Joey responded. "How did they get in? The door is shut, and they did not use the train tunnel."

"That we know of. Who knows how long they've been in the room," Tom bent down to pet them and looked from whence they came. "There's an opening in the back corner. I'd guess that they have freedom of the shop."

"They do," John chuckled. "My wife and I come here for different programs. These two have Mavis wrapped around their little paws. Don't accidentally step on one of them," John rolled his eyes, "Mavis will light up big time!"

"Sounds like a voice of experience," Joey grinned.

"Let me introduce Murdoch and Julia. Murdoch is the black one." John saw Tom's mental gears spinning and chucked, "I'll save you some mental strain there, Tom. They are named after the main characters in the *Murdoch Mysteries* written by Maureen Jennings. Mavis and Milo love the show. My wife and I checked into them and now we're hooked too. The writing is excellent and the characters are great."

"I think that these two have taken up enough of our time." Shortly after returning to their monitors, Tom spoke up again, "I found Mr. Goatee numerous times."

"Same here," Tom heard the others speak up and the sound of footsteps as the two other men joined him.

"At first, he just enters the store like a casual visitor, and then after coming out the hallway, he seems to be focused on someone. He just seems to be watching whoever it is."

"And thinking," Joey added.

"Then his attention seems to turn quick, I believe that's to check on the commotion around Ronnie."

"Watch his face stiffen," John adds. "That is one hard man. He leaves almost immediately and in the opposite direction. So did anyone figure out who he was observing?"

"I'm not sure," Tom stated. "But, it may be Mavis." At the two men's questioning looks, he continued, "The place is pretty crowded and maybe I am wrong, but let me show

194

you something." He quickly shot to four different places and pointed out where he thinks the man was looking. "I may be wrong, but it was after Mavis came out of the hallway ahead of them. I think Mr. Goatee is watching her. I think we should ask her what she was talking to them about."

John left the room briefly again and returned with Mavis. Tom brought her up to speed and waited for a response. "I didn't talk to them."

"Not at all?"

She thought a minute, "No. Well, not really. I had come back here to check on something. I had something on my mind when I left the room, and forgot to check the peephole to see if the coast was clear. I jumped a wee bit I'll tell you, when I came out of the room and found two men in the darkened hallway. I said excuse me or such as I passed by and came back onto the floor. To be honest, I didn't give either a second thought." She looked at the men, "Is there a problem?"

"Not sure," John answered. "Do these two look familiar at all?"

"Yes and no. One is Bruce and the other one I don't know."

"Which one is Bruce?" Tom asked.

She pointed at the man in the hat, "that one. That's Bruce McDavy."

"I know Bruce, but can't tell that that's him in this video," John stated.

"The hat does make it hard to see, but I passed right by him, so I saw his face clearly." Mavis answered casually. She suddenly stood straighter, "Is that going to be a problem? What exactly are you all looking for here?"

"We are just investigating and checking ideas and leads," Tom answered. "However, I think that you should get Milo here so we can advise you both on something."

Mavis reached for the phone on the wall and quickly dialed her husband and asked him to join them. She chuckled as she hung up the phone, "We both have cell phones, Joey. My husband just doesn't like to use his and mine is out front charging."

Joey smiled, "It wasn't cell phone usage I was looking odd about, it's the phone you used. It's a bit on the antique looking side."

Mavis grinned, "I absolutely love older things. You should see my Victrola!" She cackled with glee.

Milo showed up in a few minutes and the detectives thanked him and her for their cooperation. "We don't have all the facts, but we want you two to look at this man with the goatee. Memorize his face and if you see him anywhere, please contact us. Please, don't challenge him or ask him questions."

"Does this man intend to hurt my Mavis?" Milo asked with concern.

"We honestly don't know. If he doesn't know of these cameras, then he shouldn't know that we have discovered him. It may be nothing but we would be foolish not to warn you two. Also, I know that I shouldn't need to say

196

this, but please do not tell anyone about what we have discussed," Tom instructed.

"And we need a copy of this recording," John added.

"Of course, no problem," Mavis assured them.

As the detectives were leaving the bookshop, Joey said, "Thanks for including me in this. My partner couldn't make it again due to her kids, but I really appreciate it."

Chapter 60
Sunday Afternoon

Alex grabbed the ringing phone and was surprised to hear an old friend from the neighboring town. "Morgana, how nice to hear from you!"

"Unfortunately, I have a huge huge favor to ask of you."

"Of course, ask away, although I can't promise you a 'yes,'" Alex said truthfully.

"I fell Christmas shopping yesterday…," Morgana started.

"Oh, no! How injured are you?"

"I sprained both my wrists," she replied.

"Sorry, to hear that. How can I help?"

"Since we are pretty close to the holidays, I don't have a ton of cake orders. The few I have, my staff feel they can handle fine. This year, we created some cool petit fours, and they have taken off big time. My staff will handle any orders that come in. But, cookies are another matter. I have a few cookie orders where I believe I can cover, however, I always get some last minute ones, and I will not be able to handle those."

"Tell those customers to contact me, but no promises. I will take it day to day and take what I know I can do."

"Excellent, Alex. You are the best. If I may, one of my best customers already called, and I took the chance that you would be able to cover at least one of mine and already gave them your number. At the risk of losing them permanently to you, I told her about your Todede's. She would love to give them a try. I just wanted to give you a heads up. I know that they are not your favorite by far, but a lot of us love them, even Cat, as if I have to remind you," she laughed.

"Thanks for the warning," Alex chuckled. "Can you do much decorating-wise?"

"Some. Slow and careful, and you and I know that this is not the season for that," she replied. One more thing, if a family by the name of Snyder from this town calls, be careful of anything peanut. Feel free to tell them no. There is one super strong peanut allergy running in that family, nothing to mess around with."

Alex listened carefully and took notes, "Thanks for everything. As I said, we will take things one day at a time. No promises. Hope you heal quickly!"

"Thanks, me too! And if you have any questions, please don't hesitate to call."

Chapter 61
Sunday Evening

Mike and Cat were enjoying their mini get-away in the Pocono Mountains. They were lounging on a soft leather couch enjoying a fire in a huge fireplace in their suite. On either side of the fireplace were two large windows that allowed them to watch a colorful sunset among some snow covered mountains. Just as the remaining sunlight disappeared and the stars were starting to shine, Mike reached down beside the couch with his left hand and picked up a box. "Cat, I bought you something, but I don't want to scare you, it's not what you might think it to be."

Cat straightened up a bit as he gave her a wrapped gift roughly the size and shape of a shoebox. She opened the box and found another wrapped box inside. She shot him a quizzical look as she lifted that box out and unwrapped it. "Really?" She said as she lifted another wrapped box out. He snickered and smiled as she continued to open four more boxes. "You having fun yet?"

"Yes, as a matter of fact, I am," he stared into her brown eyes and smiled again.

Cat opened another box and found a black velvet box. She opened the box and her eyes widened when she saw a beautiful ring. It was a white gold ring with three small white diamonds in a line in the center of the ring. A wave of blue small diamond accents started on the top of the left diamond and curved to the right over the next two diamonds and down into the ring band. Another wave of blue small diamond accents started at the bottom of the right diamond and curved to the left under the next two diamonds and up into the ring band.

Mike reached over and gently held Cat's hand with the ring box. He felt her stiffen a bit, "This is not an engagement ring." He smiled as she relaxed and turned to look him in the eye. He arched his right brow briefly, "After our camping trip at Mr. and Mrs. J's campground, I figured that you might freak if I asked you to marry me. I know that marriages have not exactly been successful in your family," Mike said.

Cat shook her head, "No, they have not."

"But, I figured you could handle this for now."

"What exactly is this?"

"Cat, one day I do want to marry you. I'm willing to wait for a bit on that for now. However, I was wondering if you would accept this promise ring."

"I'm not real familiar with promise rings," she looked at him.

"I researched into this a bit. I am serious about spending my life with you. Any time I approach the subject of marriage, I can feel your hesitation and sense of panic. What I would like to hear from you is, do you hesitate because of me or because of your family's issues with marriages?"

"The latter," Cat replied. "I do love you and we have been dating for quite some time. And after that aforementioned camping trip, I know that you are the one for me. I just still kind of freak over the 'forever' and 'til death do you part' idea." She shrugged slightly, "Sorry."

Mike smiled, "Then, would you please accept this, shall we call it, pre-step to an engagement and wear this promise ring? I want you to know that I am quite serious about you and I have never felt this way before about anybody. The three main diamonds represent our past, our present, and our future."

Cat looked at him and then down at the ring and thought for a few minutes, enough to make Mike slightly squirm. She looked back up at him and smiled, "Yes, I believe I will."

He gave her a huge hug and a deep kiss, "I'm glad you sexy woman!"

Once she got her breath back, she asked, "On what finger or hand do I wear this?"

"It's basically up to you. There is conflict in my research on that point; however, I would suggest not the normal ring finger on the left hand."

Cat thought briefly before sliding it onto her right hand, onto the finger beside her pinky, "It fits perfectly."

"I was hoping that you picked that one." She looked at him with a questioning look and he continued, "That's the one I measured the one night while you were sleeping."

Cat laughed. Then she rolled into Mike a bit closer, ran her hand lightly over his groin and asked, "How about consummating this agreement?"

"You betcha sexy!"

Chapter 62
Dec 18
Monday Very Early Morning

Alex woke around three in the morning to a phone call from the police, "Ms. Applecake?"

"Yes."

"This is Sasha at Custom Alarm. An alarm is going off at your shop. I tried calling your shop and no one answered, so I called the police and they are on their way."

Alex sped toward her shop. She slowed as she saw the police cars in her driveway. She passed the shop and came in through the back alley and into her back parking lot. She jogged up to her building and searched the officers for a familiar face, "Buck! What's going on here?" He looked at her and smiled. She glared at him, "Don't judge me, Buck."

The officer held his hands out in a calming manner, "I'm not. Everything seems okay, Alex. We'll need......"

Buck was interrupted by a car with flashing lights sliding into the driveway to a halt. The door flew open, "Alex! Are you okay?" Tom asked quickly and flew to her side.

"Yes, I'm good. I just got here after receiving a call about an alarm going off at my shop."

Tom took a deep breath, looked at Alex, and smiled, "You're in your pajamas."

"Yes, I am," she tilted her head at him. "And your point? The phone call I got about a break-in at my shop did wake me up." She quickly looked down and double-checked her outfit, "At least I'm decent." She looked up at a smiling Officer Buck, "As you were saying?"

"We checked the building and it looks fine, except a broken window on this outside door that leads into your office. We figured that is how someone entered, but I can't tell what the person or persons did once he/she/they entered the building. I suggest that you enter and look around. Maybe you will see something we didn't."

"Sure," Alex and Tom walked the building from top to bottom and found nothing out of sorts. As Alex talked to the officers who responded, Tom boarded up the window with supplies that he found in the basement. "I'll reset the alarm. If I find anything later, I'll let you know."

Chapter 63
Monday Morning

Carsenia hustled through the front door of the bakery after Maggie opened the shop, "I got a lead on Thaddy!"

"Fantastic!" Maggie half-shrieked. "What is it?"

"A neighbor boy told his uncle about a friend's cool drone. The uncle is about to ship out in the military for something-or-other and wanted to give his nephew a gift that would not be easily forgotten, so he got him a drone with night vision and a camera. They have been playing with it for the past week. Last night, they were reviewing some of their recordings with friends. The one friend got all excited and said that people at the bakeshop would want to learn of their findings. So the boy's Uncle Tyrod contacted me. Doodles was the dog that dug up Thaddy," she smiled.

Maggie was doubtful, "It's been almost a week. Do you really think Doodles' owners still have it?"

Carsenia shrugged, "We can only hope. I'm meeting up with Doodles' owner in," she flipped her wrist over to check her watch, "twenty minutes at Connie's place, Eats Galore. Letitia, Doodles' female owner, was in a bit of a rush when I talked to her this morning and didn't have time to talk to me. So, wish me luck!" Carsenia left the store with Maggie doing just that.

Chapter 64
Monday Morning

"Any idea why anyone broke in here?" Jo-Jo asked Alex.

"None whatsoever," Alex replied. "If you find anything, please let me know." Alex and Jo-Jo were almost done decorating cupcakes for a couple of different events, when someone knocked on the office door.

Alex answered it and was surprised to see Tom, "I come bearing donuts."

Her eyes lit up, "Fantastic! Any Crullers?"

"I think there's at least one in here somewhere," Tom looked in the bag in his hands.

He walked over to see what all they were working on. "It's interesting that you guys can get totally different looking cupcakes, but not totally switch out the types of decorations used each time that you change orders."

"We use a little of this and a little of that. While it's true that we are using the same glitter, sprinkles, novelty sugars, and icing. We vary them up and use them a bit differently."

"I'm taking a quick breakfast break, if you all have time. I have enough for all," he said looking toward Jo-Jo.

"Of course, I do," Alex smiled. "Jo-Jo?"

"I'm just finishing up and I will be over, thanks!" She smirks a bit.

"What's with the smirk?" Tom asking knowingly. Jo-Jo's face reddened some, "I know, I'm a cop, and yes, I do like donuts." They chuckled.

"Sure don't look like it," Jo-Jo said under her breath as she concentrated at the job at hand.

"I'm sorry, I didn't quite catch what you said," Tom walked toward her.

Jo-Jo smiled at him, "It was nothing, I'll be over soon."

"Let's sit at this table and I'll get some drinks," Alex suggested.

"Alex," Tom waited until he had her full attention, "I believe that you need to keep on guard right now."

"Something else happen?" Alex asked concerned.

"John and I could only locate a couple of cameras in the area where you fell and that Marshall guy helped you. The one camera has not worked in quite some time. The other camera works, but the angle's not good. It's an older one and the clarity is not the greatest either. We agree that it was no accident, but we cannot identify the guy. You were standing with a bunch of other people around you during the actual attack, and that kept us from getting a clear view of the man's actions. He did not turn in the direction of the camera and he was wearing a hoodie. He also had a cane with him, but did not seem to really need it for walking purposes. With the break-in this morning, I'd be a fool not to worry." He hugged Alex, "Promise me that you will keep aware."

"I promise I will try," Alex replied. "This season can get hectic, but I will try to be extra cautious."

Tom looked at her a moment and slowly breathed out, "I hope that you do." Tom and Alex sat down to enjoy the donuts.

"The burglaries seem to be pretty complicated to figure out," Jo-Jo stated. "Is that normal?"

"Not really. We feel it's the same burglars, but we have only a few eye witnesses. When we compare the witness testimonies, we don't seem to have a lot of similarities. There is no steady pattern in the attacks: the burglaries happen on different nights of the week, sometimes even during the day, nobody agrees on the vehicle used, nobody can give us a head count on the number of burglars, and they are hitting three different towns. Someone has put a lot of thought into this. Sooner or later a mistake will be made and we will get them."

"Are you sure it's the same group?" Alex asked.

"Yes, we are pretty sure. The methodology of the actual burglaries is the same, if that makes sense."

"I'm sure being low on man power is not helping," Jo-Jo commented.

"You got that right. The flu this year is a real bugger. That's why Joey is helping here so much. Both of the other police forces are also having flu issues, just not as severe yet. That's why I was working on Alex's murder case. I think the boss was too sick to care and that's also why he agreed so easily with the DA on arresting Leroy Winchester."

"How are you and John faring, flu-wise?" Jo-Jo inquired.

"So far, so good. I use an herb for increasing the immune system that my sister strongly believes in, and John's wife has him using essential oils or such, neither of us really understand them, but they seem to be working." Tom finished a donut before continuing, "My main reason for being here is that I'm following up on a weird message that you left me late last night. It was garbled and I'm not sure what you were trying to convey," Tom replied.

As Alex was trying to remember what all she had wanted to ask Tom, she finished her Cruller. "I was just asking about that dog head I found. Were you able to find out anything interesting?"

"We're still working on it. Your mechanic guy, Sedge, wasn't the easiest man to track down. You told me Thursday night and Friday I went to the garage, but Stan did not know which vehicle Sedge found the dog head in. Sedge was off on Friday, something to do with the wedding. It had been pre-approved, so nothing suspicious there. Stan checked his records. Sedge had worked on five vehicles on Wednesday and helped with three others. So we followed up on each of the car owners and everyone had a good alibi. I know it sounds bad, but I talked to the young man on Saturday, just before his wedding." Alex looked dumbfounded at him and just shook her head. "What? I needed some information. He told me a Mr. Wixford was the owner of the vehicle where the dog head had been found. Apparently, Mr. Wixford was away on a business trip a couple of weeks ago, but his car was here. His wife's car was in the shop, so she had the use of his.

His daughter borrowed the car to go camping for the weekend with her boyfriend. Shortly after his return, he noticed that his ABS check light was flickering. He finally took it to the shop and had some work done. Apparently, the daughter had run over a log or such and damaged something under the car."

"Camping? Now? Who does that?" Alex asked.

He laughed, "Some people don't mind camping in the cold."

"That's nuts! Then, it wasn't tent camping."

"I believe it was. We checked with the campground, it's a piece away from here, and the attendant confirmed that they were there."

"Wow, tent camping at this time of year," she shook her head. Carsenia entered the room.

"Sorry, for interrupting, but I have a question. But first, if you don't mind, who was tent camping recently?"

"A Melanie Wixford," Tom replied.

"No way," Carsenia commented adamantly.

"What? Why do you say that?"

"There is no way Melanie went camping, especially in a tent, at this time of year. She's too much of a priss. I know, she went to school with me."

"Her mom described her as a tomboy when I had asked," Tom replied.

"She would, the woman is delusional. Just because she used to help her grandpa on a dairy farm when she was small, doesn't mean she would still do that now. She still thinks her daughter is a virgin, for Pete's sake. My mom can't believe that she doesn't have at least two or three kids by now."

"But, she's what? Nineteen or twenty?" Jo-Jo asked.

"Exactly. She couldn't find a good boyfriend if she tripped over him. Melanie has always allowed guys to talk her into anything and everything, usually trouble."

Alex glanced at Tom and saw his mental gears spinning. "Carsenia, did you mention a question?"

"Oh, crap, you're right," she glanced behind her quick and back to Alex. "Mrs. Cannon is out there and wondered about that item she asked you to order her."

"Remind her it's for Valentine's Day, and I placed the order like I told her, it should be here next week. I will call her when it arrives." Alex watched Carsenia hurry off and turned back to Tom. "What's up? Figure something out?"

"I just might have. A while back, I was at The Mechanicsburg Mystery Bookshop for an author talk. A man, who had written a book about a sniper, talked about how cops have to protect themselves from getting tunnel vision. I had noticed that can occur, but he's right, we must keep that in mind in investigations."

"Tunnel vision about what?"

"They figured they were looking for a white van for the culprits, but they should have kept an open mind about it. Everyone kept looking for a white van. They ended up catching the guys in a blue car. I believe that's kind of what I, or we, have been doing."

"You mean the burglars are using different vehicles."

"Yes, and not necessarily their own," Tom got up and started cleaning up the table. "I will need to contact that campground again."

"I can get that if you want to leave," Alex spoke up. "So, Melanie or her beau ran over Libby's metal pole and not a chunk of wood," Alex said getting excited. "That's how the dog head got stuck under the vehicle."

"The evidence would seem to indicate that. Except, Mrs. Ferrara's house was not robbed, and neither were her neighbors. Unless, hitting that library box scared the burglars off." Tom observed Alex's change of expression, "You know something."

"I believe I do. I think the burglars got scared when a dog was where he wasn't supposed to be. I bet that they left in a hurry and destroyed the box in the process. You need to talk to the Birkmans." She gave him the information as Jo- Jo asked a question.

"Have you figured out how the burglars are figuring out which houses to hit?"

"Not yet," Tom answered.

"I'm sure that you've already checked it out, but could it be something simple, like someone knowing when the mail or newspapers are being stopped or held?"

"No real pattern there either. Different post offices, not all the same newspapers, people have their lights on changing timers, no common dog sitters, etc."

"I don't mean to be accusatory or anything, but what if it's a little of this and a little of that?" Alex inquired.

"What do you mean?"

"Like those cupcakes," she pointed to the table where she and Jo-Jo had been working. "We use each decoration a bit differently, but the result is still a pretty cupcake, just a different way of getting the job done."

Tom started to speak, but stopped. He quietly looked at Alex and Jo-Jo, walked toward their decorating area, and then looked around at the cupcakes and decorations. His eyes wandered back and forth between the culinary items. He looked at Alex, "I have to go." He grabbed his things and started to leave.

Alex and Jo-Jo looked at each other and then at him. Alex shrugged her shoulders, "I'm guessing you figured something out."

Tom came back and kissed her quickly, "Yes, I did. Thank you very much. This has been a very informative donut break," he glanced with a smile at Jo-Jo before leaving.

Chapter 65
Monday Afternoon

Carsenia, came in for her shift just after lunch. When she got Maggie alone for a few minutes, she explained that Letitia had dropped off Thaddy at the local pawn shop just yesterday. Doodles had damaged him and she fixed him up. "Damaged him?" Maggie was horrified. "How bad?"

Carsenia put her hand out, "Just lightly. His shirt was scraped up and a chunk of his nose nipped off. Letitia was surprised her Husky/Big Swiss Mountain dog didn't do more damage. She fixed him up and then sprayed him with something to protect his changes. Letitia didn't want him and didn't realize that people were looking for him, so she donated him to the local pawn shop, Misfits."

"Great! Did you check it out?"

"Yes, but a little boy beat me to it," she said dejectedly. "The guy working there would not give me his identity."

Maggie checked her watch, "I leave in fifteen minutes. I'll give it a try."

Chapter 66
Monday Afternoon

Tom was discussing with John his visit with Alex, and what he had been thinking about how the burglars were pulling their jobs, when Joey popped into the police station. "Hey, we might have gotten a weird stroke of luck."

"What do you mean?" John asked.

"The farmer had a critter cam on that pond," Joey replied.

"How'd you find that out?" Tom inquired.

"I stopped by the farm and asked the farmer if there was any particular reason that he was at the pond yesterday morning. He has a lot of acreage and a lot of fencing to check. Why there?"

"And his answer was?"

"Apparently, local kids like to skinny dip in that lake. It's outside the fence row, so no cows get in and around it to muck it up."

"It's winter time," Tom stated.

He held up a finger, "Yes, the perfect time for polar bear plunges."

"You mean going in the water with only a swimsuit on?" John asked.

"Or less," Tom added.

"That's majorly stupid," Joey commented. "In the city, you would need some major tetanus shots.

"Agreed. Now, about this critter cam?"

"I just got back from getting a copy of the time frame in question. I didn't get a chance to look at it yet. The farmer doesn't keep track of this, his son, Greg, does. Greg called a few days ago and told his dad that the critter cam's viewing area had drastically changed for the worse, and wanted his dad to fix it. His dad forgot. Greg had called his dad to remind him and that is the main reason that Mr. Anderson was out at the pond yesterday morning. He had reminded his dad that New Year's wasn't far off and that kids may be striking in force around that time."

They all watched the footage, "Crap, I agree the critter cam's viewing area stinks! No way would the farmer be able to identify any kids cavorting, except by their feet!"

"Let's watch it again. I think we can pull out some useful information."

"Dang it! I can see just a small section of a vehicle. It's black."

"I believe it's a truck."

"I concur."

The men backed up the recording again and watched two sets of cowboy boots walking. Each person was also dressed in blue jeans. A set of black boots were walking in a determined manner, some brown ones were hesitating. Brown boots slipped, and for a moment they saw a man hit the ground, and then a hand jerks him back up. "Did anyone recognize who just fell?"

John checked his notes, "It's a bit blurry, however, Ronnie was wearing brown boots when he was pulled from the pond, so I feel pretty sure that that was Ronnie we momentarily saw. Didn't the clothes look right for him?"

"Yes, I agree."

"So, we need to keep a look out for someone wearing black boots driving a black vehicle, probably a pick-up truck, in the country, in the winter. Piece of cake," Joey finished sarcastically. "I'm not sure how well that's going to go."

"What were you expecting, a clear video of the murder?" Tom inquired.

"Yes, I was, or at least hoping for," Joey replied. "Wait, don't you mean alleged murder?"

"Not anymore," John replied. "The coroner's report came in and indicates that while Ronnie had plenty of alcohol in his system, he didn't drown. He died of strangulation."

"So, it is murder now," Joey stated.

"Yes, and we have a few clues to work with. The black boots aren't just boots. They are black square-toed cowboy boots with an antique silver toe accent, and decorative black stitching," John clarified.

"Guys, catch the hand coming down to yank Ronnie back up. The yanking man was not gentle and he's wearing a ring." Joey backed up the video, "Watch for the ring. Even though it's blurry, you can tell its silver. It's not flashy, but does have a squarish shape on top."

"There are two people walking, only one slipping, I believe the black boots have a tread. We need to see if anyone caught those bootprints and took molds of them for evidence. If not, then we should go out to look for them."

"If the area was released, anybody could have walked around in that area. Any chain of evidence would be broken and we would not be able to use what we find in court," Tom commented.

"Maybe not, but it might help us pinpoint the guy we are looking for," John responded.

"The critter cam did come in handy. I'll lay odds 'black boots' doesn't know about it. Whereas, this video wasn't as perfect as we'd like, it has given us some clues and directions to follow up on."

Chapter 67
Monday Night

Tom stopped by the bakery to eat supper with Alex. He walked into the back area of her shop just as she was setting the Chinese take-out on the table, "You read my mind, I was in the mood for General Tso.

"Then it's a good thing I got some," she smiled.

"So what's on your mind?"

"Why does something in particular have to be on my mind? Can't I just want to see you?"

"Yes, you could, but during your phone call, I got the feeling there's something else," he grinned.

She laughed, "You guessed it," she turned a bit red. "There is something else. I have been thinking about Leroy Winchester. Now, don't get me wrong. I did not kill Alex Sr., but I find it hard to believe Leroy did it. I realize anyone can kill, but I don't see him as the one for Alex Sr."

Tom's smile disappeared, "I agree. I'm not saying he's innocent, I just think it's premature, but the decision was made over John's and mine objections. The chief and the D.A. see: motive, his wife was sleeping with the victim, opportunity, he has no real alibi, he says that he was in seclusion working on a wood project, and means, a tool with Alex Sr.'s and Penny's blood was found among his woodworking tools. The captain's happy and said that I should be too, because you're in the clear."

"You found the murder weapon, a wood carver's tool at Leroy's place?"

"Yes."

"Why would he keep it? Surely he'd think the cops would check his tools."

"I don't think he would, but I've been overruled. The D.A. is right in one respect, people can be stupid. I pointed out that wood tools are sharp, the whittlers knew each other, so Alex Sr.'s blood could be on the tool for a totally innocent reason, as well as Penny's."

"He told me that the case was solid and to let it go. He ordered me to keep my hands off of it. With the flu hitting the station so hard, I should be happy to clear this case off my work load."

"But, you have your doubts," Alex said.

He nodded, "I certainly do. From what I have found out, Leroy was probably happy that Alex Sr. was sleeping with his wife. This is a very busy time for him business-wise. Leroy told me that all of his tools have his initials inscribed on them. The alleged murder weapon does not have his initials on it, even though the rest of his tools do. I truly believe that reasonable doubt exists." Tom just looked at her for a few moments. He put both his hands flat on the table in front of him and wiggled them a bit as he talked, "This is really out there, and I have absolutely no proof, but I swear the D.A. and chief are way too happy to end this case."

"Shouldn't they be? Isn't that normal? You know, part of the job and all?"

"There's more to it, and I can't quite put my finger on it. They seemed relieved or something."

"Why do you think that?" Alex inquired.

He shook his head slightly. "Just a feeling I've got, nothing more…….at least not yet," he locked eyes with her briefly. Tom stopped talking and finished the food on his plate. Alex noticed the bags on his face and glanced at the clock. "Do you have to go back to work? Remember, I keep cots here. If you want to sleep for a bit, I will make sure that you get up at your designated time."

"I think I will accept your offer, but only for an hour. First, I want to bring you up to date about something we found out earlier."

"So you want me to keep a look out for black boots with a black pickup truck?" She asked somewhat skeptically after he had finished briefing her.

"I know, it's slim, but who knows. Just be careful," he gave her a kiss and an intense hug and went to lie down.

Almost to an exact hour later, Alex came to wake him, "John just called, there's some kind of major issue at the other end of town. It's all hands on deck. He said for you to call him when you got out to your car."

Chapter 68
December 19
Tuesday Early Morning

Mike gave Cat one more long kiss before turning towards the door, "I have to go babe."

She gave his butt a quick squeeze, "Do you have a guess for your return?"

He turned back with a big grin, "Probably this weekend. I worked extra this summer so I could have more 'home' time during December, I made a deal with the dispatcher. And I'm holding him to it."

Cat watched him drive down her street. She was about to turn to go inside, when she saw him veer into a driveway down a bit. "Crap, now what?"

Mike grabbed his cellphone and called Cat, "Cat, I need you to call 9-1-1. Tell them to get to Alex's place for a possible break-in. Tell them that an armed civilian will be inside."

Cat did as requested, slid into some shoes, grabbed her keys, and ran down to her friend's house.

Mike carefully jogged up to Alex's front door. He examined the broken glass and determined that someone had broken it inward and noticed that the front door was ever so slightly open. He carefully and quietly slid into her house and took note of the situation. There was an umbrella cone with a couple of umbrellas tipped over and lying in the hallway, otherwise, everything seemed fine.

Mike raised his gun in front of him and surveyed the room. He canvassed the house from one room to the next. He knew this house was almost a duplicate to Cat's, but couldn't remember which bedroom Alex used as her own. "Alex," he called out low a few times. Hearing nothing, he raised his voice, "Alex? You here?"

"Halt! Stay where you are! Stay where you are!" Rang out strong in the room.

Mike turned slightly to his right and listened as the bird in the cage repeated its message. He grinned slightly as he continued his search. "Alex?" Mike said a bit louder as he walked toward the main bedroom.

The door at the end of the hallway, which had been slightly ajar, opened a wee bit more, and he saw an eye looking at him. The door flew open as Alex realized who he was, "Geez, Mike, you scared the crap out of me! When did you get back? What is going on?"

Mike looked to the ground briefly and back up, "No, not literally," she grinned.

"Are you okay? Anybody harm you or in the room with you?"

Totally confused, she answered, "I'm fine and quite alone." Her focus changed to somewhere behind him.

Mike swung quickly with his gun in front of him. "Whoa, Mike! It's only me," Tom said with his hand on his own gun.

Seconds later, an officer approached from the side, "Everything okay in here sir?"

Tom looked at Mike and then Alex, "I'm not sure. Mike, is everything good?"

Mike relaxed his gun and handed it to Tom to defuse the situation as quickly as possible. He looked at the officer and said, "I have a carry permit and I thought a friend could be in danger."

Within seconds, Cat walked into the house and observed Mike giving Tom his gun. The officer turned quickly, "Miss, you can't be in here."

Cat quietly looked at Tom. "It's okay, officer. She can stay." Tom looked at Alex and Mike, "So what exactly are we all doing here so bright and early?"

Mike gave a quick rundown on seeing the broken front door and checking on the house. He had just found Alex when everyone in the world appeared. Tom got things moving with calling in a crime team to check for clues, and having officers patrol the front area to the house to keep people at bay.

After some time, Tom came to the group that had settled at the table and explained that it looked like someone had tried to enter the house, but was stopped by someone or something.

"I choose something," Mike replied. "Alex might not have a dog, but she does have some protection." Everyone looked around and then back to Mike, Alex grinned. "Her bird yelled quite loudly, 'Halt, stay where you are,' when I came in the room. I believe that he might have yelled it to whoever broke in. Then, I believe someone knocked over the umbrella stand."

"Who?" Cat asked looking around.

"Micky!" Alex answered. "He likes to protect me."

"I wonder when this all went down?" Tom commented.

"I would say around two twenty three this morning," Alex replied.

"Can you get a bit more specific?" Mike asked with raised eyebrows. Everyone chuckled.

"That's when Micky was going off," she replied. "Every Christmas, after I put up the Christmas tree, Micky gets upset because I can't spend as much time with him for around a month. I just thought it was him being snarky. I was warm and comfortable in bed, and didn't feel like getting up for him. My bedroom door was ajar in case he wanted to come in. I don't know if you all have noticed, but he can get a bit attitudinal at times."

"Just a bit, huh?" Tom said sarcastically. He thought for a second, "The story sounds plausible, but do you have any idea who might have done this?"

"Not really," Alex answered. "I haven't had time to think it through."

Mike checked his watch, "Hey, I'm sorry, but I have a run to do. Am I good to go?"

Tom handed back his gun and said yes. Alex gave him a big hug, "Thank you for looking out for me."

Chapter 69
Tuesday Morning

Cat and Alex were sitting at a table in the bakery taking a quick break, eating a few cookies and bringing each other up to date on the past couple of days, "That's a gorgeous ring, Cat!" Alex said as she examined Cat's right hand. She looked at her friend, "So, you're okay with it, not scared?"

"No, I'm good," she smiled. "And, thanks, I really do like it! I.........." The ringing of the telephone interrupted Cat.

"Alex! Thank gosh that you are okay," Cora gushed over the phone.

"Why wouldn't I be?" Alex asked.

"I have to warn you that you are in danger!"

"What do you mean? From whom?"

"That's just it, I don't know," Cora answered frustrated. "Late last night, my cell phone died and I had to call my husband. I found a pay phone. When I picked up the phone, I heard voices. I was about to hang up when I heard, 'Alex must die.'" Alex froze momentarily and gripped the phone harder. "I freaked, but continued to listen; it had to be a joke of some kind, right? I mean who talks about killing people on a pay phone? And just because I know an Alex doesn't mean that it's you. Then another voice said, 'That's too risky. Her boyfriend is a cop.' The first voice said, 'I don't care. That woman has a way of hearing things and figuring things out. We take her out, and then her boyfriend will be messed up in the head for a bit. It will buy us the time that we need.' The second guy spoke up again, 'Ronnie, I could see, but I don't want any part of killing a woman.' The first man got irritated and said something like, 'we'll see,' and hung up. I wasn't sure what to think. But, really, how many Alexes have a boyfriend who is a cop? That's why I'm calling you. I somehow lost your personal number when I switched cell phones, so I had to wait until this morning to call your bakery. I wanted to warn you, and let you decide the best course of action."

"Thank you Cora!" Alex replied. "I will take it under consideration. And, I will be careful. Just please answer me one question, where in the world did you find a pay phone?"

Cora laughed, "I know, right? I used the one on Matterhorn Road by the laundromat."

Maggie entered the backroom as Alex and Cat were discussing the warning. "After this morning, I believe what she heard was definitely real."

"I agree," Cat replied. "But, I never heard of picking up a pay phone receiver and hearing someone else's conversation," Cat replied. "Have you?"

Alex was in the middle of shaking her head, when Maggie chimed in, "Yes, it can happen." Both ladies looked at her. "My daughter and I were at the Park City Mall in Lancaster some time ago. She saw a pay phone and got excited. She had seen one in a movie one time and had questions about it. She asked if she could check it out, and

I, of course, agreed. I thought it was a hoot! She picked up the receiver, put it to her ear, and got a quizzical look on her face. After she replaced the receiver, she asked me if she should hear voices. I said no. She said that someone was talking on the phone. So I picked up the phone to listen, and sure enough, there was a masculine voice reading off a credit card number to someone. I replaced the receiver quietly and we walked away. Alex, this could explain what happened this morning. I am truly worried for you." She looked at Alex, "You must call Tom!"

"Oh, definitely," Alex assured her.

Maggie reached for her coat, "Don't forget, I'm only working half a day today. Carsenia's out front and handling things, Jo-Jo should be showing up in about five minutes."

"Okay, see ya tomorrow," Alex said as she reached for her phone.

Chapter 70
Tuesday Noon

Carsenia was happy to see Jo-Jo, "Maggie has the boy's name who had gotten Thaddeus. She's going over now to see if she can retrieve him."

"I'm glad to hear it, Christmas is getting close," Jo-Jo replied.

Ten minutes later, the phone rang and Carsenia answered it. It was Maggie, "Just letting you know, that I am hot on Thaddeus's trail. The boy is at school, but he already gave Thaddy to his aunt this morning."

Cat had just plunked some supplies on the counter for Carsenia when the front door was opened by a woman followed by a teenager. "I'm glad that you are here, Cat. May I please speak with you?"

"Of course, Mrs. Sweeney."

They walked off toward the back of the front room, "I believe it's important to set a good example for children, don't you?"

"Of course."

"You are identified in this town with Alex and this bakeshop. I think you need to keep this in mind," Mrs. Sweeney emphasized self-righteously.

"I do keep it in mind," Cat replied confused. "What exactly are you trying to get at?"

"I hate to critique people, but I believe it's important to dress correctly at all times when out in public, especially when people are well endowed on the top like you and me."

"O…kay," Cat stated and looked at the woman with confusion written all over her face. "I'm not sure what you're getting at," she checked her watch, "and I have things to get done."

"Well, I am watching Essie for a day or two and last night she had friends over for a sleepover. We saw you running down the sidewalk to Alex's place around three this morning, and your chest was bouncing up and down considerably. I believe that you might even have been in your pajamas!" the woman finished shocked.

Cat just stared at the woman for a minute, "What were you doing up at three in the morning with a group of girls? Should they not have been in bed? Why is Essie not in school at this hour? You know, to set a good example."

"It was a fluke, they were asleep shortly thereafter. I can assure you," she sniffed. "Her school is having some kind of water issues, so her Christmas vacation started earlier than expected," she sniffed again. "But, nonetheless, Cat, you need to be more careful," the woman replied.

Cat had a lot of smart aleck comments shoot through her mind, but because she was working, she tempered herself, "I thought my friend was in trouble, but I will try to dress more appropriately. Thank you for the reminder." She checked her watch again, "I must get back to baking."

Cat was hightailing it to the back of the building when a voice stopped her, "Miss Cat?"

"Yes, Essie?"

"Is Miss Alex alright?"

'Yes, she is," Cat responded, "Why do you ask?"

"Real early this morning, I saw you run to her place. Mr. Mike was already there. His truck was parked a bit crooked. A bit later, there were some cop cars, and I saw Mr. Tom run in with some officers. I talked my Aunt Roz into coming here. I looked for Miss Alex, but I didn't see her."

Cat smiled, "Thanks for the concern. Alex is on an errand, but she is quite alright." Essie started to turn away, "If I may ask a few questions?"

The girl turned back, "Of course."

"What were you girls doing up at three in the morning?" At her surprised look, Cat continued, "I just got done talking to your aunt. She's different, isn't she?"

Essie giggled, "She's definitely that. As to your question, I was waiting for a pizza delivery. I was the look out."

"At three in the morning?"

She nodded, "Yes, there's a new place in town. They are staying open 24 hours from now to Christmas Eve to try to build up business. I had some friends over for a movie marathon and we decided that we were hungry for pizza."

"What movie marathon?"

Essie smiled, "The *Die Hard* movies."

"Awesome Christmas movies huh?" Cat returned the smile.

"You bet! Not everyone agrees. Please don't tell Aunt Roz, she would not approve."

"Your secret is safe with me," Cat chuckled and then thought of something. "I never saw a pizza delivery guy."

"He came after you were in Alex's house. I heard Mr. Mike's truck and looked out to see you running down the sidewalk," she smiled knowingly.

"You sure it was just pizza, nothing else?" Cat queried her with a slight steely look

Essie stood up straight. "It was just pizza," Essie assured her. "I plan on becoming a police detective. Drugs of any kind could screw that up and that is not happening."

"Did you happen to see anyone else over at Alex's before Mike showed up?"

She nodded, "A dark vehicle, the kind that looks like a car and pick-up combination. At first I thought the pizza man stopped at the wrong house, but then I realized that he didn't have a lit sign on his car roof. It did have a business decal on its side. I could not read the decal, but it had a strange shape. If I figure out the decal, I will let you know. The vehicle moved slowly and without any headlights. My one friend, Marina, came over to see what I was looking at. A person, I believe it was a man, got out and went to Miss Alex's front door. He was not carrying anything in his hands. A short time later, he came running back to his truck and took off. A few minutes after that, Mr. Mike stopped and ran to the house."

"You are very good with details, keep this up, and you will make a great detective." The girl's face lit up at the compliment and she turned to find her aunt.

Chapter 71
Tuesday Afternoon

When Alex entered "Passages of Time," she found both Mavis and Jayne at the front counter. "Are you going to the Ice Fest tonight at the park?" Mavis asked.

"Yes, I am. Out of curiosity, did Tom or anyone else call you about black boots and a black truck?" When they shook their heads, Alex clued them in. There was a major incident last night and everyone got called to help. I figured that I would come over and make sure that you got the information."

"Thank you! There is a lot happening in this town lately, more than the usual nuttery. I fear our police are getting worn out." Mavis looked at her friend a moment, "You must take care of your man."

"I'm trying, Mavis," Alex replied. "You guys did a fantastic job on the 'Christmas Passage' this year!"

The ladies looked at each other and simultaneously said, "Thank you! We like it!"

Alex laughed, "I have one question. When Tom and I came to check out the passage, we heard an exquisite voice singing. I went to find the source. There was a young woman beautifully dressed as a Christmas angel. Her outfit and make-up were very good. She seemed to be a street performer and worked along flawlessly with the music you all had playing in the 'Passage.' Did you hire her?"

Mavis shook her head, "No. As you said, she seems to be a street performer. She's not on my land, so who am I to say anything?" Mavis' eyes twinkled, "She does compliment the ambience of the 'Passage' very well. Jayne saw her across town and complimented her. Now, she's here."

Alex glanced at Jayne, who smiled, "I did not lie. She is good."

"Yes, but did you suggest that she come here?"

Jayne looked around to make sure no customers were close enough to hear, "When I saw the meager amount in her collection hat, I merely supplied a few locations that I felt that she might do better."

"Do you know her name?" Both ladies gave her a strange look, "She would do very well at weddings."

"Martiya," Jayne replied. Alex repeated the name. "Before you ask, I don't know her from anywhere else, and I don't know if that is her real name or not. I do know that she dresses in at least two other costumes that are equally nice and always wears a lot of makeup."

"She only seems to appear at night," Mavis added.

"Interesting," Alex smiled. "I will have to think on her."

"Do me a favor please?" Jayne requested.

Alex eyed her warily, "If I can."

"If you find out she's a wanted criminal or such, as long as she is not an endangerment to anyone, please wait until after the holidays to turn her in. She is very good for business." Jayne responded, and to which Mavis heartily agreed.

"Changing the subject totally, Alex, I have to get something in the back. Please walk with me," Mavis requested. "Jayne, please give me that item under the counter that we discussed earlier." Once Mavis had the item, she preceded Alex to the back of her store.

When they reached the computer room, Mavis shut the door and gave Alex a wrapped gift, "Merry Christmas!"

Alex smiled, "Thank you! My gift for you is back at the shop, I'm planning on bringing it by a bit closer to Christmas."

Mavis waved her hand in the air, "That's fine. Open what I found for you!" Mavis eyes lit up as she spoke.

Alex did as requested and studied the book cover as she read the title, "*A Dictionary of Flowers and Gems*," to herself. "This is beautiful!"

"The author is the daughter of some friends of mine. As soon as I saw the book, I figured that it could help you." She smiled as Alex looked a bit perplexed, "I know of the bouquets that you periodically receive. My mom knew your aunt well and told me about her knowledge of the flower language. I thought it a bit hokey, but mom corrected me. I'm laying odds that sometimes you get flowers that cause you to do research. I believe that this book could come in handy."

Alex gave her friend a hug, "Thank you so so much! You are right about it coming in handy. I was never as fluent as my aunt, but I've been getting better," she smiled.

Mavis changed the subject, "Alex, as to the subject you mentioned when you entered my store, we need to contact Tom." She was quiet for a moment as she searched her mind, "Do the, the, the, things, that we-are-to-keep-a-look-out-for have some fancy stitching on them, or are they plain?"

"Black boots," Alex helpfully reminded her.

"Yes, boots," Mavis agreed.

"There is some kind of stitching, why?"

"The one guy that your man was telling me to keep an eye out for, had those kind of boots."

"You sure?"

"Yes, after I came out in the hallway, I jumped a wee bit. I was embarrassed. I mumbled sorry or such and looked down as I passed them in the hallway. I didn't want to stare at their faces, but I ended up taking note of their footwear. The black boots I saw were worn by the guy I did not know the name of."

"I agree, we need to tell the guys."

When Alex was about halfway through the store, she heard someone calling out her name. Alex looked around and saw Mavis' mom, Sylvia, sitting in a comfortable chair. She had a drink on a side table and a book on her lap. "Hi, Sylvia," Alex walked over to the older lady. "Did you want me for something?"

"Yes, dear," she smiled. "Please look out for my Mavis. She's my little girl, and I worry so."

"I will do my best, Sylvia," she bent down to give her a hug and wish her a great Christmas.

"I know that you will," Sylvia replied. "Thank you for your help."

Chapter 72
Tuesday Evening

Maggie burst into the bakeshop right before closing. "Girls, come here!" She said with a huge smile. She reached into her jacket and pulled out a wrapped figure, "I got him!"

"Oh, thank the Lord!!" Jo-Jo said.

"Ditto," Carsenia yelled, "Let's see him!"

Just then, Alex came into the room, followed by Cat, "What is all the racket about ladies?"

Maggie looked at her co-workers and friends and they nodded their heads quickly, "Alex, with everything going on, I don't know if you realized that Thaddeus had left the building for a while."

Alex swung around to the tree in alarm and saw that her friend was right, "What happened to him? How long has he been gone?"

"For a bit, but we have a Christmas surprise for you!" She gave Alex the package.

"What is this?" she curiously opened the package. "Holy cow!! It's Thaddeus!!" She turned him over a few times in her hands, "It is him, but different."

"Improved a bit," Cat added. "Alex, these three ladies have been hot on his trail for weeks and have been triumphant, I am pleased to say!"

She looked expectantly at the ladies and they took turns regaling her with his many travels and some tribulations. "I will have to thank Letitia for fixing him up. I love the new look. Let me return him to his rightful spot." Alex walked over to put him back in her tree and the ladies followed. She turned and hugged each of her friends, "Thank you so much for everything! This is a fantastic present!"

Chapter 73
Tuesday Night

Alex took a deep breath of the cool night air as she exited her car. She looked at the park full of people and activity. She was quite a bit early to meet her friends at the opening gate of the park, so she decided to do a quick peek at some of the ice sculptures.

Mavis came up and lightly tapped Alex on the shoulder, "What do you think of all of this?"

Alex had a huge smile, "It's fabulous! Have you gotten around to all forty ice sculptures?"

"No, not yet," Mavis smiled and looked off toward a food truck. "Milo loves hot chocolate. We have seen about eight so far. My favorite is the Victrola. I love old things." She winked at Alex, "That's why I love my Milo." Both ladies laughed. "Do you want to look at the next one with me? I told Milo that's where I would meet him."

"Sure, Tom is scouting around checking a few things out. He will call me when he's done. Let me text Cat and let her know where to meet us."

Alex and Mavis went over to check out the photo event ice sculpture. It consisted of two figures made out of ice that looked to be dressed in winter clothing. Each figure of ice had a circular opening for the face. One could stand behind the figures and put one's face partially through the opening and make whatever facial contortions one wanted. A huge growling polar bear finished the piece. It was slightly off to one side of the ice figures. It stood about six foot high and looked threatening. Alex nudged Mavis, "Want to get a picture taken?"

"Sure, let's get about three or four and change our expressions," Mavis suggested.

"Sounds good!" Alex agreed

About ten minutes later, while checking out their different photos, Alex looked up to see Jacob starting to pass by, "He's doing carriage rides again this year! Very cool!" Just then, she caught motion off to her right side. "Mavis!" she yelled as she watched her friend pitch forward and slam her wrist onto the passing carriage. Before she could react, she saw Mavis moving straight backward and upright again. She looked just past Mavis and took a deep intake of air, "Ben, thank the good Lord that you were here!"

"Mavis, are you okay?" Milo half-shouted as he arrived on the scene with hot chocolate dripping off his hands.

Mavis had been cradling her wrist and arm, "I'm not sure, I hit my wrist on the carriage, but it could have been much worse."

Milo, while tenderly looking at her arm, glanced upward briefly and stiffened, "Alex and Ben, please help Mavis get medical attention. I will be back." Milo took off running before anyone knew where he was going.

"Milo?!" Mavis shouted and turned to watch her unathletic husband run toward a man who quickly turned and also ran.

Alex looked around quickly and saw Cat and Mike. She yelled their names to get their attention, "Milo needs help!

He went that way," she pointed with her left hand while grabbing her cell phone with her right. Alex made a quick call, "Tom! We need help in the middle of the park!" She gave a quick description and he said that he was already over that way and would see what he could do." Alex turned her attention back to Mavis, "How are you doing?"

"I don't know what the heck is going on around here!" Mavis answered exasperated, "My wrist feels like it's on fire." Tears welled up in her eyes and started to run down her cheeks.

"I called 9-1-1," Ben spoke up. "But if we can, let's get you to the west side of the park so that they can reach you easier. Let's also get you closer to a light so that we can see your hand better." Instantly, a light lit up their immediate area. "Thanks, Alex, for your phone light." He checked her over briefly, "There's a little blood, but I think if you cradle it close to your body, like you were a few seconds ago, you will be alright, for now. Let's get you to the side of the park."

"May we be of assistance?" Jacob inquired. "I heard some commotion and the couple that had just been enjoying their ride informed me of the mishap. I apologize for our part in your injury Mavis."

"It was not of your doing, someone pushed her into your carriage," Alex explained. "But, yes, we will accept your offer of service. We need to get her to the west side of the park."

Meanwhile, Cat and Mike were having a bit of trouble catching up to Milo and his quarry. "There are a ton of people here! I lost sight of Milo!" Cat cried out.

"Cat, follow me!" Mike yelled over his shoulder as he swerved around a group of people checking out another ice sculpture. "I see them up ahead a bit."

Cat pulled up aside Mike as he slipped on some slush and ice, "Where?"

The two looked up and gasped as they saw Milo approach his quarry. There was a quick exchange of words and the men tussled a bit. The brown-haired man pushed Milo over the wall, but Milo held tight, and both disappeared from sight. "Damn, that's not good!"

"There's a good eight foot drop off that bridge!" Cat exclaimed.

Tom looked around as he put his phone away. He saw Mike and Cat stop and followed their direction of attention. He observed Milo and a man go over a bridge. He was about to head for the bridge, when he observed two men standing together in the opposite direction looking out-of-sorts. One pointed at the bridge and spoke quickly to the other. Both men looked around hurriedly and once they saw Tom, they took off running. Tom grabbed his phone, "Joey, I was where we planned to meet, but I don't see you. I'm in pursuit of two men in the park."

"I'm behind you." Tom turned to see a motorcycle coming straight at him. He stepped off to the side to give him room. "Wait and literally jump on the seat behind me when I pull up beside you. Hunker down and hold on to me and the back of the bike to balance yourself, jump off when I catch up to them."

Tom had just shoved his phone in his rear pocket, when Joey pulled up beside him on his motorcycle. He blew his horn continually as Tom stepped onto the seat, thankfully covered in a sheepskin seat cover. Tom yelled the direction the men had taken. Joey goosed the bike as Tom held on tight with his left hand on Joey's shoulder and his right one low on the back bar of the seat. People scattered as they passed through the park. At a "Y" in the pathway, one man went left and the other right. Joey turned right. Within seconds, he was parallel to the man and Tom jumped off the bike, and flattened the man on the snow covered grass. He got off the man, cuffed him, and read him his rights as people clapped. "Awesome jump!" One bystander yelled. "Great job!" Others yelled.

Joey went down the path a piece, turned around, and came back to stop beside the detective and his perp, "That was fun!"

"Yeah, it was, but we still have one more guy to track down," Tom noted.

"No, we got him too," Joey grinned and then chuckled at Tom's questioning look. "I was late getting to you because I saw my old partner, Rico, and stopped to talk to him for two minutes. I had asked him to hang around the side of the park in case we needed back-up. When our guys split up, I turned to the right and called Rico to catch the guy who had gone left. He literally ran right into Rico and Rico collared him."

"Fantastic!" Tom's face lit up and he briefly looked around the park. His face changed quick as he noticed flashing emergency lights along the side of the park on the main roadway, "Crap, please take this dude while I check on the mess at the bridge." Joey got off his bike and held onto the bound man, while Tom grabbed his phone to learn of the bridge happenings.

Chapter 74
Tuesday Night

"What the heck! Get off me old man!" the goateed brown-haired man demanded

"You hurt Mavis! I don't allow that!" Milo replied with a controlled fury.

The man took a second to reply, "So, you're the husband. Tell her to forget what she heard and she'll be fine."

"If not?"

"We might tangle again," he pushed Milo off and started to move, but stopped. "Damn, what did you do to me?"

Milo was trying to figure out his own source of discomfort and tuned the other man out. He sat up as Mike and Cat arrived on the scene, took one look at his knee and paled. Mike instantly assessed the problem, "Lay back down Milo, I got this." Milo did as requested as Mike quickly checked him over, "Medic!" he yelled and then shook his head once, "Cat, call 9-1-1, tell them we need two ambulances."

"What about me?" the brown-haired man said.

Mike looked over at him, "I will get to you in a minute. Do you have any pain?"

"I think he broke my ribs," the man complained.

"Stay there and we will get you help. Don't move! Since you were on the bottom when you landed, you might have hurt your back. We will need a backboard. One of the ambulances will be for you."

A disheveled man appeared by Mike's side in less than a minute, "Here, Sergeant, what do you need?"

Mike looked surprised for a moment, "Doc, this man needs your help. I know we have no supplies, just tell me what you need." He leaned over so Milo could see his face. He touched the injured man on the shoulder, "Hang in there, Milo. This man is a military medic, he will be with you, while we get supplies." Milo grimaced and nodded his head.

Doc checked Milo out. "We need to stabilize the knee area and get him to the hospital stat."

With one look in the medic's eyes, Mike knew time was of the essence. "Cat, help me find some sticks and give them to Doc here. One look at Mike's face and Cat didn't ask questions, she just complied. In a few minutes, they returned with the sticks. Mike stripped off his belt and handed it over with them. "Cat, give him your scarf too please. We need to get him to the side of the park for a quicker pickup." While Cat handed over her scarf, Mike looked up and saw Jacob Carpathian and his carriage pulling up to the bridge. He ran up and flagged him down.

"Are you in need of aide?"

Mike quickly looked the carriage over and nodded, "This will do. Mavis, Milo has injured his knee pretty bad and needs to get to the hospital. You and Alex are fine where you are. Jacob, please lower the back gate door on your carriage and help me get Milo loaded up."

247

"I can get the door and there will be room for him, but I cannot help with Milo. I injured my back," he replied apologetically.

"I'll get the back gate for you, Jacob. Stay where you are," Alex said as she jumped from the carriage.

"Okay, that will do. Do you have a strong blanket?"

"Yes," he reached for one beside him and tossed it to Mike.

"Time is of the essence. Be ready when we get him up here." Mike ran back to Milo. "How we doing?"

"Fine, captain. Do you have transport?"

"Here's a blanket, help me lay it out and move Milo onto it."

"Mike, do you need more help?" A voice called out.

"Yes, I do. We could use three more volunteers. I want three people per side of the blanket to help haul Milo up this embankment and into the back of the carriage. People quickly took up the requested posts.

"Oh, Milo!" Mavis cried out when she saw her disheveled husband. "What happened?"

"Time enough later for that," he cracked a faint smile. "Mike got me temporarily patched up. Are you okay, honey?" Milo asked with concern.

"Yes, Jacob is taking me to an ambulance. Now, we can ride together," her eyes watered.

In a few minutes, a brief controlled pandemonium broke out at the side entrance to the park. Some people were upset that the entrance to the park was closed down during the ice festival. They quieted, and started to get nosy, when the ambulances that had been parked a bit down the road, pulled up to meet Jacob's carriage and loaded up Milo and Mavis. Two police cars pulled up to take on the prisoners. Tom was met by the attendants to the other ambulance and took them to the bridge for the brown-haired man. Alex followed after she assured Mavis that she would meet her and her hubby at the hospital in a little bit to see if they needed a ride home or anything.

When Alex reached the bridge, she found that the brown-haired man had been loaded onto a stretcher and was being hauled away to the awaiting ambulance. She joined her group of friends. "I believe this might take care of the burglary ring," Tom hypothesized.

"You think?" Alex asked as Joey arrived on the scene.

"We were to the point that we thought Xavier," Tom tilted his head in the direction of the man that had just been taken away, "That brown-haired man, was the mastermind. He had help, and we were thinking two or three men. We just caught two men here tonight, elsewhere in the park. Once we take care of interviewing everyone, and searching a few of their houses, we will know for sure. If we don't have everyone, we will soon enough, on that, I feel sure."

"That will make our mayors happier," Joey contributed.

"Definitely," Tom laughed. He turned to Alex, "I already called John and will meet him at the precinct house. We will see where we stand on all this."

Alex looked at Joey a moment, "I heard how you and Tom captured the one guy. If I may ask, why were you on a motorcycle in December?"

249

Joey laughed, "What can I say? Sometimes a guy gets bike fever." His eyes sparkled with joy, "I was in the garage working on my bike when Tom called me. And I thought, why not?"

Alex laughed, "Yeah, why not?"

"Alex, are you done here tonight, or staying longer?" Cat inquired.

Alex glanced at her watch, "I think I will stay a bit longer. I would like to see a few more ice sculptures," she smiled and her eyes lit up briefly. "And, I believe the hospital will need some time to check over Mavis and Milo."

Chapter 75
Dec 20
Wednesday Morning

Cat burst through the bakeshop's office door, "Alex, has the phone been ringing off the hook?"

Alex looked up at her, "Yes, a bit, but it's to be expected. Everyone's calling in with last minute orders, questions, and requests. Did you forget, tis the season and all?"

"Have you been answering the phone at all?" Cat persisted.

"Nah," she shook her head. "We open in an hour and I've been finishing up that huge Thompson order."

"Much more to do?" Cat asked as she approached Alex's work area.

"No, I'm just writing the names on each one now. I think I was nuts to take this order, but I thought the idea of super-personalized petit fours was cool. And," she smiled, "the money is good."

"Wow! Alex, these are gorgeous!" Cat gushed as her eyes scanned the chocolate covered mini cakes. "The different shapes are neat too. The triangular trees look very festive!"

"Thank-you! Originally, I was going to keep them simple, but they're for the children and I decided to have some fun. The round wreaths and triangular Santa faces are for the ladies. The squares with hollies and ball-ish snowmen are for the guys. Eighty in total." She glanced at the clock, "I'll have these done very shortly." She squinted at her friend, "Why did you ask about the phone?"

"This," Cat waved a newspaper in the air. When she realized Alex had no idea to what she was referring, she continued, "A new comic strip came out today!"

"Okay, now who's being crucified?" Alex inquired as she approached her friend laying the paper down on one of the tables.

"We are!" Cat exclaimed and pointed to the comic strip on the page. "You picked a fine week to stop being nosy!"

"What?" Alex stared at her friend as she reached the table and quickly looked to where her friend was pointing. "Holy crap!" she exclaimed. "This is so so wrong!" She bent closer to examine the comic. There was a drawing of a house that looked like Alex Sr.'s in the middle of the frame. A woman was walking out the front of the house carrying a box toward a VW bug, another woman was walking out the back of the house, and both women were wearing aprons. "It's obvious to me that this is supposed to be us, but do you think others will think so too?"

"Most definitely I do, and we won't have to wait long to see what others think."

"Dang it, Cat, we could be in a spot of trouble here." Alex commented as she continued to study the drawing.

"Spot? Spot, of trouble you say?! Alex, we are going to be in a whole flipping ocean of trouble." She quieted as she watched Alex look around the room and briefly battle with herself. "I know that you don't like extra trouble

252

around the major holidays, and that you will swallow a ton of crap in order to avoid conflict, especially at Christmas. But, someone has thrown down the gauntlet and has challenged us big time. What do you really want to do about it?"

Alex looked at her old friend and her face hardened, "We are going to pick the darn thing up, clear our names, and shove it down whoever's throat."

"Awesome," Cat smiled shark-like, "where should we start?"

"At the newspaper. We need to find out who gave it this information."

"You mean talk to Steve. Alex he's not going to talk to us."

Alex looked at Cat, "But, that is where we start. I can't help it if he doesn't like us."

"You have a skewed memory. He doesn't like me, because he doesn't like you. He doesn't like you, because you were quite vocal about him being the worst person in the world for Mr. Cutter to sell his newspaper to."

"I believe that I have been proven correct," Alex responded. "I will call Tom and Ben on the way to the newspaper and give them notice before they are blindsided."

"If I were them, I would start being afraid to take your calls," Cat commented.

"Look at it this way, they will never be bored. This is an added headache to an already hectic season. I'm going to kill Steve!"

"You are going to have to watch that kind of talk," Ben said as he entered the bakery. "Especially now, please."

"Ben!?" Alex and Cat exclaimed simultaneously. "Did I forget that you were coming by this morning?" Alex asked.

"No, you didn't," he replied. "When I saw my newspaper this morning, I figured that I should swing by here on my way to work. Judging by what I just heard, I was correct. You two had best be careful today."

The two ladies looked at each other and then at him, "Of course we will," Cat responded.

Ben stared at them a second longer, "I hope that you do." He turned to go, "You have my number in case you find yourselves in need."

"Ben, hold up," Alex said. She walked over to him, "I have a small holiday gift in the office for you."

He gave her a hug with a huge grin when he saw his gift basket, "Thank you, it's very cool!"

Alex returned to the petit fours, "Let me finish these up quick and then we must take a quick road trip."

Alex parked the car in the newspaper's parking lot and turned to Cat, "While I talk to Steve, please look around the newsroom. After I ask him about the origin of the comic strip, see if anyone looks odd or uncomfortable." Cat nodded in agreement.

They entered the front door of the brick building to find themselves in a rather modern looking foyer. "This used to be more homey or welcoming," Alex commented. "Even the Christmas tree looks odd."

"Yeah, I know what you mean. I liked the country feel," Cat concurred.

"Mr. Gunderson will be out to speak to you in a few minutes," the young, perky receptionist responded to Alex's request to talk to the owner of the newspaper.

"We could just go inside and talk to him there, to make it easier on him," she suggested. "We only need a few minutes. I'd hate to pull him too far away from whatever he is working on." Alex pointed to the only doorway that went further into the building.

"Well, he would not......." The receptionist started to say, but stopped as the door opened.

".....like it at all," the man who had just entered finished her sentence and glanced at the cowed girl. He turned toward Alex and Cat, "Ladies, I believe that I know why you are here. Follow me to my office for just a few minutes, but only a few."

The man escorted the ladies to his office and shut the door. He sat in a big chair behind his large uncluttered desk and waved them to the two chairs in front of his desk. "I see that you did quite the renovation on this room," Alex stated as she looked around. "It used to be so..."

"Old is the word that you are looking for," Steve Gunderson supplied. "I don't like antiques, I like a newer more contemporary style." He noticed Cat's antsy behavior and glared at her, "What is wrong with you woman?"

Cat was momentarily startled at his loud inquiry, "I need a bathroom. I'm sorry, but......"

He shook his head with irritation and waved a hand toward the door, "Fine! I believe that you know where it is. I didn't renovate those just yet."

"Planning more changes?" Alex asked as she gave a quick glance toward Cat, who as she closed the door, rolled her eyes toward the heavens. Alex turned her full attention back to Steve.

"Definitely, just like I did with the newspaper itself. I assume that is why you and your friend are here. I knew that you two would show up, but I am a bit surprised at the speed."

"I was wondering if you would be willing to explain where you got the idea for this week's comic square?"

"I still call it a comic strip, and no, I'm not going to tell you where I got the information," he assured her.

"It's a lie. Don't you check your level of accuracy?"

"I did a quick check and my police guy told me that you all don't have alibis. I was on a bit of a time crunch, so I just went with it. Besides, all the other comic strips have been totally accurate, and they are just comic strips, so accuracy isn't really needed."

"But, you are seriously messing with people's lives!" Alex responded with some heat. "It doesn't bug you at all does it?"

"Not really, in fact, I love it! When I bought this rag, it was floundering, since these strips have started, my sales have skyrocketed. People love them, and people love to give dirt on their neighbors, and supposed friends. I have a ton of material to work with. In fact, I might start putting two strips in each paper," he beamed.

Alex shook her head, squinted her eyes slightly, "So, if I ask you to do the right thing and print a retraction, you would say..?"

Steve laughed, "That ain't happening. You two deserve all that's coming your way," he sneered. "You guys think that you are so wonderful, but I know better. Now, leave..." He looked over his reader glasses at her and waved his hand dismissively, "...you know the way."

Alex turned to go and saw Cat leaving the bathroom. Cat followed her from the building. She got in the car with a smile on her face. "What's up? I believe that you didn't really need the bathroom."

"You are right about the bathroom and I don't want to risk jinxing anything," Cat answered. "Someone should be calling the bakery somewhere around noon. Whoever answers the phone should give the caller named Willy, my cellphone number. 'Willy' will then call me and give me some information."

"Why the 'cloak and dagger' treatment?"

"Not sure, I will ask if 'Willy' actually calls. The person waited until I was in a stall and spoke thru the crack of the door after making sure no one else was in the restroom. She also let me know that she wasn't trying to be creepy and assured me that she wasn't looking, just talking."

The women returned to the bakery and got busy with work until the anticipated phone call rang. Maggie who had been fielding a ton of calls since the bakeshop opened, answered the phone and followed what she had been asked to do. Within moments, Cat's phone rang and she went to the basement to talk without interruptions.

Cat re-entered the bakery approximately twenty minutes later to share the results of the phone call. "Do you remember an Allie Caruthers from high school?"

Alex thought for a few minutes, "Was she on the smaller size, thin, brown hair, glasses, a bit shy, and on the school newspaper?"

Cat nodded her head, "That's her. Well, she works at the newspaper, and saw our arrival. She's not happy with the comic strip, and how it was handled, and wanted us to know what happened. Allie said that our comic strip was not the planned one. She said that the boss got a phone call not long before the print deadline, set up a meet with someone, and left the building for a time. When he came back, he was all excited. Gunderson demanded that the strip be switched. He put a rush order on it, so that our strip would be in this week's paper. Allie asked about the accuracy. He assured her that his police contact insisted that we did not have alibis, and that the police thought we were serious people of interest in the whittler's death. Besides, he hates us and relished the idea to skewer us in print. It's a comic strip and therefore accuracy was not super important. She added that if she could help in any way, to just contact her at the number she called me from."

"Did Allie say why she was helping us?"

"She believes that we helped her in high school and she's trying to return the favor."

"We did help her," Alex squinted at her friend, "but you didn't confirm anything did you?"

Cat's eyes got big, "No! That would not be a good thing to get out. I told her that I wasn't sure to what she was referring. She hesitated a second, then suggested that if she was mistaken, and she didn't truly believe that she was, that we just pass it along and help someone else out of a jam."

"Why the 'cloak and dagger' spy routine with the phone and such?"

"Allie said that she wanted to think things through one more time. She really loves her job, she just doesn't like the new boss. Mr. Cutter was fabulous, Steve rots. He has poisoned the atmosphere there. She didn't want anyone seeing her talk to me or you or hand us anything. She is just as concerned outside the building and that's why she didn't want to meet me. He has informants everywhere. Apparently, a lot of our townsfolk like to dish dirt on others."

"I'd like to think it's more like ten percent. Every job, culture, etc. has ten percent of people who ruin it for everyone else, and unfortunately, they are the ones that get the attention." They continued getting holiday work done for a time when Alex looked up at Cat, "I been thinking about this comic strip. I believe someone saw something or I should say someone, just not you, that night. We need to figure out whom that someone was. They saw me leave out the front, apparently he or she saw someone leave out the back."

"Wasn't that Penny?" Cat inquired.

"We know that she left sometime after me. But, if she was being truthful about not killing Alex, and seeing him dead when she was leaving; then, someone else left before her. We need to figure out who this witness is and hear his or her side of things."

Chapter 76
Wednesday Night

Alex grabbed a few light bulb replacements and walked out to the front lawn of the bakery to check her Christmas light displays. She had driven past the other night and took note that a couple of lights were out. Alex noticed that the halo on top of the one angel was slightly askew. As she reached up to fix it, she glanced toward her three kings and realized that each king had a light out. She walked over to them and shook her head, "You guys are odd. Each one of you has the top light out. I guess I get to stretch tonight." She reached up to loosen the one light bulb and accidentally dropped it. "Crap!" As she quickly bent down to fetch it out of the wintry mix on the grass, a sharp noise rang out, and splinters exploded about her. She looked around confused and started to rise back up, but a large body tackled her. She started to scream when a large hand clamped over her mouth, "Shush, Alex, it's Mike. It's me Mike." Her terror subsided as the man's words sank in.

Mike released his hand when she stopped squirming. He looked around as a cop car pulled screaming into the driveway. His attention was focused momentarily at a distance spot, when Alex asked, "What in the world is going on?" Mike re-focused on her and helped her to her feet.

"Someone took a shot at you," he replied. "I came to pick up Cat and something caught my eye." He was examining one of the Wise Men, Balthazar, and looking off in the opposite direction. "Your fast drop to the ground was very fortuitous."

"My what?" She inquired and then nodded her head. "I just dropped a bulb and bent down to retrieve it," she said.

"Well, it was perfect timing," he repeated.

Tom and Cat came running around the corner of the bakery. "Is everyone okay?" Tom asked as he observed Alex brushing herself off of snow and debris.

"Apparently, being a klutz at times is a good thing," Alex answered. Her voice had shaken a bit and Tom stepped forward to envelope her in his arms.

As he hugged her, he looked past her toward Mike, who quietly pointed to the hole in one of the Wise Men, and then pointed toward Alex, and tapped the back of his head. Cat caught all the hand signals, "Holy crap! That was no accident! Alex, you're going to have to be extra careful of your surroundings until this killer is caught."

"Which killer? Supposedly Senior's and Penny's killer is behind bars," Alex replied.

"But, we don't believe the right man is in jail for that, and then there is Ronnie's killer, and the pay phone killing squad." Cat said irritated.

"How did the person know where to wait for you?" Tom asked perplexed.

"It's not like Alex announces when she's going to check her lights and décor," Cat added.

Mike was quiet as Alex mulled the question over. Mutely, she just looked at her friends and around a bit. She shrugged, "I have no idea."

"Alex, I believe that you are a creature of habit," Mike stated and caught everyone's attention. "I'll lay odds that you do this every Wednesday night. Am I correct?"

"Yes," she nodded. "If I set a routine I don't forget to do things. Wednesdays are our latest nights and its dark out when we leave. It's the best night to do it." Cat nodded her head in agreement.

"How many Wednesdays do you think you've been doing this?" Mike asked.

"I believe this is the third one."

"Someone has noticed," he said soberly. "You'll need to adjust your regular routines in everything that you do. No patterns. Alter everything," Mike recommended.

Alex's eyes started to well up, "That's not going to be easy. That's how I keep sane and make sure that nothing gets missed or messed up. This season is especially hectic."

Cat hugged her best friend, "I'll help, and you know that the rest of the gang here will help too!"

Tom spoke up, "For now, please give me the extra bulbs. Mike and I will finish up out here." He turned to Mike after the ladies went inside, "Will you please take care of the decorations and I will check in with my guys across the way."

"Sure," Mike agreed and took the replacements bulbs.

Tom rejoined Mike a little bit later, "What's up? I believe that you only fixed the one Wise Men."

"Before I answer that, if I may inquire, what did your boys find out over there?"

"Not much. They checked the area, especially concentrating where you saw movement. They found evidence of someone waiting for some time, but nothing conclusive. They were no bullet cases, no trash, no cigarettes, and no solid footprints, because the ground was mushy from melted snow. It does look well trampled."

"Why do you ask?"

"I think that this was a set-up from the beginning," Mike said. "Except for one other light, only the top lights are out. I think that you might be able to get fingerprints from the bulbs. I only touched the first one, but so did Alex. You could possibly get fingerprints from the Wise Men, but they are made of roughly sanded plywood. I believe that you are looking for two people."

"Why two?"

"One organized and one not. I believe that someone prepped for this attack. Someone put the time in to study Alex and figure out how to get her into a vulnerable position. I believe that the person, who planned the attack, did not actually carry it out. This attack seemed rushed. It may be dumb luck that the person who carried this out did not leave any clues from his shooting location. Do you mind if I go over and take a look?"

He shook his head, "Let's go over and see if they're done." Tom talked briefly to the men and nodded to Mike.

Mike closely observed the ground. He slowly walked away from the policemen as he widened his search area. He tensed momentarily as he observed a disturbance in the weeds that led away from the bakery. He started to follow other disturbances in the tall grass and brush and disappeared from Tom's sight. Tom followed. He had just caught sight of Mike squatting down and checking the ground, when he noticed some movement slightly in front of Mike and to his right. Before he could speak, Mike had risen and attacked a figure heading his way. In a matter of a minute or two, if even that, Mike had a man pinned to the ground begging for help. Tom jogged down the hill and arrested the mud covered man.

A mud spattered Tom and Mike entered the bakeshop triumphantly, "Tom arrested your man! Mike caught the guy!" They spoke simultaneously. Tom turned to Alex, "It was the last burglary guy trying to complete his task. He's on his way to the station house now."

"He has a black eye and not from us," Tom said. "I believe he's the man who brought Ronnie into the burglary ring. I think Xavier showed him his disapproval."

"Thank you both!" Alex exclaimed and gave each man a hug.

"Thank Mike. He's the one who tracked him down."

Cat walked over to hug Mike, "That's my man!"

"I hate to tell you Alex, your Balthazar is the King that got shot out front." Tom pointed to Mike, "He took some holly off one of your bushes and gave him a boutonniere."

Cat and Alex looked at Mike inquisitively. "What?" he said. "It's very festive."

Tom laughed, "Totally holiday. I'll help you fix him this summer."

Chapter 77
Dec 21
Thursday Morning

Cat came in the delivery door and saw Alex looking thoughtfully at her desk. On the desk lay, a basket, a baggie with three Welsh cookies in it, and a small bouquet of pretty flowers. "Another surprise flower bouquet?" When Alex didn't respond, she continued, "What's up?" Alex looked up at Cat, "You seem deep in concentration."

"I am a bit."

"So what you thinking, boss lady?" Cat persisted.

Alex flourished her right hand toward the desk, "I found these this morning by the door."

"O…….kay," Cat replied, "and…..?"

"Everything was in the basket," Alex said, "In all the years that I have been receiving anonymous flower bouquets, I have never received one in a basket, have I?"

Cat thought for a few seconds, "No, you haven't, but there is snow on the ground and there are cookies this time. Maybe the person thought a basket would be best."

"Exactly," Alex held up her right index finger, "I have never received food of any kind before.

"No, but it is Christmas," she supplied.

"There's been numerous holidays and never anything but flowers. I think someone wants me to think that this is my mystery person," Alex replied. "And, another thing…."

"Yes?" Cat rolled her eyes when Alex didn't say anything for a while, "You planning on telling me?"

"Of course, silly," Alex chuckled, "We briefly have discussed this before, but there were footprints to and away from this bouquet."

"Now, that's a big change," she concurred. "We have never seen footprints, animal prints, wheel tracks or anything that would give us a clue as to how these things appear. Yet another creepy thing about these bouquets."

Alex got up, walked to the door, and opened it, "Take a look at the ground. We got fresh snow last night. I see yours, mine, and a third set of foot tracks. I took pictures too, but I don't know if they will help us at all."

Cat walked out quickly and compared her footprint to the unknowns. "Mine is smaller," Cat observed, "so I believe we can guess that this person is taller than you and me."

Alex laughed, "You just described three quarters of the planet."

The ladies returned to the warmth of the building, "Do you think it's a copycat? Maybe even Tom?" Cat wiggled her eyebrows up and down and smiled. "Maybe he's jealous and wanted to surprise you. The flowers are really good looking. What do they mean?"

"And that's another thing. They're random flowers with random meanings with no one general message." Alex pointed as she went, "That one means love, that one means disappointment, that other one speaks of rejection or indecision." She flourished her hand, "and the greens have numerous meanings. It's really odd."

"If you ask me, these bouquets that you have been receiving have always been odd."

"Tom agrees with you. I would be highly surprised if this was him, but at least that's an easy puzzle to solve. I'll just call him. In the meantime," Alex stood up and placed everything back in the basket, "I'll put this in the safe, so no one accidentally eats a cookie."

Cat did a double-take, "You think someone tampered with these?"

"I think it's a distinct possibility," Alex replied seriously as the office door swung open and more employees entered ready for another day of fun.

Within the hour, Tom and John showed up for the basket, "I don't like this at all, Alex. I'm going to figure out who's been doing this, and no it was not me." He gave her a big hug, "We'll take this to the lab and see what they say."

"Hey, before you leave, can you two tell us anything about that guy who injured Milo and the men who did the burglaries?" Cat asked

Tom smiled, "Maybe I could be persuaded to talk."

"That's your turf, Alex!" Cat laughed as her friend turned a bright shade of red and John grinned.

"We made pecan sticky buns yesterday, let me warm some up and you can fill us in on some details," Alex offered.

"Deal," John replied.

After everyone got comfortable, Tom started talking, "Xavier Scott Pierce was the leader. His gang was a

268

precision machine until one of the guys decided to go rogue and had Ronnie fill in for him for one night. It did not go well. The remaining guys were less than pleased and made him the driver, he ended up smashing Libby. The Birkmans were supposed to be away. Xavier's gang had two more houses to hit yet before Christmas: the Birkmans and one other family and then they were going to disappear. Xavier had a great plan: use three guys and their girlfriends, all who just happen to have jobs that provide the times when customers will be away and leave their houses vacant. The informants were in three different towns. They changed things up by using different peoples' vehicles. The main problem was Ronnie, he could not be controlled. He refused to allow Xavier to intimidate him and Xavier killed him. They just needed to buy enough time to finish the planned jobs. Xavier's gang followed y'all at different times. One of them pushed you into the street, Alex. Two members of the gang broke into your bakery and were scared off by a person dressed in black with a bat. They swear that they were sober and the person was really there," he paused and looked at Alex for a moment. "One broke into your house, but that was thwarted and I'm really glad. The man who did that was one nasty piece of work." Tom smiled, "He firmly believes that a cop was in your house."

"But, why come after me and Cat?"

"It was the drone recording. Xavier heard all the talk of the fairies and since his gang was pulling a job that night, he figured his gang was the fairies. When he saw you leave the Ballantines, he surmised correctly that you had a copy of the drone recording. He decided to eliminate the problem, but it was more complicated and harder than he expected. Xavier got highly irate after he said that his men did not use headlamps or flashlights, and we informed him that the drone footage had absolutely nothing to do with him."

John continued, "Xavier tried to keep his hands clean in case things went sour and they did. We have proof on him for killing Ronnie, but nothing concrete to tie him in with the burglaries."

"Yet," Tom added while cleaning up his table area.

John nodded in agreement, "The girlfriends supposedly are innocent. The men just plied them for information."

"And the attack last night?"

"Xavier and two of his gang, a Brick Oglby and a Bryce Fencer, were arrested in the park. Last night was an attempt by the third one, a Bruce McDavy, to get back into Xavier's good graces. He was still sporting a black eye from Xavier for bringing in Ronnie and royally messing up Xavier's plans. Originally, Brick Oglby was to do the shooting, but he was arrested that night in the park," Tom reported.

"Brick, Bryce, and Bruce? Seriously?" Cat asked.

"Yep," Tom grinned, "You can't make this up. Truth is stranger than fiction." They all laughed.

John looked at Alex, "I believe the 'pay phone kill squad,' I think that's what Cat named them, and Xavier and his gang of merry burglars are the same people. Per the chief and the D.A., Alex Sr.'s and Penny's killer is behind bars, so perhaps you are safe now," John explained. "But...."

"Per the chief and the D.A.," Cat repeated sourly.

John inclined his head briefly, "They say the case is strong, but I would still watch my back if I were you. Because, yes, as you know, Tom and I have doubts about Leroy's guilt."

"As do Cat and I," Alex responded.

"You know, that Xavier had a great plan going on. His fault was that one of the men he chose thought he could tweek the plan without messing anything up," Tom said.

"If he would have chosen someone else, it might have worked out," Cat suggested.

"Who? Xavier? Or Bryce?" Alex asked.

"Either one, really. Think about it. His plan was great. He really did use a 'little of this and a little of that' to achieve the results he wanted. Xavier's plans varied the vehicles, the towns, the weekdays and time frames of the days. He had three guys with different jobs and each guy had a girlfriend with a different job. The jobs covered a range of areas that provided a lot of information about the people in these towns and when they would be away for an extended time frame. He was only one week away from finishing his jobs and disappearing from this area. He just messed up when he let his emotions get the better of him."

"And killed a guy," John said.

"Yeah, he killed a guy and that's how we got on his trail."

"You sound like you admire the guy," John observed.

"Admire him? No. Just saying that his plan was very good. It almost worked, and messed up our case completion rate." Tom replied.

John's phone started ringing and he answered it, "We have to go." He nodded to the ladies as he listened to the phone and headed out of the building. Tom gave Alex a quick hug before leaving with the basket he had originally come for.

Alex turned around and caught her friend staring at her, "What?"

Cat looked around briefly and then back at Alex, "They say that there was a figure in black inside this bakery and that kept the burglars from doing any real damage."

"I heard. But, no way, who would the figure had been? Tom and John also figure the burglars got some liquid courage before coming here, got scared, and were seeing things."

"I don't know about that," Cat held up a hand to stop Alex. "Hear me out. This past fall when we got back from the campground, after your Linden tree blew down in the storm, you found a rolled up parchment on your desk. Remember that?"

"Of course I do. You were there with me when I unrolled it. It was that cool poem about Lindy. I framed it and have it hanging on my wall at home."

"Exactly, we never did find out who put it there."

"We didn't look too hard. We always get busy doing things."

Cat pointed at her briefly, "But we did ask everyone who works here and everyone we thought who had even a passing chance of leaving it here. Alex, we always joke about the weird noises in this place around two in the morning and say 'there's our ghost again,' but what if there's more to it? It's creepy!"

"You mean a real ghost?" Alex looked at her friend incredulously.

"I know, I know, we have always said that there are no ghosts, everything has an explanation, but there are lots of people who do believe in them. And sometimes, I have to wonder." She stopped and looked at her friend and held up a finger, "Case in point, that white flash that helped Tom find you at the campground. Don't they call her the 'Lady of the Lake?'"

"Yes, they do," Alex said. "But here, in my building? I really don't think so. There is a rational explanation. When we get some free time, I know, hah, hah, who knows when that will be, we can check into things, but not now. Whether it's a ghost or a real person, it has never caused us harm and if the burglars are correct, it protects us. So for now, I'm letting it go. Agreed?"

"Agreed, but just for now," Cat emphasized.

"Alex! A Mr. Ballantine is heading your way. He said it was imperative to talk to you," Carsenia called back on the intercom.

No sooner had Alex thanked her friend and opened the door, the man stood before her. "Come in Mr. Ballantine. You requested an audience?"

"Yes, I did, and it's Tyler, please. My wife is extremely irritated with me right now, she demanded I come over and talk to you."

"Okay, you're here. So, please take a chair and start talking."

He sat down and looked chagrined, "It's my fault that you're in the newspaper, in that comic strip."

She straightened up in her chair, "Come again? I don't even know you."

"Exactly," he took a deep breath and rubbed his hands through his hair. "I'm friends with Steve Gunderson. We were drinking one night and shooting the breeze. I said that we were a bit tight money-wise this year and I was upset because I wanted to get the kids a few more gifts. Somehow, talk switched to those comic strips and he said that he wanted a really juicy one. I suggested Alex Sr.'s death. Witnesses put you coming out the front of his house and I saw something at the back of his house on my son's tablet. Steve got all excited and said that he could use that. That he would pay me to be an informant. I don't know you, so I figured what the harm. You have been in trouble in the past and have always escaped. He paid me pretty well. I insisted that I would not, and could not, swear to the actual people who had entered and exited that house in a court of law. He said it didn't matter; he does not give out his sources. It's a comic strip and accuracy didn't really count, but that he would check with his police source first. I asked what he was actually paying me for and he said for the tip. Some tips are good and some are bad, but this would pave his way to pay you back for whatever trouble he feels you have caused him. I used the money to buy some gifts for the kids and two for my wife. When I explained where the money came from, Emily went ballistic. She demanded I come and apologize to you. You have been real kind to Tommy and her, so I thank you for your kindness and apologize for my actions. If there is anything I can do to fix things, please do not hesitate to ask."

Alex looked at the man for a minute or two and asked him for the amount Steve had given him. "Wait here, please." Alex went to her office and returned shortly thereafter carrying an envelope. "I want you to pay Steve back. There is some extra money there for you to use, however you honestly see fit."

He looked at her confused, "But why?"

She smiled, "Your son was a big help and I like your family. Please take good care of them."

"Sure, no problem," Tyler replied. "Thank you! Again, I'm very sorry!"

"Also, I will be telling the police what you said. They may have additional questions."

As the man left the room, Cat came out from around the back, "Seriously Alex? He's scum! He'll probably just keep the cash."

"Then, it will be on his shoulders." She looked at her friend shake her head, "The boy was a big help and I do like the family. I just pray that he does the right thing."

Chapter 78
Thursday Late Afternoon

Mr. Cutter walked into his old building and quietly looked around the foyer until the receptionist, a young snippy girl, finished a phone call, "Yes, may I help you?"

"I hope so. I'm here to see Steve Gunderson."

"Does he know you're coming?"

"I'm not sure, I called earlier, he seemed a bit distracted, but did agree he had a few minutes. I will need more than just a few minutes though."

Just then the door opened, "I am sorry, Mr. Cutter, I will see if I can find a few more minutes, but I am quite busy, it being Christmas and all," Steve murmured. "Please follow me to my office, errrrr, you're old office."

As they were getting settled in the room, Mr. Cutter asked, "Where's Mrs. Rutner?"

"I let her go," Arthur simply answered.

"She was a dependable and quite capable woman who was great at her job."

"I'm sure that you have noticed, I'm freshening up the building and office in all manners of speaking, including personnel," Steve replied as the phone rang. "Please excuse me, I am expecting this call."

Mr. Cutter looked around the office while Steve was talking on the phone. He was about to confirm an order for something when Mr. Cutter waved his hand to get his attention, "You might want to wait to place that order."

"But I want this order to arrive before the actual holiday, so I need to order now."

"Is it personal or for this business?" Mr. Cutter carefully asked.

"For the business," Steve curtly replied.

"Then, I repeat, you might want to wait."

"Why!? Give me one good reason," Steve demanded.

"This is not how I wanted to discuss things, but alright, I am here to take back my business," he evenly answered.

"Excuse me!?" Steve snidely asked. After an increase in volume and activity from the phone, Steve glared at it a moment before commenting, "No, not you, apparently I will have to call you back." He hung up the phone without waiting for a reply. "Why would you think that was even possible old man?"

Mr. Cutter raised his eyebrows slightly at Steve's choice of words, "Because I can." He waited a heartbeat before continuing, "I'm exercising the 'morals' clause."

Steve's mouth dropped open, "What 'morals' clause?"

"I suggested that you read our contract carefully, and apparently you did not. I have found out that you have your 'fingers in a lot of different pies,'" Mr. Cutter responded. "I asked that you get a lawyer and double-check the contract and you refused. I can only guess that you do not take your different business ventures as seriously as I do. I had a morals' clause added so if you went for sensationalism over accuracy and truth, damaging this paper's good reputation, I could get it back. Preserve what I have carefully built."

"This paper was barely getting by. Now it's thriving."

"At what cost? You are hurting people!"

"Only those that have put themselves into a position that have allowed me to benefit," he snarled. "Who cares?"

"I do!"

Steve's mouth dropped open and spittle flew, "I don't think so old man. You're crazy! I'll get Ben Gifford, the lawyer; he'll fix me up right!"

Mr. Cutter smiled and slightly shook his head.

"Now what?" Steve seethed.

"Who do you think put that morals' clause into the contract? You signed the contract and took over without issue. Are you going to leave without issue or do we need to involve the courts and the police? You have definitely violated the morals' clause with your comic squares that you have been running."

"But they have been accurate and sales have greatly improved!"

"Some might have been accurate, at least one was vastly misleading, and this last one was totally wrong. You are messing with people's lives and talking about money. You don't really care about this paper or this community."

Steve thought quietly for a few minutes, "What if I decide to challenge the contract in court?"

"You'll lose," a new male voice spoke up as a tall dapper gentleman entered the room. "Sorry, I didn't knock before entering," he grinned at Mr. Cutter and shook his hand. "I take it you didn't wish to wait for me before confronting Mr. Gunderson."

"No, I hate waiting. Glad you could make it Ben. Do you have the papers ready for signing?"

"Indeed, I do," Ben replied.

Chapter 79
Thursday Night

Alex was slowly driving down the road by the lake, trying to see some of the ice sculptures on the left while trying to keep an eye on the right for anyone backing out. She caught an ice sculpture of a gingerbread man giving a high five. She laughed as she watched a man jump up to return the high five. Just as the man landed on his feet, Alex's car was hit on the back right side, and the front of her car ended up pointing toward the right. She slammed on her brakes as she felt the front of her car turn toward the right. "What the he......?"

She put the car in park and surveyed the immediate area before getting out of the car. She recognized the big boat of a brown Lincoln Town Car that hit her and rushed to check on the driver. She knocked on the driver's glass window. The older woman inside rolled the window down. "Are you okay Mrs. Morelander?"

The shaken woman looked at her, "Oh, I am so sorry Alex. Did I hit you?"

"Not me, personally, but, my car, yes."

"I'm sorry. I hit the pedal before I was really ready. It has been a long time since I have been in an accident, what do we do now?"

"First, I want to make sure that you're okay. Are you injured in any way? Does anything hurt?"

The woman waved her hand, "I'm fine. This old car is like a tank."

"Well, next we need to find a cop," Alex said as she reached for her phone.

"That would be me," a masculine voice spoke up from behind Alex.

Alex turned toward the speaker, "He's going to walk us through the process, Mrs. Morelander."

The officer straightened up a bit as Alex spoke, "I heard how she is doing, and how are you Ms. Applecake?"

She was momentarily thrown for a loop, "I'm fine, officer."

About thirty minutes later, Alex was on her way with a crunched up fender. She was thankful that the officer was able to pull her fender away from her tire and that the tire was fine. She checked her watch and headed for Tom's house. Her errand to the florist and post office would have to wait.

"Alex, why did you go the way you did? Didn't it take you the opposite way that you told me you were going?"

"Yes, but I remembered I needed to go to the post office for a second and then to the florist," she mentioned matter-of-factly."

Officer Moorly called Tom later to inform him of Alex's accident, but he had already learned of the issue from her. "Sorry, I didn't call sooner Tom, but I was called to another incident."

"That's quite alright. I understand," he walked out of earshot of Alex, "but I do have a question."

"Sure."

"Do you believe that this was just an accident, or could it have been a threat to Alex?"

The officer thought it over, "Just an accident. Do you know Mrs. Morelander?"

"Not at all."

"No disrespect meant, but I believe she is getting a bit old to be driving, especially the ocean liner she has."

Tom laughed, "Thank you Oscar. I get the picture."

Chapter 80
Dec 22
Friday Morning

Carsenia came into the bakery, "Alex, I think something odd occurred last night."

"What's that?"

"Someone called in to add to a previous order. They knew the name and had details on the order, so I took the order change and attached it to the old one."

"OK," Alex nodded and semi-listened as her mind ran to the things that needed done for the day. Her full attention snapped back to Carsenia and she raised a hand, "Whoa. Stop and please repeat the last two sentences. My attention was pulled momentarily, I'm sorry. This is our busy season and I have to really work on that."

Her young worker smiled, "That's alright, I took notice. Maggie warned me about that."

Alex's face reddened, "Sorry, I didn't realize how bad a problem it was. Please repeat those earlier two sentences."

"Sure. The person said that the order's name was Snyder. He went on to say to add two dozen peanut butter cookies, the exact type didn't matter because he just loved peanut butter. He said to mix the cookies up because they like a variety."

"No, no, no," Alex muttered. "That's not possible."

"I thought it weird, because I asked if anyone in the family had peanut allergies. He said yes, but that they had cancelled out of the festivities, and it was totally cool to

283

have peanut butter this year. I said no problem and hung up. But, when I went to add the change to the order, I saw your peanut allergy warning attention label. I attached the change, but it didn't set well with me all night."

Alex went to the orders and pulled the Snyder family's out. "I'm very glad that you said something, Carsenia. You have great instincts. I will just double-check things before we fill this."

After her employee returned to the front room, Alex called Mrs. Snyder and found that neither the woman nor her husband changed the order. "The allergies run to the extreme in this group. I don't know who that person was, but I thank you for contacting me," she said gratefully.

After ending the one call, Alex made another, "Morgana? Please tell me how you got injured again."

As Alex slowly put her phone down, Cat entered the office, "What up?"

"I don't believe our troubles are over yet."

"What? Why not? Penny's husband was arrested for her murder. The burglars have been caught and are sitting in jail or in the hospital."

"Someone called here and tried to mess up an important order in a way that could have ended in someone's death and me in a legal nightmare. I talked to Morgana again. She believes that she was pushed into the road, just like I had been. I just got off the phone with Tom and he's going to question the burglar guys to see if they hurt Morgana. Tom says that the cookies that someone left in that basket were poisoned. He didn't tell me what kind of poison, and

I don't really care. The footprints were of no help like we figured. The basket and flowers were generic, so no real help there either. We need to keep on our toes for a while yet."

"For how long?"

"No idea, but we definitely need to keep aware," Alex warned.

Chapter 81
Friday Afternoon

Cat entered the bakery and told Alex that Mr. Cutter was here and would like a chance to talk to her in total privacy. "Sure, bring him back, we'll talk in my office, and please guard the bakery entrance door so I don't have any interruptions."

"Sounds like a plan."

Alex had just placed another chair in her office when Mr. Cutter entered. "I promise to keep this brief, because I know that this is a busy time for you."

"Sure, how can I help?"

"I want you to know that yesterday I took my paper back from Steve Gunderson. I also want to apologize for that comic strip that he published on Wednesday."

"That's wonderful! That newspaper needs you. And thank you for the apology, but that was not of your doing." She was going to stand up, but realized that he had more to talk about.

"I have something in my possession that I do not want to have," Mr. Cutter said as he removed a box from a canvas bag that he had carried in with him. "Thankfully, my lawyer, Ben Gifford, had Mr. Gunderson leave the newspaper office without taking anything non-personal with him. He tried to take this box with him and Ben said no. These contain the horrible leads that people submitted to the paper for those horrid comic squares. I just told you that Ben is my lawyer, and due to some recent legal matters, it's been highly publicized that he is your lawyer. So, I asked him some questions of you."

Alex arched her brows, "I'm sure that caused him some discomfort." She laughed. At Mr. Cutter's questioning look, she continued, "He doesn't like to talk of his other clients, especially given your profession."

Mr. Cutter grinned, "You are quite right on that. But, he very carefully said enough to make me feel comfortable with what I am about to do. You have the right to refuse and I will come up with another idea." Alex was intrigued and leaned a wee bit closer to the man. "You were quite correct that Steve Gunderson was not the person that he led me to believe. I would like you to review these papers in this box. I did start to go through them, but quite frankly, I just don't have the heart to know some stuff about my neighbors and friends. I don't want any news decisions to be made or altered because of these," he tapped the box. "You can destroy any you believe to be out and out lies, others that are just meant to hurt people, or even all of them. But, maybe you could do some good with the knowledge of some, and help a few people in one way or another." He stopped talking and let Alex think for a minute or two, "What do you think?"

"Why me?"

"I have heard many things about you and your friend Cat, especially due to my profession. I honestly believe you to be a good and helpful person. I have asked a few people, that I trust implicitly, for their input of you. No one else knows of the contents of this box, except you, me, and of course, Steve."

After a few thought battles in her head, Alex replied, "Yes, I believe I will take it. I will do my best." He handed her the box.

The older man smiled, "I know you will. Thank you very much. I just hope that it won't burden you too much."

"We'll see. As soon as you leave, I'm placing this in my safe." Alex put the box in a desk drawer. "So you got your paper back, now what?"

"I have a lot of work to do. Steve made a lot of changes. I have to sort out what and who to keep. I like the comic strip idea, but will have entertaining ones. I also thought it might be fun to add a craftsman/hobbyist section." He took a deep breath and released it, "I am especially thrilled that my reliable receptionist, Mrs. Rutner, has agreed to come back."

"That's fantastic!" Alex gushed. "You sound like you have an excellent start on things. If I may, I'd like to suggest someone on your staff there that I believe is a great asset. She has the newspaper's best interests at heart." Alex provided the name and Mr. Cutter smiled. "Thank you Alex! I will think on it." He wished her a great Christmas and went on his way.

Chapter 82
Friday Evening

After telling all her employees that they could leave a bit early, Alex prepared to close her shop for the night. She walked past her Christmas tree, stopped and walked back. She knelt down and removed Thaddeus. "How are you doing? I haven't gotten a chance to give you a good look over until now." She sat on the floor and turned him over as she checked him out. "I like the new shirt color. You still look tough, but nicer with the new nose." She slid her right hand down his back and was puzzled, "You have a small rough spot." She got up and walked back to her desk with a brighter light.

She looked closer at the troll's butt. For some reason that she never knew, the pants had a rectangle with two buttons on it, looking almost like "drop drawers." There was a small nick along the top line of the rectangle. It looked odd. While looking closer at the line, she pushed kind of hard on the one white button with the one finger of her right hand and heard a very small "tick." She felt the candy cane in the troll's hand move a wee bit with her left hand. Repeating her past movements, she definitely felt the candy cane move minutely. She turned it on its side and wiggled the candy cane again with her left hand. As she wiggled it, the red sack in his right hand moved a tad in her right hand. Now, she turned it over and examined the red bag closer. As she tried to wiggle it, she heard another minute "tick" sound again and the butt rectangle opened a bit at the bottom. She turned him over on his right side and with her right thumb pried the butt door open a bit more.

She lowered the desk lamp closer to the ornament in her hands. She saw the light glint off of something. She tapped him against her left hand, and a piece of jewelry fell out. There was a thread tied to the jewelry with one end of the thread connected to something in the troll. She slowly pulled on the thread and a note fell out. Alex took a pen and tapped it up inside the opened hole, nothing else seemed be in it. She picked up the jewelry item and examined it, it was beautiful. She then picked up the note and carefully opened it; two smaller notes fell out of that one.

"Hello, Alex!

Merry Christmas to my favorite niece! I knew that you would find this surprise. Wasn't it fun? I stumbled across Thaddeus' hidden compartment many a moon ago. I do not know how long he has been guarding his jewels, but I thought it a marvelous surprise. I found an older note and included it with mine. It gives us knowledge on how Thaddeus came to be, but no real clues as to his hidden treasure. I left the one that I found for you to find, but I don't know who placed it here and if it's the original treasure or a replacement. I have no idea if any other relative found this hidden compartment. I had never been told of it. I hope that this note finds you well and that your life is good. I believe that you may know where I am or who knows, maybe not! Please do what you want with it. Use it, wear it, sell it, whatever you want, just do not let it be a burden. I thought it was a hoot, and felt that if I were in financial straits, I would sell it. But, thankfully, I didn't have to, so I passed it along. I wish you a fantastic holiday season, and I do so hope that you still feel the magic!

Your loving aunt,
Gertrude Applecake

P.S. Don't worry about the smallest note, you know me, always with a back-up plan. That is to the lucky bugger who would have found the blessing, if you hadn't. Notice which note was bigger and on the outside. Love ya, honey!"

Alex laughed and wiped some tears from her face, her aunt had been quite the character. This note made her miss her more, but now she understood the unique look her aunt would bestow on her whenever she talked of Thaddeus's hidden beauty. She opened the second note,

"Hello Future Relative or Friend,

I made this troll guy to last through the years, to pass down through the generations to remind people of the simple fact, that it's the inside of a person that matters most, not the outside. You take care of him and he has the potential to take care of you.

A person's worth is not based on the outside looks or appearance, but, on what's inside the heart and the head, which is where we truly live and think.

Take care of my guy and of yourselves,
Hubert Carlton Applecake

She picked the jewelry back up and admired it for a few more seconds. She reached in her bag for a fingernail file and lightly filed the spot on Thaddy's butt that had gotten her attention. She frowned at a small beige spot that appeared when she was done. She thought a moment before searching her desk drawer for a dark green marker. She tapped it onto the beige spot and smiled at how well it blended with Thaddy's pants. She replaced the jewelry and notes back inside Thaddeus for some future decision time. Alex looked at her watch and cringed. She jogged to the front of the shop to put him back in the tree, before jogging back to the back again and leaving.

Chapter 83
Friday Night

Alex was on her way home after a quick stop at the post office and a longer stop at the local florist, The Happy Plants. She felt her car pulling to the right, she lightened her grip on the steering wheel and the car pulled harder to the right. She lowered the driver's window and could hear a slight thump, thump, thump. "Crap!" She pulled off to the side of the road and put her hazard lights on. She got out of the car and walked to the right side of her car and frowned and then looked upward to the heavens and all around. "Cold and dark is not the best for changing a tire," she grumbled. She looked up again, "But stars are better than clouds," she spoke out loud again to herself. She got out her car jack and needed equipment and started to set up to do a tire change, another vehicle pulled in behind her shining its headlights on her and her car. The door opened and Alex tightened her grip on her tire iron, "Who's there?" she called out.

"Reed. Reed Wolf. Alex, is that you? I'm Heather's husband, from Happy Plants," he clarified.

Alex released the breath that she did not know that she was holding, "Hi, Reed. Sorry, I didn't recognize you immediately."

He chuckled, "Totally understand. You don't have AAA?"

"No, I keep meaning to. This is a simple tire change. Won't take long."

"Do you want me to do it for you?"

Alex smiled, "Thanks for the offer, but I can do this, and you're dressed in fancy duds."

"I'm on my way to a party, but I feel odd not helping."

"I tell you what, please let your car where it is, it's giving me a lot of great light. If you can, take a flashlight and warn people coming that we're here. I don't want anyone running into us."

"Sounds good."

Alex looked at her watch, "When do you need to get going?"

He smiled, "Whenever you're done. I'm not leaving until you are good."

Fifteen minutes later another car slowed down and then pulled off the road in front of Alex's car. "Alex, how you doing?" a familiar voice spoke up as Reed came back to investigate.

She smiled, "Almost done, Tom. What brings you out this way?"

"A special delivery, I'm just returning from Black Water." After a few minutes talk, Tom shook Reed's hand, "Thanks for watching out for Alex. I got it from here and you can go join the party, unless you don't want to. This would be a good excuse to get out of one."

Reed laughed, "I'll remember to use it at a future time. This party should be a fun one. Take care and you are quite welcome."

"Alex, want me to finish up?" Tom asked.

"No, I'm almost done, but thanks."

"Well, I'll put the bad tire in your trunk," he replied. As he did, he examined the tire with his light, and ran his fingers over the slit in the tire. He closed his eyes briefly and shook his head. Tom stood back from the car trunk and slowly looked around the area and up and down the road. Nothing appeared odd or out-of-place.

A few minutes later, Alex knelt to get the jack out from under the car. Tom came back and offered his hand to help her back up. When she rose, he gave her a hug, "You're hot! I didn't realize how sexy it is to watch a woman change a tire." He kissed her and smiled. Out of the corner of his eye, he watched a dark car pass by on the road.

"Down, boy," she laughed. "I'll have to make sure I have a flat tire after we're married. Somewhere far off the beaten path, so that we can celebrate the tire change completion properly, without someone passing by."

He squeezed her butt, "Sounds perfect to me. If you're ready, we can finish cleaning up and then I'm going to follow you home."

"Afraid my tire's going to fall off and beat me home," she laughed.

"I'm sure you put it on tight. I just don't truly trust these little 'donut' tires that are used for spares. After the holidays, I'm going to get you a proper spare tire."

"If that will make you happy, go for it," she laughed.

Chapter 84
Friday Night

After Tom made sure Alex got home, he headed for the
police station, checked the police log and found another
incident that occurred the night before. He double-checked
the location and lowered his head. He noted the
investigating officer's name and went in search of the man.
"Mack, you investigated an issue last night on Latimore
Road, do you mind running through the details for me?"

"Sure, no problem. We got a call from a couple whose
car got a flat tire. The woman said that there were things
on the road and whoever came should look out for them.
She said that her husband was changing their tire and was
concerned that it was so dark out because the street light
was out. I had been on that stretch of road the night before
and it was lit and the road surface fine so I was really
curious. I got there and some idiot scattered some kind of
metal tacks on the road. These people were lucky that they
only had one flat tire. I put up caution cones and watched
for traffic. She was right about the light, so I lit the
immediate area with the lights I had in my trunk. Someone
from maintenance came out to clean the road. It took a bit
of time because the tacks were super sharp."

Tom thought through the summary again, "Anything
else happen before you got there?"

"I'm not quite sure what you're getting at," Mack stated.
"Neither the lady nor the man said anything, but maybe it
slipped their minds. He was busy with the tire change and

she was worried someone would hit him. They were also concerned about the time, and being late getting home, because the babysitter had to get home to study for a school test."

"Would you mind if I questioned them?"

"Not at all," Mack replied. "Let me give you their information."

Tom knocked on the Wycoft's door, "Thank you for allowing me to stop by at a later hour."

"Sure, no problem, how can I help? My husband is at work."

As they got settled at Crystal Wycoft's dinette table, he explained why he was there. "I'm not sure that I can add anything to what your officer probably told you. He said that it was probably some stupid prank."

"Did you notice anyone walking by while you were stopped there or did either of you wave off any other vehicles?"

She nodded, "Now that you mention it, someone did head toward us on the road." Tom straightened a bit as she continued. "I was wondering if I should risk getting out of the car to try to warn him, when the car pulled over and parked about six car lengths away. I lowered my window and heard the man yell if we were ok or needed help. My husband yelled back that we were fine, that he should not come any closer, and that we had called the cops. I'm sure that I heard him swear something before reversing and leaving."

"Did you get a good look at the car or the driver?"

She shook her head, "It was too dark. The street light was out."

"Are you sure it was a man?"

The woman thought a moment, "Now that you ask, no I'm not one hundred percent positive. I believe it was a man, but it could have been a woman with a cold or just a deeper voice."

"This person stopped before either you or your husband said anything?"

"Yes," she nodded, "I thought it a bit strange, but maybe his headlights caught the tacks on the street. Conrad and I had been talking before the flat tire and I was facing him so I didn't see them, maybe Conrad did."

"The man didn't offer assistance of any kind?"

"No, but I can't fault him for that. He did not sound familiar to me, so we probably didn't know him. It's not really all that safe to help strangers anymore, even in a small town like ours."

"Unfortunately, you're quite correct. How certain are you that he swore after your husband replied to his question?"

She laughed, "Quite certain. Because it was quite clear. I don't understand why he did it, but he did not sound happy at all. Maybe he had to get somewhere quick and since the road was messed up, he had to detour another way."

"That sounds like a viable explanation to me," Tom replied, but figured that it was totally wrong. He thanked the lady and gave her one of his business cards in case she remembered anything else.

Fifteen minutes later, he was sitting on the couch with Alex watching her train run around her tree. When it had finished, she turned to Tom, "You seem to be mulling something over. Have you had a chance to talk to Ben?"

"Excuse me?" Tom came back mentally from wherever he was.

Alex misread his reaction, "I know that a lot has been happening, but did you get a chance to talk to Ben?"

"Yes, I did a couple of days ago. In fact, I must apologize, with everything going on, I almost forgot," Tom answered.

"Oh, you didn't say anything. Did you need a few days to think things over?"

He turned to her, "Alex, you seem very worried over this. Please don't be. I did not need time to think it over. I admit I was totally surprised, but I think it's cool. Ben explained everything to me, including a very detailed confidentiality agreement." Alex reddened a bit. "Relax, honey, I totally understood and agreed with Ben and I signed it without hesitation." He touched her arm, "Just an idea that's really out there, but because of this 'Dove' thing, could someone financially gain in any way if something should happen to you? Your ex-husband, David, maybe, or a family member whom you might not get along well with?"

Alex thought it over for a few moments, "I don't believe so."

"What happens to it when we get old? Or Ben gets old?"

She shook her head, "Those are excellent questions. I'm not sure. I will have to ask Ben about it sometime after the new year." Alex took a sip of cocoa and smiled, "Thank you for my new Christmas mugs. They're really cute." She looked at the smiling brown teddy bear head with a Santa hat and a small holly."

Tom grinned, "You're welcome. I prefer drinking from a bear's head over drinking out of Santa's pants." Tom turned real serious, "You were quite right earlier. I was mulling something over, but a totally different subject. Let me ask you a question, if you would not have had the car incident with Mrs. Moreland last night, what roads would you have traveled to come home?" After she responded, he filled her in on his findings of the tacks attack. "Alex, you are in danger. I am really worried. Someone is seriously intent on causing you harm or worse. I don't know who it is and it's very frustrating," he finished in a growl.

"You will figure it out," Alex assured him. "In the meantime, I will try to be on guard and be much more careful."

"You need to be, I plan on marrying you in two days," Tom replied.

"And I, you," she smiled. "I believe that you'll be sleeping in the spare room again tonight?"

"You bet!"

Chapter 85
Dec 23
Saturday Morning

Alex and Cat had just finished their final baking for the day, when they decided to take a quick break with a few of their favorite cookies. Alex went to her office for a minute to make a phone call. She leaned out quickly, "Cat, can you please go out to the front and help the ladies for a few minutes. They sound quite busy out there."

"Sure, no problem."

Alex ended her call and after listening to the intercom, decided Cat might be a few more minutes. She opened her safe and retrieved the box that Mr. Cutter had left with her. Alex figured that she'd do a hurried search through the papers and see if someone could use some help before Christmas. Alex was disheartened at a few by the lack of compassion some people had for others. "These can be destroyed without problem," she mumbled under her breath. "This spring I'm having a bonfire," she grinned at the thought. One gave her pause, she might not have time to help a family before tomorrow night, but should be able to by New Years. She shook her head at the one that told of gargoyle cameras at the bookshop. She decided she would keep this one and try to figure out who turned it in.

"Alex," Cat's voice rang through the intercom, "Turn the oven back on. Carsenia will be back to explain.""

Alex hurried to return all the papers to the box. As she picked up the one, she froze momentarily, "Oh, crap! Tom has to see this one!" She had just finished putting the box in the safe, when Carsenia entered the bakery crying, "What's wrong?"

"Alex, I'm very very sorry, I must have misfiled an order. A lady came in to get her cake, and it's not ready. Cat told me privately that we don't even have it baked, because she didn't know of it."

"May I see the order?" Alex requested, "Oh, Mrs. Carbuncle," she muttered as she reviewed the paper, "It's alright, they don't really need it until tomorrow night. We can get it done by then, and deliver it before the party." She looked at the girl for a second, "It's just a cake, no real reason to cry Carsenia."

"She is a horrid woman! She screamed that she knows you and she'll have you fire me," Carsenia croaked out. "I like this job a lot and don't want to be fired! Especially at Christmas."

"Calm down. I'm not going to fire a great employee like you over a simple mistake that any one of us could make, especially at Christmas. It's a simple fix and I'm sure Cat is handling it fine. Besides, I don't take firing orders from customers, especially ones I'm not real keen on."

Cat came in the door just then with a very irritated look on her face, "That woman is horrid!" Alex and Carsenia looked at each other and started laughing. "What?"

"You both have the exact, and I do mean the exact, opinion of her," Alex remarked. "Work everything out?"

"Yes, we are to have it ready for tomorrow and will deliver it by four o'clock for free," Cat said.

Alex looked at her friend's face, "But there's more, isn't there?"

"Oh, yeah," Cat continued, "At first, Mrs. Perfect wanted Carsenia fired. I told her that was not happening." Cat grinned, "It looked like she was about to say something, but I guess she read my face correctly, because she shut up. But only for about two seconds, when she suggested her order should be free." Alex's eyes got wide. "Relax, I told her that wasn't happening either. I informed her that the cake would be ready for her party, as she had planned it to be, and we would deliver it for free. So that's the plan."

Carsenia went to the bathroom to wash her face, and then returned to the front to do her job. Alex reviewed with Cat Tom's worries about her being in danger. "I think we need to figure out who wants you out of the way," Cat said.

"Actually, I have been thinking it over quite a bit. That's why I look like crap this morning, I didn't sleep well last night. I believe this person to be Alex Sr.'s and Penny's killer. I think the killer is from Black Water."

"What's you're reasoning?"

"Morgana is from Black Water. Whoever instigated the cookie order change is probably from there, because they would know the family with the peanut allergy. Apparently, they either don't like them or don't care. Whoever this person it, must know that I'm Morgana's back-up when needed. The person has killed twice, I don't

303

think it mattered to him or her if she was just injured or died."

"So either the killer is from Black Water or just lucked into the needed information and situation," Cat said. "I'm leaning toward the former and not the latter."

"I agree," Alex replied. "I'm also thinking it's another wood whittler."

"Why? Walk me through your thoughts on this," Cat asked.

"It goes back to Alex Sr. He stole designs from others and benefitted from it. He slept with whomever he pleased, whether it was a wife of a supposed friend or not."

"Why Penny?"

"Because she was there and maybe the killer knew it, or she might have tried to blackmail the killer."

"Possible, but why you?"

Alex shrugged her shoulders, "Maybe the person thinks I saw something, or possibly Penny said something that led the killer to believe that I know something. For some reason, this person sees me as a threat."

"There are a lot of maybes in there, Alex," Cat commented.

"But…..?"

"But, I believe that you may be on to something," Cat replied.

Alex looked at the clock, "We need to get back to work. I have that Sparrow cake to finish and we need to review things and make sure that we are caught up." As Cat stood up, Alex finished, "If you think of anything else, please let me know."

"You bet," Cat smiled and dove back into the work at hand. A short time later, Cat asked, "What if Alex Sr.'s killer is just a jealous husband and not a whittler?"

"If that's the case, then we're toast. Not sure how we could figure that out," Alex replied. "I think we have to look closer at Gray Sommerline and Lizzy Barnstable."

"I'm sure that there are other whittlers and craftspeople that Alex Sr. could have majorly irritated."

"Yes, but these two are part of Alex Sr.'s whittling group, so let's work on them first."

"Okay. As Tom and John reviewed the burglary group's actions against us, mainly you, most if not all were caused by that group. Why did Alex Sr.'s killer wait until now?"

Alex shook her head, "Not sure, but he or she has struck with a vengeance recently and we need to catch this person before someone gets seriously hurt!"

Cat checked her watch, "Hey, we have to get going. Don't forget, we need to be at the park soon."

Chapter 86
Saturday Early Evening

Joey finds Tom and John at their station house and asks them if he can talk to them in private. "Sure, what's up?"

"Wait until you hear what I found out," Joey replied. "I looked a bit more into the evidence at Alex Sr.'s house and the glass that was found on the floor had some kind of residue in the bottom of it."

"More than just alcohol I could guess."

"Definitely," Joey answered solemnly. "It was Vicodin, a type of painkiller that can be highly addictive. Apparently, the Vicodin had been crushed up and applied to the inside of the glass. A glass that was Alex Sr.'s favorite. When alcohol is taken with Vicodin, it can cause dizziness or drowsiness. I think that might explain what Alex saw."

"So we need to find out who is using Vicodin," Tom said.

"Done," Joey answered. "Three out of the local whittlers group uses it. Alex's observations about Black Water makes sense to me, so if we go with it, we only have two candidates: Gray Sommerline and Lizzy Barnstable."

"Out of curiosity, who's the third person?" John asked.

"Leroy Winchester," Joey answered.

"So, we need to inquire of the first two first and then possibly Leroy."

"They will both be at the ice sculpture fest in this town tonight," Joey responded. "Apparently, the local whittlers group is doing some kind of demo tonight."

Tom glanced at his watch, "Alex had planned on going tonight. She's probably there right now. We need to find her." He grabbed his cell phone and tried to reach her, "That's odd, all circuits are busy and I can't get through."

"Out of curiosity, why and how did you get the glass examined? We were ordered to let the case go because a suspect was charged with the crime already. Any more inquiries could damage the case," John asked.

"Like you two, I don't like innocent lives to be wasted in jail. Besides, you were ordered; I wasn't in the room at the time, and like you, thought Leroy innocent.

Chapter 87
Saturday Night

Alex wandered through the ice sculpture fest in the park. There were a number of sculptures that she had missed earlier. As she passed by an ice sculpture involving an eagle and the American flag, she took a double look at someone walking in the opposite direction. "Why is my ex-husband David here tonight?" She mumbled to herself. She came across the booth of a local wine shop and her face lit up. Instead of a table or such to serve samples of wine, there was a bar made completely of ice. The base was made up of three independent sections. The middle rectangular base was made of clear ice with the wine shop's logo somehow embedded in the center. On either side of that base was about a three inch open space, and then a smaller rectangular clear ice block with white pine trees and a mountain scene embedded. An ornate eight inch ice slab lay on top of the base to serve as a countertop, and complete the bar. On each end of the counter were vertical rectangular ice hollowed blocks to hold and chill wine bottles. Thankfully there were no ice stools for patrons to sit on. Two lights just under the bar provided light for the servers to do their jobs. Victorian streetlights added ambiance lighting for the customers. There were regular tables and chairs scattered about for patrons to take advantage of.

Alex noticed a man standing at the bar that she thought she recognized, so she walked up closer. Marsha Winters' husband, Derek, was asking the bartender for another drink. "I think that you had enough to drink, sir. That drink in your hand will be the last from us."

"What right do you have to say that? I'm tired of having to fight for everything. Even my own wife has been embarrassing me. She needs to stop sleeping with other men! First, at least to my knowledge, it was that Alex Sr. and then with Lincoln George. Make no mistake, I will not be the passive husband just standing in a corner." He started to step away from the ice bar, and stumbled. Alex caught him quickly and kept him from falling, "Be careful there Mr. Winters."

"I don't need your help Alexandra! I took care of that Alex bastard and next will be that Lincoln fellow." He cleared his throat and lumbered off with his drink to sit at a far table.

As Alex watched Derek sit down, she tried to decide if she should call Tom. He didn't look like a killer, but she heard Tom's voice in her head asking her what a killer really looks like.

"Some people cannot handle their liquor," a familiar masculine voice stated.

Alex turned back to the ice bar, "Reed! When did you get here? There was just some other dude here a minute ago."

"You're quite correct, the local whittler group is doing something with the ice sculpture people and I had to help with something there. I just returned to relieve Torrence."

"Did you hear what Derek just said?"

"Not all of it. The ingrate doesn't realize that you kept him from faceplanting just now. After that, I had a customer to tend to. Is there a problem?"

Alex turned to glance back at Derek again, "I'm not sure." She turned back to Reed and smiled, "Thanks again for helping last night. How was your party?"

"You're welcome. It was great, I'm glad that I went."

"You didn't run into any issues for being late?" Alex inquired a bit worried.

"Nah," he shook his head. "On the contrary, it scored me points with my beautiful wife. Heather thought I was quite gallant." He flourished his arm over the array of different wines, "Can I get you anything?"

"Reed, I don't drink, but I have a few questions about wine."

"Sure, no problem. Would you like to taste any?"

She shook her head, "Sorry, not really, but thank you anyway."

"Go ahead and ask away."

"Are all wine bottles the same size?"

"No, there are full size bottles and half size bottles."

"Do you have any of those half size ones?"

"Sure," Reed replied, "Let me get one." He reached over and pulled one out of an ice block. "This is an ice wine. It's a dessert wine and it's a bit more expensive than other wines. We are giving small samples out to the public."

Alex picked up the bottle and looked it over. "Wow, I didn't know that wine bottles came in this size. It's unique.

She held the bottle up in the air a bit, and the liquid has a nice golden color." She looked at Reed, "Do you know of any that come with something red lying in the bottom of the bottle?"

He gave her a quizzical look, "For someone who doesn't drink, you have some particular questions. Yes, I do know of one, there may be more, I just know of the one."

"That's alright, do you have one here that I can look at?"

"Sure," Reed put the first bottle back and handed her another one.

Alex turned the bottle around and saw what at first looked like a finger lying in the bottom of the bottle. She held it up in the light a bit more, "It looks like a type of pepper," she observed.

He smiled, "It's a red cayenne pepper. When you first drink this wine, you get a super sweet taste and then the spice and heat kick in."

"I think if I were to try a wine, this would not be the one to start with," Alex commented.

"Totally understand," he flourished his right hand toward the ice blocks, "I have a variety here if you ever want to give it a try."

"One more quick question, on television, people don't pull wine out of freezers and such. Does all wine have to be chilled?"

Reed shook his head, "No, there are many different wines. For example, dry red wine is good at room temperature and needs to breathe. The two bottles I have shown you are ice wines. They are chilled and do not need to breathe to drink. I could go on for hours about wine," he smiled.

"I bet that you don't have to explain much to the local whittler group." Alex commented. "They all drink wine."

"No, they don't," he replied.

"Yes, they do. I was at each of their houses recently and they all had wine bottles in their homes at one place or another," she refuted.

"Tis the season, I guess. A lot of people give and get wine for presents. That's probably what you saw." At her questioning glance, he continued, "Alex, I just got back from doing a toast earlier with that group. I took wine along for it, the way I was asked to. Two of the group stated that they don't drink alcohol, so I got them a soda to toast with instead."

"Which two didn't want any alcohol? If I may ask."

"Gray and Lizzie," Reed answered. "Have any other questions?" He smiled.

Alex shook her head, "Not right now." She tilted her head toward the end of the ice bar, "You have people coming. A big thank you Reed," she shook his hand and slightly dipped her head briefly.

He laughed, "Any time, Alex."

As Alex walked away from the wine booth, her mind swirled with Reed's information, thoughts of David and her earlier discussion with Tom, and Derek's comments. She turned and noticed Derek Winters had left his seat. She was trying to figure out her next move when something clicked. She reached for her cellphone and started dialing. An arm reached around her and pulled her hard against a body. "Put it away!!" a voice hissed in her ear. She did as instructed, but hit the "call" button as she did so. "I knew that you couldn't let things drop and would keep at it until you figured everything out. Now, walk with me quietly. You make one loud noise and I will shoot someone in the crowd. Do you understand?" She felt something hard jab into her side.

"Ow! You are hurting me!" she hissed. "And yes, I understand," Alex replied as her mind raced for an escape plan.

Meanwhile, in another part of the park, Tom and Cat are waiting to meet up with Alex by one of the temporary stages set up for various performers. A duo of performers took to the stage and started to sing a cover of the David Bowie/Bing Crosby song "Peace on Earth/ Little Drummer Boy." "Crap!" Cat murmured and started to look around the park.

"What?" Tom inquired.

"Alex loves this song," Cat checked her watch. "She should have been here by now, I hope everything is o….." Cat scanned the park and saw Alex walking in the opposite direction with a man bundled up in winter gear to her right. As she watched, Alex looked her way briefly. Thankfully, the two passed by a park light and she looked downward briefly, so Cat followed suit. Cat watched the two disappear into a darkened area.

"Tom!" She grabbed his shoulder, "She needs our help!" Cat took off after Alex and the man.

Tom quickly caught up, "How do you know?"

"She signed. She asked for help," Cat answered and then broke into a light jog.

"I didn't know that you two could sign," Tom replied as they rounded the corner where Alex and the man had gone. The two stopped dead. The park was filled with people and with all the different activities taking place, it was filled with noise.

"I'm really beginning to hate this park!" Tom huffed.

"Do you see her?" Cat asked alarmed.

"No......." Tom scanned the crowd. He leapt up onto a streetlamp base and held onto the post and watched for a second, "Yes!" He pointed off to their left. Tom saw Alex trip and get yanked back up. Tom reached for his phone and it was dead, "Damn it! Cat we need to get over there." He dropped back down and started running, weaving among people. Cat hurried to catch up.

Meanwhile somewhere in another part of the park, Jacob and his mule were providing carriage rides. "Rastus, why are you fidgeting?" Jacob asked as Rastus glanced back and pulled to the right. Jacob looked over and saw Tom and Cat running. He looked ahead of them and saw Alex and another person pulling her. Jacob glanced back at his passengers, "Hunker down and hold onto something! We're going to help a friend in need!" Jacob had Rastus pick up his pace, and trotted off on a path that would put them ahead of Alex and whomever.

The man pulling Alex started to breathe a bit heavier. "You are dragging! Move it! My car is not much farther. When we get there, you will get inside without a fight or so help me, I will shoot someone!"

"I'm tired! I've had a long day and I believe I've just twisted my ankle, you jerk!"

"All you do is whine. Don't worry, I'll be relieving you of your pain shortly," he growled. "Now move!"

Alex's phone started ringing, "Don't you dare answer it!" He brought them to an abrupt stop, "Give me your phone," he commanded. She hesitated, he tipped his head to their right, "Do you want to see that little girl bleed?" She reached into her pocket and handed over her phone. He tossed it to the side and started walking again.

"Alex!" A voice yelled from a distance.

Gray turned to see the caller, "Hurry up, your friend is getting closer." All of a sudden Gray stopped again. He smiled a slow evil smile, "Better yet, we'll let her catch up." He moved to stand behind her.

"What are you doing?" Alex cried out.

"You two have been a pain in my butt. Those idiot burglars were trying to take you out and failed. You obviously didn't enjoy the Welsh cookies that your mystery person left you."

"It wasn't my mystery person, the delivery was flawed big time and I'm not into rat poison. It does the body bad!"

"That's what I was counting on," he huffed. "Then each time I carefully planned your demise, something prevented it. I'm done with you two! When Cat gets

315

closer, she's done. You make a move or a sound, I will shoot someone else. Your choice Alexandra! And then your end." He hissed.

Alex freaked inside, tears ran down her face as she watched her best friend jogging her way. Alex turned her head slightly as she caught movement to her left. She watched as a group of kids were innocently fooling around and blocking Tom from reaching her. She saw the frustration in his face change as the sound of hooves penetrated her head. Alex and Gray separated and went flying to the ground as John rolled between the two and bystanders screamed.

Gray started to get up and heard someone wheeze, "Don't move or I will freaking shoot you!"

Cat ran up to her friend and bent down, "Are you hurt anywhere?" Alex mumbled. "I'm sorry, what did you say?"

Alex lay on the ground, "I said, please give me a minute." Cat had just helped her stand up as Tom reached them. Alex's legs gave out and she started to fall. He caught her before the she hit the ground and steadied her. The three turned around to tune into the mess behind them.

Joey was trying to catch his breath as he held a gun on Gray Sommerline. John's wife was helping him get up after taking a hard hit on the ground. John's daughter was making sure everyone was okay on the carriage and staying put. Joey's friend, Rico, was calming the bystanders who had been screaming. Jacob was praising Rastus and making sure that he had suffered no serious injuries on their

316

hurried journey. Tom made sure Alex was okay, asked Cat to keep an eye on her, and walked over to help Joey arrest Gray and get him off the ground.

Chapter 88
Saturday Night

Tom turned to Joey as they entered the station house, "Did you have enough time to catch your breath?"

John chuckled as Joey gave a questioning glance, "When you had Gray down on the ground and told him to freeze, I wasn't sure you had enough oxygen to pull it off."

Joey laughed, "Hey, when I realized what was going down, I ran across that park as fast as I could. I just missed jumping onto that blasted carriage!"

"I'm glad that you joined the party when you did," Tom replied and John agreed.

Tom, John, and Joey entered the interrogation room where Gray Sommerline sat waiting for them. He had been Mirandized and refused a lawyer.

"An officer told me, that you muttered something about killing Alex Sr. because he stole your designs?" Joey asked. "Really?"

"Yes, if it had only happened once, then I would have let it go. In fact, I already had. But three years in a row was, and is, too too much. I took precautions of weird proportions but he still got them. Then I found out his mistress was in on it and then I knew how he got my designs."

"How?" John asked, but had already guessed.

"She was my mistress before his," Gray answered with pride in his voice.

"But, is it really a big deal?" Tom inquired.

"Hell, yes!! He entered a competition and won with a design that I was going to enter. He got some money, but more important, his name got out big time and he got some very lucrative work because of me. Talk to Leroy Winchester. I heard he won a competition recently. I am very happy for him. He won it fair and square."

"Being arrested for a killing that you committed did not help," Tom said.

"Well, what can I say, self-preservation stepped in. I was hoping that he would be found not guilty and beat the charge," Gray replied with some embarrassment.

"Couldn't you have pointed out what Alex Sr. was doing?"

"How? My word against his. He had more money to fight. Why injure myself because of him? I took precautions and he did it again. He even won one year by combining a couple of artists' designs into one design. He had no morals, no honor, and he didn't care. But, I did. If I lose honorably, I can take it, but I was losing to my own work! It was hard not to hit him, not to lower myself to his level. If I would have said anything, it would have looked like 'sour grapes.' I would look worse and him better. When I found out he stole the wives of others, it bothered me, but I figured it took two to tango, so to speak, but stealing others' designs too!? When I stopped by his house, I was planning on just talking. Then I saw the ornaments that he was going to hand out to the carolers, and I lost it. Once again, he was ripping me off. It was too much, so I removed the problem. If I got caught, I would handle it, at least others would be spared."

"But, you went after Alexandra," John stated.

"Not at first. I saw others going after her and hoped that they could and would handle her. She was the only real threat to me. When they were stopped, I stepped back in. Your Alex is one smart lady that somehow learns too much. I knew that she'd figure it out and she did. Unfortunately, she is not one to let things lie. I knew that she would soon remember the item that would give me away, so I had to try to stay free. It was her or me?"

"What item?" Joey asked.

"A stupid wine bottle," he answered. "I don't know why I kept it. When she came by to drop something off for me to work on, it was on a counter in plain sight. Then I overheard her talking to Reed at the ice bar in the park, she was asking about the difference in types of wine and shapes of wine bottles."

"And Penny?" Tom inquired.

"She betrayed our group, then she tried to blackmail me. She was as bad as Alexander, so I removed her too. Before I did, she said that she had told your Alex everything. I had a feeling that she was lying, but I couldn't chance it. Penny's comments actually sealed the deal on Alexandra for me. I had gotten rid of the wine bottle, so if she had remembered something, it would be he said, she said. But if Penny had actually talked to her, who knows what all she would have had against me."

"So you're the one who coated Alexander's glass with Vicodin," Joey stated.

"Yes, I figured it was a safe glass to use. It was his favorite. No matter what he drank, he used that glass. He could have quite the temper. No one else was allowed to use it. I didn't want anyone else to get sick or anything."

"Why the Vicodin?" Tom asked.

"Because Alex Sr. was a taller and stronger man than I. I figured it would level the playing field so-to-speak, and it did."

John nodded his head to the officer in the room with them, "You will be charged with numerous crimes, this officer will take you from here."

After the officer led Gray away, Tom turned to John, "It was very fortuitous that you and your family were taking a carriage ride tonight. Thank you for helping Alex." Tom shook John's hand.

"You should thank my wife, she's the one who had insisted," John smiled.

"I will," Tom responded with a grin.

Chapter 89
Dec 24
Sunday Late Morning

Alex and Cat arrived at the bakery at the same time. They parked in the lot behind the store. Cat saw the bouquet in the crook of the tree first. "Alex, your holiday mystery bouquet is here."

"Awesome!" Alex said and picked the beautiful bouquet from the tree. They walked to the office door. She unlocked the door and they entered the shop.

"I still find it creepy. Merry Christmas from a ghost," Cat snickered.

"I think it's neat. It's a gift from my aunt and whomever, I'm sure. I just hope that I find out before the person passes, so that I can thank them for his or hers thoughtfulness."

"This one has a message I presume," Cat said hopefully.

Alex smiled, "Yes, it does. It wishes me love, faith, and peace."

"Now that's a great Christmas message!"

"You bet!" Alex agreed, but felt a bit giddy inside also, for the bouquet also wished her happiness in marriage.

Cat touched Alex on her arm, "Remember, when the burglars said that when they had entered this building, someone was here that scared them away? Do you think this flower person and the building protector are the same person?"

Alex thought it over briefly, "Why not? Nobody has come up with a better explanation for an unknown person to be in the building. Joey postulated that it was another burglar but there was no proof of another break-in. While it is possible that the two burglars destroyed any evidence left by the first guy, I don't really believe it."

"But, how does your flower person get inside? You had the locks changed a while back after Abrahms was killed.

"I don't know. We still have some wrap-up Christmas activities to handle today. Let's figure out that mystery in the new year."

"Speaking of mystery, did you find out why Derek Winters insisted that he had taken care of Alex Sr.? It sure sounded like he confessed to you at the Ice Bar last night."

Alex nodded her head, "I agree, that's one of the things I was mulling over when Gray grabbed me. Prior to that, I was being better at keeping an eye on my surroundings. Tom said that Derek has paid Steve Gunderson to make a comic strip that showed Alex Sr.'s house and numerous women coming in and out of it: some by walking, some by climbing out windows, that kind of thing. It could have caused a lot of problems, because he wanted the women to be drawn realistically. Apparently, there were quite a few. A number of relationships, in this town and nearby towns, would have had more than the usual holiday friction. Chances were high that Alex Sr. would have been dead by New Years, one way or another."

Cat walked over to the one table, "What about this one cake? I thought the bride was going to pick this up yesterday."

Alex looked over to Cat, "She had car trouble. So I agreed to deliver it today when I deliver Mrs. Carbuncle's cake."

"Are we still delivering this other order to the church so they can celebrate Jesus' birthday tomorrow?"

"Yes, you will need to take the delivery van at around two and deliver those three sheet cakes and the eight inch tier cake to Grace United. I'm going to ask Carsenia to go with you to help, because that's when the bride wants her cake at the other side of town. I'm going to use my car for the cake and the boxes you all are going to make for her."

"That's when we close. I can do it alone if you want and if she can't spare the time."

Maggie, Carsenia, and Jo-Jo entered the room together in a jolly mood. "What are we making for whom?" Jo-Jo inquired.

"Just before closing yesterday, my one bride's dad dropped off a last minute request," Alex walked over to another table. "The big boxes here are chocolate-covered pretzels. In this other box, we have blue candy boxes." Alex pulled out a box to show them. "I love the silver snowflake pattern on these. We fill the boxes, close them, use these elastic ties to attach homemade tags and to help ensure that the boxes stay closed. This needs done by one forty-five. Any questions?"

"Yeah, who drops something like this off on us just before Christmas? Like we don't have enough to do?" Cat inquired.

"That's why I was truly grateful that Jo-Jo had a couple hours to help out."

Chapter 90
Sunday Early Evening

On Christmas Eve, everyone gathered at Alex's house to celebrate Christmas. "Hi, everyone! I am glad that you all could make it today. As I told everyone about two weeks ago, this year we are going to do things a bit differently. We have a few family members and friends coming later and I don't want that to interrupt our gift exchange, so we will start with that and then turn to the food. I hope that you can stay later, but it is not mandatory of course. I think that you will have some fun though, if you do stay. I ordered a bit more food to cover the extra people. So, since everyone but Mike is here, I believe we should get started."

As people went to get their gifts, Maggie walked over to Cat, "Hey, where is Mike?"

"He's running a bit late. Some trucker friends of his were involved in a slight fender bender, not of their own fault. They have to get the truck fixed before they can move on, so he called and asked if it would be okay to bring them tonight and give them a good Christmas Eve. Of course Alex said yes. They are going to stay at his house tonight and come to my house tomorrow morning for breakfast. The mechanic figures the work will be done by the early afternoon. It could have been earlier, but Rufus, Mike's friend, said no. The holiday was important, enjoy family first and then give a call when it's ready."

A "U-shaped" table that had been set up in the dinette was full of food. Everyone had brought one item with them to contribute to the feast. This year, Alex kept one end bare except for a tablecloth covering the table. A small note on it read, "Reserved space for a special surprise dessert. Please save some space to share and enjoy it!" People were enjoying their selections of ham, potatoes, gravy, pickled eggs, bread-n-noodles, applesauce, salad, rolls, vegetables, finger food snacks, and various beverages, when Mike showed up and introduced Becky and Rufus Bridgewater, a truck driver team that he knew.

"Welcome, Merry Christmas! Please let me take your coats and things to my spare room. Welcome to my house and as they say, 'My house is yours.' Please join in and enjoy the evening," Alex suggested and then went to the door to let Joey and John in.

As the evening progressed, conversation flowed to all topics including guesses to the surprise dessert food. Extra chairs and tables were set up in the living room for everyone to enjoy their meals.

"So does anyone know if Alex Sr.'s dog, Carver, found a home?" Maggie asked.

"I heard a woman artist over one town took him in. Apparently, Carver didn't take to a lot of people in Alex Sr.'s whittler group. But whenever the woman would stop by for a visit, being a fellow artisan, he was okay with her. She's a Pepsi lover and apparently so is Carver. He took a taste of her drink one night, after moving in with her, and instantly fell in love," Jo-Jo said with a smile.

"Is the woman's name Sadie by chance?" Alex inquired.

"Yes, yes it is," John replied.

"What about that homeless veteran guy, Diesel, that helped Milo in the park? Does anyone know what happened to him?" Tom asked.

Mike laughed, "Doing very well at the present." Cat, along with a number of others, looked questioningly at her man, as he continued, "There was no way that Mavis, her mom Sylvia, and Milo were going to let Diesel return to the park. Milo's knee was worst then we thought, and Diesel's efforts helped save his leg. He's living comfortably in Mavis' 'Visiting Artist' guest house in their backyard, and will be joining them for the holidays!"

People clapped and some hollered, "Alright! Awesome!"

Becky found Alex, "Thank you for opening your house to us." She gave Alex a quick hug, "We had planned to be at home by now, but that's the life of a trucker." She smiled and shrugged.

"I have known Mike for a quite a while and I understand to a point. I would think that the holidays are the hardest."

"Can be, although with some guys we know, they love the excuse of not having to hang with relatives," she chuckled. "Your place is lovely. Thanks again."

"You are quite welcome." Alex touched Becky's arm lightly, "I was wondering if you and your hubby could do me a favor. Feel free to say no."

Becky listened to her request and smiled, "We can certainly handle that. Where is the item?" Alex handed her an envelope. "I believe that I will go find my hubby."

Additional friends and some family arrived around five thirty and Alex welcomed them. Around six, Alex looked around for Cat. From across the room, Becky noticed that Alex seemed to be getting anxious about something. Without really thinking, when she caught Alex's eye, Becky used American Sign Language to ask if Alex needed any help that Becky could assist with. Alex was momentarily surprised, but smiled, and signed back asking Becky to help find Cat and let her know that she was needed. Becky agreed and went off in search of her quarry.

Within a few minutes, Cat was asking Alex what she needed. Alex asked Cat to follow her to her bedroom, "I need your help with something."

"Okay, sure," Cat replied.

People looked around and wondered when everyone heard Cat yell, "Awesome!" Momentarily, Cat opened the door, gave everyone a small smile and called for Mike to join her and Alex. Shortly after that she exited the bedroom wearing her coat and a big smile and carrying a small Christmas tree decorated in silver and blue ornamental balls. "If everyone would please grab your coats and meet me at the door to the patio, I would really appreciate it."

In the hustle and bustle and noise of everyone's bewilderment and curiosity, Tom, John, and Pastor Daniel exited the house by the side kitchen door. Soon everyone was bundled in their winter garb and waiting for Cat to give them more guidance. "I am going to place this tree just outside these doors. Please take an ornament as you pass the tree, it's filled with bird seed. Welcome to an awesome surprise! It is my great pleasure to invite you all out to the backyard to find a seat, and enjoy yourselves as we watch Tom and Alex get married!" Cat announced enthusiastically. As everyone cheered, she flipped a switch and opened the door. People oohed and aahed as the backyard lit up with a glow of white Christmas lights. It was magical. Putting his cell phone in his rear pocket, Rufus touched Becky's sleeve and tilted his head back toward the inside of the house. Curious, she followed his lead.

Cat placed the three foot tree that she had been carrying on a table just outside the doors. As people walked through the doors, they picked an ornament off the tree and were awed. Lights filled the trees and bushes, some twinkling, some not. Rows of chairs faced the opposite end of the yard. A single aisle split the seating area equally in half. A rope light laid on the ground to mark each side of the aisle walkway that led to a light filled arched trellis. Pine garlands and silver-tipped pinecones entwined about the trellis. Two gorgeous white porcelain doves with silver accents were poised in the center of the top of the arch.

Cat looked around and noticed the outdoor heaters that had been set up unobtrusively. She also noticed some people seated who had not been in the earlier gathering in the house. She walked over to them, "You have been very busy Christmas elves!" She smiled at the ladies of the Happy Plants florist company as she went back inside the house.

"Yes, we have," they laughed.

Pastor Daniel was standing at the back of the archway area. Mike, Rufus and Becky silently slipped out of the house and found seats to use a short time after everyone got seated. Tom and John appeared at the right side of the archway. They waited quietly with smiles on their faces. Soft music started to fill the air as a friend started to play "To Have and To Hold" on his flute, and soon Ben joined in. His voice blended beautifully with the flute. Everyone's heads turned back toward the house in anticipation. A young girl came out first. She held a basket full of white and red rose petals and slowly scattered them as she walked down the aisle. Next came Cat, she was wearing a dark blue velvety dress with white fur trim and cuffs. She was carrying a small bouquet of Stargazer Lilies, Stephanotis, and Purple Sweet Pea. Shortly thereafter, Alex glided out of the house in a white velvety dress with dark blue fur trim and cuffs. She wore a mini veil and carried a bouquet that matched Cat's, except that it was larger. Her dad smiled as he walked his daughter down the aisle.

When they reached the archway at the end of the aisle, Carl hugged his daughter, shook Tom's hand, placed Alex's right hand in Tom's left, and turned to join his seated wife. Alex and Tom stepped up on the platform together. The actual ceremony lasted only about ten minutes. As Pastor Daniel announced that Alex and Tom were man and wife, a slight snow started to fall. Giggles arose from the crowd. Tom gave Alex a short, but passionate kiss. They turned toward the guests and everyone clapped and hooted. Tom announced, "Thank you to all for being here and sharing this moment with us. Please join us back in the house for some more festivities." The couple walked back down the aisle as everyone tossed birdseed at them.

As people re-entered the house, they congratulated the new Mr. and Mrs. and noticed that the mystery spot had been filled on the food table. A three tiered stacked wedding cake had appeared. It was a navy blue-iced cake with white snowflakes of various sizes randomly placed all over the cake. Each tier was centered on the one below it. Each tier had about a one inch margin all around it and that was filled with icing to look like snow. As one looked at the front of the cake, there were a couple of chocolate pine cones and small pine branches placed on the top left, middle right, and bottom left tiers of the cake. The whole cake had been elevated two inches above the table and additional larger pine branches had been splayed out under the cake to finish off the decorations. The wedding cake was topped with a statue consisting of two glass doves edged in silver   Alex rapped a spoon on a crystal glass to catch everyone's attention, "Please stow your coats and get comfortable. Since it's starting to snow, Tom and I are going to have a few photos taken outside. It shouldn't take more than fifteen minutes.

Becky used that time to find the flute player, "You played beautifully."

"Thank you very much. I thoroughly enjoyed it, especially when Ben joined in."

Becky glanced down at his cane, "Am I mistaken? I believe you used your cane as a flute."

He smiled, "You are quite correct. A Native American friend of mine from out west makes these and gifts me with a new one every now and then. I really like them."

"I know someone who would really enjoy one of these." As Becky got information from the gentleman, Alex and Tom came back inside.

Shortly thereafter, the happy couple was standing by their cake. John gave a quick toast to the happy couple. The cake was cut and all enjoyed a piece. Alex made sure no one ate a pinecone.

Alex found Maggie and her daughter, "Thank you for loaning us Carol for a short time." She focused in on the mature young lady, and handed a card and a small wrapped box to the happy girl, "An additional thank you to you for doing such a great job on such short notice."

"It was fun," she smiled and ran off to find her dad. She stopped quick, turned back toward Alex, held the box briefly in the air and said, "Thank you too."

Maggie watched her daughter turn again and hurry off, "This was a great night, Alex. Congratulations on your wedding! I just wished that I had been able to help you prep for this," she waved her hands lightly in the air. "Especially after all that mess of me being a witness against you, and all the added involvement with the police."

Alex looked her friend in the eye, "I told you, that's all in the past. Besides, you did what you had to do. Exactly what I would have done in your place. You were honest to the police. No harm to me. Besides," she gazed toward her new husband briefly before turning back to her friend, "I believe that I will now have a lifetime of involvement with the police." They laughed as they hugged briefly.

Alex's mom found her and gave her a huge hug. "You are gorgeous! And your new husband is very handsome."

Alex's dad nudged her mom and gave her a look, "Okay. Okay." She looked at her daughter, "I heard that you saw David in the park. That was my doing I'm afraid, and I want to apologize."

Alex just looked at her mom a moment, "Why on earth did you tell him?"

"I felt he should know, in case he wanted to say or do anything. You really haven't known Thomas long."

Alex's dad spoke up, "I told her that she should not have done it. You are a grown woman and can make your own decisions."

"Mom, we know people who have dated longer than we have and are now divorced. We also know people who have dated shorter than we have and are still happily married. Thank you for your worry, but I believe that Tom will be staying 'til death do us part.' I love you both, thank you for coming," she hugged them before they prepped to leave.

Tom and Alex thanked their families for making it to the wedding and staying for a while. Each had been very happy to be invited, was glad that they could make it, but needed to leave soon to get back home for the next day's Christmas celebrations. Tom's mom pulled her son off to the side and talked to him for a few minutes. When they returned and joined the group, Tom was smiling at Alex. His mom went up to Alex and gave her a hug, "Thank you for everything. I especially enjoyed the different cards that you sent me and my husband for fourteen days straight. Then, you had your friends hand deliver the fifteenth card tonight as we arrived. It means a lot to me that you made the effort to fulfill a wish and belief of mine that you did not know the reason for. Tom told me that he knew none of this, and so you did this because you truly wanted to, and not because he asked for it. I am honored that you have chosen to join our family. I believe that you will make my Thomas happy and I thank you again." After another round of hugs, they left.

Alex looked for Becky and Rufus, "Thank you for helping Mike with the cake."

"Becky decorated cakes for a number of years while our children were growing, she has a talent like yours," Rufus smiled at his wife.

Becky blushed and grinned, "Similar maybe, but you outshine me." Becky hugged both Tom and Alex, "I am glad that we could help. It was an unexpected, but very pleasant surprise. Thank you both for inviting us into your home."

Cat came up beside her best friend of a million years, "The cake was awesome! Your cover story was fantastic by-the-way." She looked down on her dress, thank you for this amazing dress. I love it. It's so not me, but is me." She chuckled and gave Alex a big hug.

"You're welcome. When I stumbled onto the dresses, I thought that you might like it."

"I knew something else was on your mind lately, but never did I think of this. I could have helped more you know."

"If you look around and think about it, I'm sure that you'll realize that you helped a lot more than you think you did. Both Tom and I very much appreciate it! In fact, we had help from various people, y'all just didn't know it. Besides, you've had a lot on your plate this season also."

"One quick question though, did you make more chocolate-covered plastic pinecones? I thought we used all the ones that you made. I did notice that no one got to eat the ones on your cake."

"We did use them all up," Alex laughed. "These were real pinecones dipped in chocolate." Alex chuckled again as Cat's eyes widened, "I made sure no one gnawed on these. That would have been majorly gross," she wrinkled up her face as she finished.

Cat just looked at her for a moment, "You used real pinecones?"

"Yes, I had a box of pinecones downstairs that were the right size. They have been down there for some time, so they were bug-free, clean, and dry."

"You're nuts!" she laughed, "But, they were cool looking!"

"Thanks!"

As the festivities wound down, more people prepared to leave. Alex and Tom spoke up, "Thank you all for enjoying this night with us and making it extra special for us."

The new husband and wife stood at the front door. As each person left, they received a hug and a memento of the evening. The memento was an ornament consisting of a pair of glass doves with silver accents. A ribbon-like banner underneath the doves stated, "Christmas is full of miracles! Merry Christmas from Alex and Tom." Everyone also received a blue box with silver snowflakes on it filled with chocolate-covered pretzels. As Maggie, Jake, and their one daughter left and received their mementos, Alex gave a warmer grin, "See, you helped more than you thought. Here's something extra for your son, I'm sorry he was sick and couldn't come. I sure hope he feels better by tomorrow."

Cat was the last person to leave, but stopped at the door and turned to the couple, "Your ride is here!" Alex and Tom looked out the door and grinned, "Get your jackets! I will lock up for you and take pictures!"

Jacob climbed off his carriage and bowed to them, "It would be mine and Rastus' pleasure to give you two a carriage ride. Congratulations!"

Alex and Tom laughed when they left the house to find that many of their friends had stayed to send them off on this ride. As they climbed into the carriage, everyone tossed birdseed and yelled blessings as Cat took tons of photos.

As the carriage started a journey through the town park, Tom turned to his new wife and with a twinkle in his eye said, "Merry Christmas beautiful!"

Todedes

(Warning - this is an ambitious recipe)

(One more warning, this makes a huge batch of cookies, feel free to make 1/3 of this recipe)

3 cups Oil

3 cups Water

1 cup Port wine

Mix above ingredients together on the stove and heat mixture until lukewarm, don't heat long.

Take off the heat and dump the mixture into a large bowl.

Add 1 cup Sugar

4 Tbls. Baking Powder – it will bubble

Gradually add approx. 5 lbs. of flour. Lay out onto a lightly floured surface and knead until no longer sticky.

Roll into 1" thick and 12" long strips. Cut into 2" pieces or 1" pieces. The larger the piece, the larger the finished product. Roll over a decorative dish*. Make the entire batch of dough. Lay on wax paper and paper towels – which will soak up some of the oil.

Two different options to make these:

Option 1- Traditional way

Put two cups of oil and one cup of Crisco in a fry pan. Heat until you see some bubbles. Won't be deep enough to cover Todedes completely. Fry on one side and then flip over. The cookies need to be cooked through and brown. Take your time. Do this part slow and fry in small batches. This takes practice. Do one as a test and time it. The cookie should stick together, and not fall apart. They can be a tad oily inside, but not mushy. As you fry cookies, you may need to add more oil and Crisco to the pan, using the same ratio as above. Lay on paper towels when done frying to cool.

Option 2 – Non-traditional way

You can bake these instead of frying. Heat oven to 325–350 degrees. Place on cookie sheet and bake for 12 –14 minutes. When done, they will be golden brown. They should look dry on top. Lay on paper towels to cool.

Eat these warm, or let cool, and store in an airtight container until ready to serve.

To eat plain at a later time, just warm up a few of them up in a microwave, or enjoy cold.

Or, when ready to eat or serve them with their coating:

Heat up a mixture of honey and water (using about equal amounts of each) in a pan. Just as it reaches a boil, drop the Todedes into the mixture and coat. Don't keep in for long, just coat the cookie. Then put them into a bowl and sprinkle or coat the cookies in sugar. Do in small batches, NOT all at one time.

Enjoy!

*The decorative plate mentioned above is one that has a textured underside, for example, some pickle plates have a textured bottom. When ready to use it, flip it over. Slowly push and roll the Todede over the textured surface, this flattens the dough piece and it may roll back over your fingers a bit.

Sheryl C.D. Ickes is an award winning author. She lives in south central Pennsylvania with her husband and daughter.

To learn more about Sheryl's books or to leave a comment: please look her up on social media or go to www.sherylcdickes.com

Made in the USA
Lexington, KY
29 October 2019